Robin Cannon received her B.A. and M.S. degrees from Fordham University, New York City, and her Sixth Year Degree in Education Administration from Southern CT State University, New Haven, CT. She has been a school teacher for 33 years.

Robin lives with her husband, Bob, daughters, Haley and Molly, and son, Colin.

Three previous books written by the author are *Tilly Fig*, *Rye Hill*, and *Fireflies at Nightfall.*

For Our Sons.

Robin Cannon

THE VANITY OF ROBBERS

AUSTIN MACAULEY PUBLISHERS™

LONDON • CAMBRIDGE • NEW YORK • SHARJAH

Ordering Information:
Quantity sales: special discounts are available on quantity purchases by corporations, associations, and others. For details, contact the publisher at the address below.

Publisher's Cataloguing-in-Publication data
Cannon, Robin
The Vanity of Robbers

ISBN 9781641823807 (Paperback)
ISBN 9781641823814 (Hardback)
ISBN 9781641823821 (E-Book)

The main category of the book— Fiction / General

www.austinmacauley.com/us

First Published (2018)
Austin Macauley Publishers LLC
40 Wall Street, 28th Floor
New York, NY 10005
USA

mail-usa@austinmacauley.com
+1 (646) 5125767

Thanks to my sister, Holly, for her invaluable input and to my daughter, Molly, for her impeccable photography skills.

Some have lavish garments, carry sharp swords, and feast on food and drink. They possess more than they can spend. This is called the vanity of robbers. It is certainly not the Way.
(Tao Te Ching, Chapter 53)

Part One

"Money is power, freedom, a cushion, the root of all evil, and the sum of blessings."

Carl Sandburg

Chapter 1
Trinity Court

It is not the man who has too little, but the man who craves more, that is poor.

-Seneca

To Miranda Grimes, there was no place more enticing than the Dakota Fetch, of this she was certain after having traveled the world over. This jewel, tucked neatly into the Black Hills, was the cattle ranch she now called home.

Her horse trotted obediently about the meadows at her command, adorned with a new leather saddle with her initials more comfortable than she could ever imagine. Although, no dream of hers had ever placed her in a saddle of any sort. Rolling green meadows, split rail fences, barns, and hay stacks abounded for acres on end, this was the stuff her dreams were made of now.

She felt pretty good too, given that only two years before her doctor had announced that she would, perhaps, be dead within six months. At the time, Miranda felt so exhausted and ill that sometimes she wished for it, but her demise, as you have probably already determined, never occurred. Perhaps it was the fresh air at the Fetch that lifted her very soul to an exhilarating height, the peace and quiet that came with every sun up and sundown, or perhaps it was knowing that within this wonderful place, she could love…and be loved.

One might ask whether she had ever been loved before. Perhaps on some level many years ago, she had been, although she had never experienced the level of passion or intimacy that defined her life now. The heavy mantle of a vast fortune, too prodigious to calculate with accuracy, had cloaked her for so long that it was now impossible to penetrate, leaving the true beauty of her soul unknown to many of those around her, even her own husband.

Admittedly, the money dominated everything she did, poisoning her life and that of her two sons, Landon and Colin. They grew up with every material wish fulfilled, shaping them into greedy young men who always wanted more than what they had. Their rampant self-indulgence usually occurred at a whim's notice, as they unabashedly lined their deep, greasy pockets without a single thought for philanthropy. Two seedy unfortunates, they had also become crooked philanderers, the both of them. If jealous husbands were not chasing them, then private detectives hired by jealous husbands were following them everywhere. Incredibly, they were both slippery enough to stay one step ahead of real catastrophe, but, nevertheless, Miranda had made up her mind to, somehow, cut them loose from the vast estate they would one day inherit and all of its nefarious entanglements, not wanting them to be ruined any further. At the time, little had she realized just how far down into that dark hole of greed and evil they had actually slipped, all the more so after having gotten wind of her idea.

So, not knowing this about her two boys and without saying anything to anyone, Miranda privately calculated the ways in which she might divest her sons from the spider web of fortune that had been woven so tightly around them. Could she get rid of the money and give them a life of normalcy? And was it too late for *her* to escape from the stronghold of her vast inheritance, from the life that had no meaning beyond dollars and cents? Her thoughts were desperate and somewhat pathetic. For a person who had everything, she really had...nothing.

As it were, fate would send Miranda on a journey of redemption, allowing her to break free from the shackles of her wealth that had encumbered her for so long. Finally, she could be the person who she really wanted to be, no longer trapped as she had been in the past. Struck as though by a rogue lightning bolt that had prompted her to think beyond the seduction of her fortune, Miranda was now ready to give it all away, for it held little meaning, especially once she was able to envision an optimistic future without it. Besides, she knew she could make a difference by doing some real good.

So, how did Miranda wind up at the Dakota Fetch, you might ask? The road that took her there was a long one that began in opulence, but in order to give the story its due, one must look to the beginning, a time when her estate, the obscenely lavish Trinity Court, defined all the facets of her life. Many aspects of the large house were still so fresh in her mind that she could sometimes close her eyes and envision those days of not so long ago when she was cocooned there, even though it was a place to which she was destined…never to return.

* * *

The magnificent drive into Trinity Court was a splendid display of grandeur and rank not known to many. One might look to the left to see the zoo of docile animals that roamed the grounds—rescues, many of them. The giraffes meandered about the bushes and trees, planted just for them, nibbling and nuzzling, as their life here gave them license to jaunt about the park-like grounds unfettered and without enclosure. Peacocks lit up the beautiful green grasses with lovely plumages of iridescent blue. How delighted was any visitor who, while strolling about the place, could gather the many handsome feathers that decorated the lawns. Lovely sheep, all of them cloaked in the black wool preferred by Miranda, inhabited one particular area of rolling green acreage, protected by the many herding dogs and keepers of the vast menagerie. Tropical birds lived in the trees, which were intricately netted for their protection, while a butterfly sanctuary housed a multitude of colorful species brought in from all over the world. Wallabies hopped about in curiosity as they watched the groundskeepers walk the expanse of the great park tending to the small animals while keeping the velvety grasses clean and trimmed. Foxes scurried in and out of their holes near the gothic-style outbuilding that lodged an illustrious aquarium fully stocked with an impressive array of tropical fish. Several large cats, tethered to their fancy leashes, stalked about the grounds with long cautious strides, seemingly ready to pounce upon any creature that might encroach upon their territory, only to skittishly shy away from the briefest flit or scamper of another animal.

To the right of the drive was a magnificent landscape of gardens, which was cultivated with a wide variety of plants and flowers. Arranged with an artistic stroke of beauty and symmetry, these plots of land were awash with glorious bursts of color that continually unfolded in elegant splendor around the main house. Trellises of clematis covered brick walkways designed to serpentine throughout the tranquil park, which were bordered on both sides by bluebells, buttercups, and pansies. The fragrance of lavender permeated the sweetened air while small gardens of impatience, forget-me-nots, and begonias surrounded the larger areas of gladiolus and sunflowers. Carnations and camellias encircled the garden benches, where one could sit in solitude while fragrant peonies, roses, and lilacs enveloped the imposing statuary with splendor. Poppies, lilies, hyacinth, and chrysanthemum abounded as red and orange hibiscus rounded out an impressive display. Trinity Court's hothouse contained some of the most exotic flowers to be found anywhere in the world, such as Dutch amaryllis, Birds of Paradise, different varieties of orchids, Asian lotus, Hawaiian musa, and a large assortment of anthurium (Lace-leaf), just to name a few. All of these sought after yet ever so fragile, and sometimes rare, varieties might be found adorning the tables and alcoves of the main house on any given day.

Also gothic in its architectural style, the main house of Trinity Court was built by ancestors of the Grimes family in the 19th century. A fortune, made in the manufacturing of textiles that went as far back as the Industrial Revolution, allowed for unabashed extravagance in the creation of this structure, a most magnificent legacy. Surrounding this large, stately home were a dozen or so smaller cottages that housed the various servants, gardeners, and business associates who managed the estate.

In addition to this vast property, were the millions of dollars that had passed down to Miranda, an only child and the latest generation to inherit one of the oldest family fortunes in the country. Having accrued exponentially throughout the passage of many years, the money drenched Miranda in great wealth, although, at times, she felt as though it were drowning her, for she often longed to come up for air.

The cavernous great house no longer echoed with the mischievous laughter of Miranda's two small boys, who were now grown, or the admonishing cries of their flustered nannies. Instead, the grand staircase, a signature feature of the stately entrance hall, crawled with the men and women of industry who conducted their business like ants at a picnic. Up and down the marble stairs they trudged all day long, with papers in their hands, under their arms, and in their briefcases; one side of the staircase leading to the west wing of the house, the other side to the east wing.

The finest marble sculptures created by commissioned artists from all over Europe had a place in every room and alcove. Magnificent oil paintings from centuries past hung on the smooth white walls, from top to bottom. Da Vinci, Michelangelo, Raphael, Donatello, Titian, Bernini, Botticelli, Durer, Caravaggio…the true masters of the house. Frescos, painted on every ceiling, collectively illustrated the stories of the Bible; tapestries in the entrance hall depicted different scenes from the Crusades. The majestic floor-to-ceiling stained glass windows, procured from cathedrals all over the world, enhanced the splendor of the grand ballroom. All the furnishings, ornately carved and centuries old, loomed large in every darkly-paneled room, as did the wood and marble fireplaces into which any person might walk. Many chefs in the several kitchens provided cooked meals and various delicacies for the entire estate, while the wine cellar boasted bottled varieties from over 50 countries.

This was Trinity Court in all of its opulence and splendor—the place of Miranda's ancestors, the foundation of her fortune. It is here where her improbable story began, steeped in the intrigues of this spectacular place. Magnificent in its beauty and grandeur but unforgiving in its suffocation of all those who entered its sphere, Trinity Court was a dichotomy of the chaste and the contemptible. What is most amazing, however, is that Miranda is here to chronicle the incredible journey that took her from the imprisonment of her empire to the wide-open skies of the Dakota Fetch. This is the stuff of which fantasy is usually made, but, as incredible as it may seem, her life was never based on fantasy. It was all too real.

Chapter 2
Madam

Not he who has much is rich, but he who gives much.
-Erich Fromm

"It's time for your afternoon pill, Madam," said the doctor. "It will make you feel better and, besides, you neglected to take your morning pill today. You must feel quite awful by now."

"I feel just fine," Miranda Grimes shot back. "I neglected to take my morning pill because it always makes me sleepy, and I have no intention of taking my afternoon pill either. I have a lot of work to do, Doctor Kessler, so please leave me alone."

"But, Madam, you must know that if you don't take your pills, you'll become sicker and sicker until..." the doctor stopped short.

"Until what? Until I die? Is that what you were going to say, Doctor?" Miranda asked pointedly.

"Well, yes, Madam...that's what I was going to say."

"I'm too busy to die!" Miranda shouted. "Do you see all of these papers on my desk?" she asked rhetorically, not giving him a chance to answer. "Well, every single one of them needs to be read and signed, otherwise no one gets paid, including you."

Miranda was tired and stressed but would never admit that to Doctor Kessler, a man who hovered around her like the grim reaper.

"Madam, it's incumbent upon me to tell you that further test results are inclined to indicate something insidious, something that may get the best of you if you don't take me seriously," said the doddering old doctor, who by now was thought to be a fool by many who lived and worked within the household.

"Oh? Something that might kill me and leave you without a job?" Miranda retorted. How jaded she had become, how cynical, but not too far off when it came to Doctor Kessler. The old man cleared his throat.

"Now, now, Madam. Don't excite yourself. You don't want to take another trip to the hospital, do you? After all, you owe it to yourself and everyone concerned to take care of yourself as best you can." The old man cleared his throat again.

"Everyone concerned? Does that mean you, Doctor? Don't worry…you'll get your money. I have no intention of dying right now," Miranda said with sarcastic assurance. The doctor seemed to breathe a sigh of relief. "And what is this insidious disease that I have, anyway?" she asked, obviously doubtful of the doctor's findings. "You were never really clear about that. Even the trip to the hospital was a folly, the doctors sending me home within 24 hours because they couldn't find anything wrong with me. What is your angle, Doctor?"

"Angle, Madam? I have no angle," he huffed indignantly, "and your father would be horrified at the insinuation that I have anything but your best interest at heart. I can assure you that you are ill, as there are issues with your blood…and your bones. Everything points towards the disruption of normal function in the marrow. I can't quite put my finger on it just yet," he said, waving a bony index finger. "But I'm hopeful that we will get to the bottom of your troubles soon."

"Soon!" Miranda blurted out with a laugh, mocking the doctor. "You've been talking about 'soon' for months now and I still don't know what the hell you're talking about."

"In my opinion, Madam, you may not have long to live if you don't take your pills; as a matter of fact, perhaps only six months. That's only this doctor's humble estimation, of course. Now, be a cooperative girl and take your pills."

Miranda bristled as Doctor Kessler's words reverberated inside her head. *What a doddering old fool.* He had been the family doctor for as far back as she could remember, treating her great-grandfather, as well as her grandfather and father, who, on his deathbed, made her promise to retain the old codger for the rest of his life, this in exchange for years of faithful service to the only patients he had ever known. Yes, that is correct…Doctor Kessler had never treated anyone other than members of the Grimes family. Miranda made that promise to her father because he was a dying man, not because she liked, or even trusted, Doctor Kessler.

He delivered her as a baby, serviced her medical needs right into adulthood, and then, in the continuum, delivered her two sons. Miranda supposed that she could have looked upon it as the natural progression of things, the circle of life, as it were, but she just couldn't. The man had recently begun to give her the uncontrollable creeps, to which he would have prescribed this pill or that if she had told him just how uncomfortable he made her feel. Also, he seemed to come around Trinity Court far too often; every day, in fact, always charging, of course, for services rendered, even if he had only observed a mere pimple. Miranda could see that he was becoming far too greedy.

After her father's death, Miranda had elevated her husband's role in the running of the family business to Chairman of the Board of Directors, giving her more time to raise their two sons. At this post, he worked all-day and halfway into the night before collapsing in utter exhaustion, only to get up within a few hours to tackle the endless work all over again. After only one year, Doctor Kessler had wormed his way into treating Miranda's husband for, what he called, a depletion of the nervous system. *Take these pills,* he would say over and over again. *Take these pills…take these pills.* Within a few short months, the utterly wearied man had dropped dead on the floor from a heart attack.

"He didn't take his pills, Madam," the doctor had said to her.

"What exactly were those pills for, Doctor Kessler?" Miranda had asked.

"For the exhaustion, Madam. I just couldn't convince him to take his pills," said the doctor.

"Wouldn't a simple vacation have solved his problem of exhaustion?" she had asked, distraught with grief.

"Oh, dear me, no, Madam," Doctor Kessler had said. "He needed to be under a doctor's care, but I just couldn't get him to see it that way."

Although she would eventually relent, giving the doctor the benefit of the doubt and reluctantly accepting his way of thinking, Miranda presently realized that her mind must have been temporarily clouded over to believe his assertion. She now understood, all these years later, that he was doing nothing more than keeping himself relevant, in other words: employed. After all, he could never have done that if a vacation, and not the pills, were to actually cure her husband's bad case of nervous exhaustion, effectually rendering his services unnecessary. Miranda couldn't help but ask herself, *Was Doctor Kessler up to his old tricks?*

* * *

"Good morning, Mother," said Landon as he strolled into Miranda's office with his hands in his pockets. "Can't get her to take her pills again, is that right, Doctor?"

"That is correct, Master Grimes," said the old fool as he shook his head. "She refused to take her morning pill and now refuses her afternoon pill. I'm afraid that she is in for quite a setback." Landon flashed a cocky smirk before sitting by Miranda's side.

"Now, now, Mother," he said with a patronizing, disingenuous tone. "Must we treat you like a child? Must we hold you down and force you to take your pills?" he said, taking his mother's hand in his and patting it with feigned concern. Miranda gave him an icy glare.

"For your information, young man, I feel just fine. I have no intention of taking pills that make me feel utterly exhausted and sicker than I probably am." Doctor Kessler and Landon exchanged worrisome glances.

"It's only for your own good, Mother," said Landon in his overbearing manner. "I must insist that you take your pills. After all, I only want what's best for you, and if you can't see that, then your sickness is clouding your judgment," he said as he lit up a cigarette and blew the foul smoke in her direction. "What will happen to Colin and me if something should happen to you? Your two boys would be so lost…and so very, very sad," Landon said in his usual phony manner, his eyes darting back and forth between his mother and the doctor.

"You and Colin?" Miranda repeated with surprise. "Frankly, I find it hard to believe that either of you would give a damn if something were to happen to me. Let's face facts, the only thing that you and your brother care about is the family's money, which seems to run through your fingers as fast as I direct the lawyers to deposit it into your bank accounts. Neither of you should worry. You'll be well taken care of when the time comes, but let me assure you that the time is not here…not yet, not now," Miranda said, spitting her words. "And, as for Doctor Kessler here—" she continued, pointing a finger in the old man's direction.

"Now, Mother, you're being unfair," Landon interrupted. "You know that Colin and I always have your best interest at heart and Doctor Kessler, well, he can only do so much. If you refuse to cooperate, then you'll never get better and all of our efforts will have been in vain. You need to see the wisdom in that. I don't want to lose you, Mother," Landon said, the insincerity oozing out of every pore in his body.

Just then, Colin walked into the room, Doctor Kessler giving him a sideways glance.

"Good morning, Mother. Giving the good doctor a hard time, are you?" he said.

"Well, Colin, I haven't seen you in nearly a week," Miranda said incredulously. "Where have you been?"

"Oh, let's just say that I needed to make myself scarce for a few days," he said with a shifty smile. "How was I supposed to know that the pretty young thing I had met in the bar had a husband?" he said while clearing his throat. "I mean, she came on to me, so I just assumed that—"

"Oh, cut the crap," said Landon. "You met her in a brothel and you know it," he said, smiling.

"What of it?" Colin shot back, not embarrassed by his brother's revelation in front of their mother.

"Enough, the two of you," Miranda coldly insisted. Unfortunately, she had become used to her sons' shortcomings. No longer able to scold them, there was nothing left to admire in either young man. As it were, they never listened to her anyway. For Miranda, the contentious relationship that she had with her sons was a losing battle. "As I told, Doctor Kessler, I have a lot of work to do, so kindly leave my office."

"Alright, alright, Mother. We can't fight you on this," said Landon, rolling his eyes. "You're a grown woman and, if you don't want to take your pills, then so be it." He threw up his hands in disgust. "Let's go and leave Mother to her work," he said to Colin and Doctor Kessler. "It seems that, once again, she's not interested in what we have to say." And, with that, the three men left Miranda's office, after having been pointedly brushed off, without saying another word.

Chapter 3
Dastardly

The person who doesn't know where his next dollar is coming from usually doesn't know where his last dollar went.
-Unknown

"Ah," Colin said, smiling, "here comes one of the servants with Mother's lunch tray. Isn't this a fortuitous situation for us?" he said slyly.

"What are you talking about?" whispered Landon. "Mother has thwarted our plan at every turn. Day after day, we lose more ground with her, and it won't be long before she cuts us off entirely. And Doctor Kessler here is on ice much thinner than ours, believe me," added the worried brother, vaguely gesturing in the doctor's direction. The foolish old man said nothing as he intently listened to the exchange, hanging on to whatever scraps of conversation he could pick up.

"Watch and learn," said Colin under his breath.

As the tray-carrying servant passed the three men, Colin placed a gentle hand on her shoulder and stopped her in her tracks. The startled young girl froze, barely looking at the handsome young master with the scandalous reputation. "Please allow me to take Mother's tray into her office," Colin gallantly requested. "We were just going in there ourselves, we three, so how fortunate for you that we met like this," he said with a dashing manner and a piercing twinkle in his eye. "I don't recall ever having met you," he continued with a bright smile, doing his best to charm the young servant. "Please say that you'll permit me to save you any further steps," he said earnestly, gently placing his two hands under the tray. "By the way, my name is Colin."

The young girl stared at the spurious young man as though in a dream. Handing him the lunch tray, she curtsied slightly and spoke in a shy whisper. "Thank you, sir, I know who you are. My name is—"

"Yes, yes," interrupted Landon. "That will be all."

The young servant girl quickly scurried off as Colin lasciviously watched her from behind.

"What are you up to?" asked Landon quietly. "Mother doesn't want to see us again. She'll only dismiss us as she did before. Why would you want to walk back in there?"

"Don't worry, I have a plan," said Colin, waving away his brother's concerns with a quick hand. "Doctor Kessler," Colin continued, "please hand me Mother's pills."

"What do you want with them, Master Grimes?" questioned the old fool.

"You'll see," answered Colin, his smile now sinisterly crooked.

As he placed his mother's lunch tray on a nearby sideboard, Colin opened the pills that Doctor Kessler had given him and dropped one, and then another, into his mother's soup.

"How do you know that she'll eat that?" asked Landon.

"Oh, she'll eat it," came the ominous assurance. "You know how Mother loves her soup," he said, pursing his lips tightly as he stirred the concoction. "Landon, you follow me, and Doctor Kessler, you stay here," instructed Colin, pointing to a chair as though the doctor were a small child. "We'll require your presence shortly."

"Follow my lead," Colin said under his breath as he and his brother made their way back into their mother's office like two chastised little puppies, tray in hand.

"I dismissed the two of you," Miranda said curtly. "What is it that you want? I'm awfully busy and have no time for any of your nonsense."

"We've come to apologize, Mother," said Colin, contrite and humble as he held the lunch tray in his hands. "We want to tell you how sorry we are for the way we spoke to you earlier and that…well…we love you, Mother. We don't want anything to happen to you, but if you prefer not to take your pills, then that is your decision and we'll abide by it."

"Please forgive us, Mother," Landon chimed in with as much phony sincerity as he could muster. "We're hoping that if you're unwilling to take your pills, then at least you'll agree to keep up your strength…please."

Miranda was flabbergasted and completely taken in by her sons' dishonest overture. "Thank you, boys. I don't know what to say."

"You needn't say anything," said Colin with a smile. "Just eat your soup."

"I believe I will. I'm a bit hungry," Miranda realized, taking off her glasses and rubbing her eyes. Tentative at first, she picked up the spoon and dipped it in the thick concoction of vegetables, noodles, and medication, sipping small amounts at first as both boys nervously looked on. Enjoying its flavor and consistency, she hungrily emptied the bowl of its contents, eating the accompanying slice of toast as well. "That was wonderful, just what I needed," she said, wiping her mouth with a napkin.

"We'll leave you now to conduct your business," said Colin solemnly. "And again, Mother, please forgive us." The two bowed slightly and left the room. Miranda was somewhat perplexed but genuinely delighted by this sudden burst of penitent behavior coming from her two boys. She hadn't seen them act so sensitively toward her, or anyone else for that matter, in quite a long time.

Colin and Landon left their mother's office, still holding the lunch tray with its empty soup dish, and walked straight back to Doctor Kessler. The old man was ever so subtly rocking in his chair while wringing his bony hands.

"Master Colin, Master Landon," he mumbled. "Did she eat the soup?"

"She did," Landon said with a grin, "and enjoyed it too. How long do you think before she…?"

"Oh my, oh dear," the old man sputtered as he stood up, still wringing his hands. "You put two pills in her soup, didn't you? Oh my. It won't take long…it won't take long at all. As a matter of fact," the doctor beckoned with a crooked finger, "follow me." The two boys smiled at one another and anxiously walked back towards their mother's office behind the teetering

Doctor Kessler. *Perhaps now,* they thought, *she would see to reason.*

As they entered the large room, Miranda was lying on one of the many couches that lined the walls. Her eyes were closed and her right hand rested on her chest.

"Mother, are you alright?" said Colin, rushing to her side while Landon and Doctor Kessler stayed back. Miranda opened her eyes and smiled.

"You were right, Colin," she said weakly. "As a matter of fact, you were all right. I should've listened…I should've taken my pills," she slurred. "I feel so sick…and so terribly tired. Where is Doctor Kessler?"

"I'm right here, my dear," he said, coming forward to take her hand. "You see, I was afraid that you were in for this setback, although we ought not continue your pills until I've had a chance to evaluate your condition," said the conniving doctor, knowing that Miranda had already ingested more than her usual dose of medication just by eating the soup. "Don't worry, my dear, Doctor Kessler will fix you up. Don't I always?" he asked perniciously.

"As a matter of fact," began Landon, finally entering the conversation, "we have a proposition for you, Mother." Colin glared at his brother, thinking that it might not be quite the right time to bring it up, while Doctor Kessler looked on with the wide eyes of an anxious accomplice. Landon returned his brother's glare and continued, "You see, we think, Colin and I, that you should enter into this special facility that we've found. Doctor Kessler has assured us that he will make certain that you're well taken care of there. We've looked into the place, Mother, and it's really quite spectacular…one of the best medical facilities in the country. Each patient has their own private doctor in attendance, while being cared for by some of the nicest nurses you'll ever meet. Really, Mother, we feel the time has come for you to know about this facility and seriously consider entering it for treatment…for your own sake and that of the business."

"Oh, I couldn't possibly consider it," Miranda said feebly. "I could never leave all…of…this." Her hand slowly dropped from her chest. Doctor Kessler lifted it gently and felt her wrist for a pulse.

"She'll be fine, gentlemen," he declared, "but she's weak. It's a good time to move her out, and I mean tomorrow," said the doctor with relish. "Now, remember our deal. I stay on as her doctor…"

"And we run the family business, which will give us complete and total access to the money," said Landon, "from which you will be rewarded a considerable pay raise."

"Let's not forget," Colin reminded them, "that we still have to convince her to…sign the papers."

Chapter 4
So Tired...so Weak

That man is richest whose pleasures are cheapest.
-Henry David Thoreau

Dawn came early for Miranda, although she was too weak to open her eyes and see it. She felt just awful, as though someone had hit her over the head with a hammer. She thought about how irrational she had been in refusing to take her pills the day before, only to prove what foolish obstinacy could do to a person. She blamed herself for not listening to Doctor Kessler when she should have as she lay motionless in her bed, far too weak to move. Was the old man correct in his assessment of her health? Did he actually know what he was talking about? The fact that she may have been wrong about the old doctor all along, boggled Miranda's mind and gave her an overwhelming feeling of guilt. She supposed that she owed him an apology, or at least the courtesy to listen to his medical advice from now on.

Her thoughts lingered more so, however, on the kind manner in which her sons had treated her the night before. It had been such a long time since they were contrite for anything, had taken her feelings into account, or had shown any sensitivity towards her whatsoever. Had they done an about face, a mea culpa, for all of their shortcomings? Miranda found it all so difficult to believe, although she could feel the smile on her lips...or perhaps in her weakened state it had only been an imagined smile. Nevertheless, distant voices caused her to stir and finally open her eyes.

"Ah, there you are," said a pleased Doctor Kessler quietly. "You have finally decided to open your eyes. Good morning, my dear. It's so good to see you awake," said the old man, patting her hand while listening to her heart with a stethoscope. "You gave us quite a scare yesterday, but you're going to be just fine, as long as you resume taking your pills."

"But they make me so tired, so foggy," said Miranda weakly.

"That's an unfortunate side effect of the cure, my dear, but you mustn't worry. Doctor Kessler will get you well, just you wait and see."

"I must apologize, Doctor," Miranda said with childlike shyness and embarrassment, "for doubting your motives. Please forgive this jaded patient of yours, because I never meant to…"

"Good morning, Mother!" Landon said in a booming voice, cutting short his mother's apology to the old doctor, as his long strides took him right to her bedside.

"Master Grimes," the doctor shushed him, "please lower your voice. After all, your mother had quite the fright yesterday and she appears, now, to have a headache."

"My head does ache," Miranda admitted.

"Oh, I'm sorry, Mother," said Landon. "I didn't intend to disturb you. I just wanted to make sure that you were feeling better," he said, taking her hand and smiling brightly.

"I'm feeling much better, Landon, thank you," said Miranda, "but I do have a nuisance of a headache," she repeated, placing her other hand on her forehead.

"Well, Mother, that is exactly what I wanted to talk to you about," Landon began. "You see—"

"And how is our sleeping beauty this morning?" interrupted Colin as he slinked into his mother's bedroom, bending down to kiss her gently on the cheek.

"Oh, Colin, I'm feeling much better," Miranda repeated to her other son, "but I still have this annoying—"

"I was just about to *remind* Mother," Landon said loudly to his brother, annoyed by the intrusion, "of the facility that can cure her of her health miseries. Remember that we talked to you about it last night, Mother?" asked Landon, attempting to jog Miranda's memory.

"Oh, yes, the facility," Miranda vaguely recalled, still feeling foggy.

"Yes, the wonderful facility," Colin chimed in, taking the cue from his brother. "What a fright you gave us yesterday, Mother, but this place can help you, if only you would agree to go there." Colin's concern was as phony as his brother's, while Doctor Kessler faded into a dark corner of the room as he relished the possibility of a grand windfall. It was so close…he could taste it.

"Before you go any further, boys, please allow your sick and tired mother to express her sincere gratitude to you for your kindness towards me yesterday. I always hoped that we could be friends, that we could be a devoted family…despite the money," she said breathlessly. Miranda's gaze became distant and vacant for several seconds before she was able to refocus her thoughts, causing her to admit to herself that, perhaps, she belonged in this magical facility if she were to get better…any time soon. "All right, boys, I'm ready to have a discussion," she finally had to admit, sounding forlorn…and defeated.

Doctor Kessler cleared the ever-present phlegm from his throat and took up the conversation on behalf of the two boys. "Miranda, this beautiful facility," he began as he walked out of the dark corner of the room, "has all of the amenities that one could ask for. You would be in a penthouse suite of sorts, my dear, overlooking a great park, and all of your meals would be prepared by some of the greatest culinary chefs in the world. You would have round-the-clock nurses and I'd be your primary doctor, taking care of you every day, just as I do now. If you should require anything further, there's a private hospital right on the premises. Oh, it's a wonderful place, my dear. Many dignitaries, politicians, and royalty visit there," he said craftily, looking at Colin and Landon with a crooked smile, for much of what he said was either greatly exaggerated or just not true…and they all knew it.

"What do I need with dignitaries, politicians, and royalty? It's they who made me ill," Miranda said quietly. "Ever since I was a little girl, I could remember the pressure…the unrelenting pressure…that people like them put on my family. It was they who demanded the most…of my grandfather…of my father…and then of me." Her gaze became distant once again.

"Mother," Landon said quietly, taking her hand, "you don't need to see anyone unless you wish it. The sole point of your stay there would be to get well. Nothing else in the whole wide world would matter."

"Mother, we would come to see you every day," Colin falsely promised, "to check on your progress, because there's nothing more important to us than your health. You *must* allow us to help you get well," he insisted.

"It *would* be nice to feel well again, to feel as though I'm healthy and rested," said Miranda feebly.

"My dear," began Doctor Kessler, "I can't imagine that you would be there any longer than a week; two at the most," lied the deceptive old fool, clearing his throat again.

"How I dreaded the way I might find you this morning, Mother," said Landon dramatically. "I hardly slept a wink for fear that your illness would take you from us in the middle of the night. I regret saying that we can no longer care for you properly here at Trinity Court. Your ill-health requires a setting more conducive to your medical needs and the convalescence that lies ahead of you."

"Mother," Colin interjected quietly, "please allow us to take you to this facility…for your own good." His pleading eyes were like penetrating, dark saucers.

"Why is it that Doctor Kessler can't just treat me right here in my own house?" Miranda asked, Colin turning her question over to the old fool.

"In this wonderful facility," said the doctor with cunning, "I would have the expert assistance of many of my most esteemed colleagues. You see, my dear, if you were to stay here, it would be dreadfully difficult for them to come out to the house to see you, but if you were in this place—this wonderful, magical place—then they would be there every day to attend to your health, as would I, dramatically speeding your recovery. Don't you see, my dear? We're trying to get you there now so that we can bring you home as soon as possible. What a wonderful prospect!"

"Yes, Mother!" said Colin excitedly. "How wonderful it would be to have you healthy again like you were when we were children…before father died, before you became burdened with running the family business. I so long for the days when we would all sit in front of the large fireplace in the Great Hall and roast marshmallows. Do you remember that, Mother?"

"And do you remember our hikes around the grounds?" asked Landon. "We would run up ahead of you and hide behind a large tree. You would then follow our giggles to the nearest mighty oak and pretend that you were a bear, reaching behind the tree and grabbing the two of us in a hail of laughter. We would scream so loudly," remembered Landon, grinning and shaking his head, "and then we would all go back to the main house and have ice-cream. What joyous days those were, when you were healthy enough to be with us." It was obvious that Landon was attempting to pull at his mother's weakened heartstrings, but, on some level, he had touched his own heart, for if one looked at him closely enough, it was easy to see that his eyes had pooled with tears, if only for the briefest of moments.

Colin, Landon, and Doctor Kessler had used their well-rehearsed powers of persuasion to such a heightened degree that Miranda wavered easily in her weakened state. They had sufficiently talked her into thinking that she needed to enter a medical facility in order to become well, a place that would get to the bottom of her troubles and cure them. But what they had actually done, unbeknownst to her, was to talk her into something far different, something far darker.

"I suppose you're all correct in what you're saying. It certainly makes perfect sense," said Miranda. "I feel so tired, so weak. I…I…"

"Now, now, my dear, it's settled," said Doctor Kessler, decisively closing the matter right then and there, his sense of Miranda's inevitable capitulation certain. "Don't trouble your mind any further. It's time now to take your pill."

"Thank you, Doctor Kessler," said Miranda, struggling to utter every word, before slipping the dubious capsule onto her tongue and sipping it down with water.

"Everything will be quite alright now, Mother," said Colin with a smile and a pat on her hand.

"Yes, it will," said Landon. "Quite alright."

As the three watched Miranda slip, once again, into debilitating cloudiness, they decided to make their move. It was now or never, for their mother hadn't the strength to object to anything. The pill had rendered her perfectly compliant.

"Will you do something for me, Mother?" whispered Landon in Miranda's ear.

"What is it?" she whispered back, sleepily touching his cheek and smiling the same way she used to before putting the boys to bed when they were little. Landon bristled and, for the briefest of moments, hesitated to do what they had planned for so long. Regaining his composure, he turned to Doctor Kessler and took a piece of paper out of his hands, placing it in front of his mother while his brother looked on. The room was rife with anticipation.

"Will you please sign this piece of paper for me?" he asked softly as he put the pen in her right hand.

She attempted to read it but then suddenly stopped, unable to bring into focus its exact meaning. Without question or resistance, she put pen to paper.

"Certainly, Landon, if you think that is what's best," Miranda said vacantly.

And with that, as her two sons and the doctor looked on in triumph, Miranda Grimes unceremoniously signed herself into a sanatorium…for the mentally ill.

Chapter 5
Goodbye

Money is like love; it kills slowly and painfully the one who withholds it, and enlivens the other who turns it on his fellow man.

-Kahlil Gibran

As the three men left Miranda's bedside, they could hardly contain themselves. Colin and Landon had accomplished what they had set out to do months before, and that was to render their mother irrelevant. As soon as she signed the paper that was so cleverly crafted by Doctor Kessler, she not only committed herself to a facility that would never agree to release her within a week or two as promised, but she also signed over control of her millions.

"As long as you remember our agreement," Doctor Kessler reminded Colin and Landon. "I stay on as your mother's physician, provided I'm given a considerable pay raise, a much more handsome sum than what I'm receiving presently."

"Yes, yes," said Colin, tired of Doctor Kessler's constant reminders. "Although, perhaps to start, we should retain you at the same fee that you currently receive. After all, what will you be doing differently that would merit an immediate raise?"

"That's correct," agreed Landon as he glared at Doctor Kessler. "The objective here is that Colin and I enjoy a steady flow of cash. With Mother gone for a while, we can do as we wish with the bank accounts without having to worry about lawyers, or doctors, breathing down our necks. If you make a nuisance of yourself, Doctor Kessler, we'll cut you loose," he threatened. "Mother was made to feel obligated to continue your services, but my brother and I feel no such duty towards you. Oh no, Doctor…you will accept what you get, or in an instant we'll be rid of you as well."

"I suggest that you step lightly, Master Grimes," hissed the doctor through clenched, yellow teeth. "Don't forget how you and your brother got to this point…this extremely lucrative point. Without my help, you'd still be begging your mother's accountants for your pitiful allowances," he said, clearing his throat.

"Don't *you* forget where your meal ticket comes from, old man," said Colin, nose to nose with the doctor.

"May I remind you that I know the truth about what happened here," Doctor Kessler answered quickly, not allowing Colin to intimidate him. "You and your brother are up to your necks in chicanery. If you choose to double-cross me, I'll report the entire sordid affair to the police."

"*You* drew up the papers, you silly old fool," Colin retorted. "We're not the only ones who are up to their necks. How long before someone finds out that Mother is not actually ill, mentally or physically? Then what? Are your wonderful papers as ironclad as you guarantee? Remember, the lawyers haven't even weighed-in on this yet, and they surely will, especially Cranston."

"They may, but it will be to no avail," spat the old man promptly. "It is I who has total control over your mother's medical needs and diagnoses. Oh no, gentlemen, you'll abide by our agreement, or, mark my words, heads will roll, and mine's shall not be one of them."

Colin and Landon looked at one another with subtle surprise. They'd always thought the doctor a fool who would accept whatever scraps he got on *their* terms. Clearly, he was craftier than they had imagined and was not afraid, in the least, to assert the power of his position. This was a problem that would have to be dealt with, but for now, it was simply time to say…goodbye to Mother.

* * *

Miranda was barely aware of what was happening as Doctor Kessler directed the upstairs maid to dress her quickly. She was utterly stupefied, as always, by the pill that he had just given her, not quite able to discern what was happening around her. The clever little farce that her sons had played with her the night before, coupled with their combined powers of persuasion that morning, succeeded in getting her to do the unthinkable, in her compromised state: to sign away her very existence. She would no longer be an obstacle to them or anyone else. The empire was now theirs, with all of its trappings of fortune and depravity. This, she would never have done willingly. But Miranda was now under their complete control as they prepared to discard her like trash, and discarded trash is never retrieved from the dumpster…not willingly.

The servants, told that Madam would be on an extended vacation to rest and relax, lined the Grand Entrance Hall to say goodbye at Colin and Landon's command. They wanted everyone to see just how awful she looked, how sick. Her skin was pale, her eyes were fixed in a vacant stare, and her mouth was slightly agape as the doctor wheeled her through the hall and towards the front door. Many of the servants noticeably gasped, especially those who had been with Miranda from the time she was a child. There were still a few of them left, the few that remembered her in her youth, a happier and less complicated time.

"I didn't realize that she was so sick," whispered one.

"Oh, how awful this is," said another, waving a handkerchief in fond farewell.

"Masters Colin and Landon are correct in sending her off," said the head chef quietly. "She appears to have rotted away. What a shame."

Of course, Miranda knew of none of it. She didn't know about the wicked plan, her sons' depraved complicity with Doctor Kessler, or the ruinous little pill that had started it all. She was even unaware of the presence of her servants.

Colin and Landon stood at attention, as though paying homage to a great world leader, when their mother passed.

"Don't worry," Landon spoke softly, indirectly addressing the line of servants behind him as her wheelchair crossed the Great Entrance Hall, "she'll be just fine. We're sending her to a place that will tend to her every need. She'll be home before anyone has a chance to miss her."

Colin agreed with his brother, smiling slightly as his mother passed him by without acknowledgement. "Goodbye, Mother," he said softly, crocodile tears streaming down his cheeks. "We'll be waiting here to welcome you home when you return."

What a grand show it was and nobody was the wiser. Doctor Kessler had wheeled Miranda out of the broad front entrance without having said a word to anyone. Of course, no one else who served within the household ever questioned the old man. He had been a fixture at Trinity Court for so long that his influence over Miranda was taken for granted and, of course, his moral compass was never questioned. Perhaps it should have been; much prior to this.

As she was being placed into the limousine, Miranda's trusted lawyer appeared in the circular drive unannounced. Doctor Kessler never allowed Miranda to be seen by the lawyers when she was in a pill-induced stupor. They would have far too many questions.

"Is that Miranda?" asked James Cranston, her faithful lead attorney for the estate, as well as for Trinity Court Enterprises, as he passed by the limousine and walked towards the front door of the large house.

"It is," answered the doctor nervously. He felt uncomfortable conversing with Cranston without the wily brothers by his side.

"Well, what's going on? Where's she going?" asked the attorney.

"She's going away," answered the doctor off-handedly. "She's not feeling well and has decided to check herself into a place that will…um…solve her problems," he said, stumbling over his words. Of course, as usual, he nervously cleared his throat afterward.

"Check herself into what place? Doesn't a person have to sign papers in order to do that?" Cranston challenged, immediately sensing that something was amiss.

"Yes, a person has to sign papers in order to do that," the doctor confirmed, "and Madam willingly signed those papers this morning."

"Why is it that I knew nothing of this?" Cranston asked angrily. "I *am* her attorney."

"I'm not obligated to share my medical decisions with you, Mr. Cranston," said the old man, "and I resent being questioned for doing my job. Perhaps we'll talk later, after I've gotten her settled," the doctor said dismissively. "At this time, I'm bringing Madam to her destination, so if you'll excuse me," he said brusquely, climbing into the limousine after Miranda.

"And what is that destination, Doctor?" Cranston called out as the limousine traveled quickly around the circular drive and out of sight, the high bushes that separated the house from the road obstructing any further view of the speeding vehicle.

"Cranston?" Landon called out as he and Colin walked out onto the grand portico of the house. "What are you doing here so early, and on a Sunday morning, no less?" he asked, wondering if Dr. Kessler had escaped with his mother unscathed and unquestioned.

"Yes, why *are* you here, Cranston?" asked Colin, always backing his brother. "Remember, Sunday is supposed to be a day of rest." The two boys were phony, for Cranston's rest was of little interest to them.

"So it is," said the lawyer, by now quite concerned, "but I had some papers for your mother to sign this morning concerning the Linwood merger. She knew I was coming."

"We appreciate your work ethic, Cranston, but really, a Sunday morning? Mother never liked to sign papers on the Lord's Day," said Colin with a playful smirk.

"Well, she was ready to sign *these* papers for me today. I just spoke with her on the phone on Thursday," Cranston anxiously replied, pushing the matter.

"Well, if you must know," said Colin, "Mother hasn't been feeling well. She'll be gone for a few days…to recover. Her illness and her nervous condition have finally caught up to her. She needs a rest and a break from signing papers," he said, still smiling. But Cranston wasn't amused.

"On whose authority?" the lawyer asked, his eyes now reduced to slits.

"On the authority of her physician, as well as her own authority," Landon interjected. "Of course, both Colin and I support her decision as well," he said in a calm, measured tone. "Now, is there anything further?"

"I suppose not," said Cranston haltingly. "You'll let me know when she has returned home. I do have these papers and—"

"Oh, yes, of course," said Landon, waving his hand as if to dismiss the bewildered attorney.

"I'll be speaking to Doctor Kessler about this as well, gentlemen," said the rankled Cranston in a half-threatening tone, his eyes piercing with resolve to get to the bottom of all this. He never liked to be left out of any conversation. '*The stakes are always far too high for Miranda,*' he would say.

"If you must, Cranston, but let me remind you, in no uncertain terms, that this is a *family* matter," Landon retorted, emphasizing the word family. "It doesn't involve the lawyers in any way."

"Everything your mother does involves the lawyers," Cranston shot back. "She's a very rich woman."

"We'll call on you when we need you," Landon said curtly, reminding the lawyer of his place. And, with that, both boys walked back into the house and shut the door.

Cranston stared at the ornate, heavy door that had just been closed in his face. He didn't know what to make of all this. What was going on here? Why didn't he know that Miranda's physical and mental state had deteriorated to such a point, and so quickly? He knew one thing, though, that he didn't trust the brothers Grimes in the least after witnessing the evolution of their disreputable characters. Miranda had certainly shared some of the sordid tales from their many shady escapades, even dispatching him, at one point, to pay-off a woman who had been blackmailing Colin. He also knew that he must, somehow, see Miranda's commitment papers. Were they legitimate? The only way he would ever find out would be to speak to Doctor Kessler—as soon as possible.

Chapter 6
Settled In

Money is like muck—not good unless it be spread.
-Francis Bacon

Doctor Kessler arrived at the exclusive sanatorium, tucked neatly and inconspicuously into the far-off hills, with Miranda in tow looking every bit the ill woman he and her sons had created. It was a select place that few could ever afford, a private operation closed to the prying eyes of all authority and the curious. This permitted Doctor Kessler to treat his oblivious charge without question or reprimand, a fine set-up for the doddering old fool of a doctor, who had duped his wealthy patient into committing herself for the wrong reason. It was he who would determine her daily routine, direct the round-the-clock nurses, and control the dispensing of…the pill.

"This is Miranda Grimes," said the doctor upon entrance, "and she's here for an extended stay under my care and my care alone. I believe you'll find that all of her paperwork is in order." In this case, Doctor Kessler was no doddering old fool. With so much money at stake, he was well aware that he had to get this right, or he would find himself banished, or something worse, by the brothers Grimes. "I want her brought to her room immediately," the doctor ordered, "and she's not to have any visitors until I authorize it," he added for good measure. "Remember, she's my patient, exclusively."

"Yes, we have the paperwork right here, Doctor Kessler, and all of your orders are clearly understood," said the compliant nurse, a somewhat shadowy figure in Miranda's confinement, the length of which was indeterminable at this time.

Miranda was immediately wheeled down the long hallway into a suite of rooms that was actually quite airy and pleasant and overlooked colorful gardens and rolling green hills. Upon entering the main room, a bright enough space where Miranda would now pass the long hours of her restricted existence, one could observe walls of stark white, in contrast to the frescos and tapestries found at Trinity Court. There were several oil paintings hung over the simple furniture, brought in from Miranda's personal collection, and a mahogany desk ordered for Doctor Kessler's private and sole use. Many green plants sat on small tables strategically placed around the room while classical music could be faintly heard over hidden speakers. The focal point of the room, however, was Miranda's bed, an all-too-familiar sight in any given hospital with the added feature of hand restraints, just in case.

The bathroom was tiled with Italian marble and equipped with ornate fixtures and beautiful furniture. Comfortable seating inside and outside the large shower enclosure seemed to invite observation of Miranda's daily toilette. An additional sitting room could be accessed through a door on the far side of the bathroom, purposely hidden behind a large exotic plant. This was a more private space that could be used by Doctor Kessler and the Masters Grimes for clandestine meetings and illicit conversations not meant to be overheard by the furtively inquisitive, namely the nurses. These women were certainly dark players too, cognizant of the fact that the patients in this facility had more than likely been admitted under profoundly mysterious circumstances. They were well aware that they worked in a unique place, one incompatible with any other of this kind, under conditions that could fairly be called sinister. Therefore, as human nature would have it, they were morbidly curious by custom, incessantly clamoring for the gossip surrounding each case. To learn of a family secret or hidden scandal, would make them privy to information fit for blackmailing purposes, and that, of course, would never do.

"You'll put her to bed and leave us immediately," said the doctor. "She needs her rest."

"Yes, Doctor, right away," said the obedient nurse as she lifted a groggy Miranda out of her wheelchair and gently placed her on the bed.

After laying her down and covering her with a crisp sheet and soft blanket, the nurse nodded slightly at Doctor Kessler and left the room. The old man quickly proceeded to lock the door.

"Doctor Kessler?" Miranda called out weakly.

"Yes, Madam," said the shady physician, taking her hand as though he deeply cared for her.

"Where are we? What is this place?" she asked, not really able to bring into focus the room, the doctor, or the short conversation he had just had with the nurse.

"You're in a place where you'll be well taken care of, my dear," he answered, patting her hand. "You're quite safe and all you need to do is rest quietly. Now, doesn't that sound easy?"

"I suppose so," she quietly moaned, putting her hand to her head. "I feel so sleepy…so foggy."

"You'll feel that way for a while, Madam. Don't let it alarm you. Until we figure out how to treat your illness, you'll be quite…indisposed," the old man said with a queer sort of smile, finding his accomplishment quite satisfying, for he had pulled it off. Miranda was now under his complete control. "I'll be back to check on you later," said the doctor, "but first you must take your pill."

"My pill? Oh yes," Miranda said faintly. "It will help…me…to…feel…better."

"Now, now, Madam, don't try to talk," said the old man. "You're exhausting what little energy you have left. Take this," he gently ordered as he picked up her head and placed the pill on her tongue. "Now, drink this down," he encouraged, slightly tipping the glass so that the water would flow into Miranda's mouth. "That will do the trick, Madam. Pleasant dreams," the doctor muttered under his breath as he turned around and slowly walked towards the door.

"Doctor?" Miranda surprisingly called out, as loudly as she was able, straining her weak voice. The doctor turned with a start, for he thought she would have lapsed into unconsciousness by now. But…she hadn't.

"Yes, Madam?" he answered warily, his heart suddenly pounding uncontrollably, as though he were the cat that had gotten caught swallowing the canary. "Is there something else that I can do for you?"

"Colin and Landon…where are they? Do they know that I'm here?" Miranda asked faintly.

"They know, Madam," said the doctor, "and they'll be here quite soon to visit you."

"I need to speak with them im…me…di…ate…ly," Miranda slurred before falling into a deep, dark sleep.

Doctor Kessler breathed an instant sigh of relief, dismissing his nauseating paranoia. As deceitful and surreptitious as all of this was, he realized that Miranda couldn't possibly understand what was *really* happening, not in her compromised state. Perhaps it wasn't really she who worried him, after all. The brothers' threats never idle, they could dispose of him, one way or another, if he didn't keep his mouth shut. The old man would have to contemplate, long and hard, his next move before they determined it for him. This, he most surely knew, for it had now become a matter…of survival.

* * *

"The old man must go," said Colin as he smoked his cigarette; the two boys were lounging around in triumph.

"I agree," Landon answered, "but how to do it? That's the question."

"It must never be traced back to us," Colin warned, stating the obvious.

"Of course not," his brother snickered, resting his elbow on the table and placing his chin in his hand, "but we need to decide what we want."

"What do you mean?" Colin questioned, not yet grasping Landon's implication.

"Well, do we want him to just disappear, or do we want something…more than that?" asked Landon haltingly while looking at his brother with dark, piercing eyes. Colin suddenly understood.

"Would you actually be prepared for…murder?" he asked with surprise, not really taking his brother seriously. "I thought we could just drop him off somewhere deep in the woods and leave him to fend for himself."

"He might make his way back…like a lost dog or stray cat," laughed Landon. "No, we have to do better than that."

"What do you have in mind?" Colin asked, suddenly turning serious.

"The doctor must be permanently removed, silenced without any indication whatsoever of foul play," Landon thought out loud, rubbing his chin with his hand.

"How are we going to do that?" asked Colin.

"*We're* not going to do anything," said Landon with a raised eyebrow, as though he had just had a great idea. "Our friendly neighborhood druggist will do it for us," he smiled, quite satisfied with himself.

"You mean Test Tube Tim?" asked Colin with a laugh. "I haven't seen him since he concocted that crazy hallucinogen that had every college student in the state tripping for months. Is he out of jail?"

"He sure is and, once again, open for business," said Landon, stroking the unshaven whiskers on his cheek. "I think we ought to give him a call."

"We're in waist-deep already," said Colin apprehensively, "having committed Mother underhandedly, the way we did. I'm still not convinced that Cranston won't unravel the entire scheme."

"All the more reason to protect ourselves from getting caught," Landon said, trying to reason with his brother. "Tim can do it, and what's important is that he has no obvious connection to us or the estate. He can formulate something for the old man that would make it look like he had a heart attack or something. Use your head, man. It can work!"

Colin looked at his brother and stood up to pace the floor. He rubbed the sudden muscle spasm in his neck as he walked back and forth in front of Landon.

"Heart attack?" he repeated after thinking about what Landon had just said. "I suppose...it's...plausible," Colin mused, wrinkling his nose. Landon smiled because he knew that his brother was relenting.

The two boys were silent for a few minutes, both deep in thought. *Could they really pull it off? Could they keep their mother under wraps while disposing of the old foolish doctor at the same time?* It all seemed so fantastic, this type of plot usually found only in the neighborhood horror flicks. But this wasn't a movie. Both boys looked at each other with dark, foreboding glances as Landon stood up from his chair and picked up the phone. The wheels were now…in motion.

Chapter 7
With Any Luck at All

Capital as such is not evil; it is its wrong use that is evil.
Capital in some form or other will always be needed.

-Gandhi

Cranston was furious. How could Doctor Kessler have made plans to commit Miranda *anywhere* without his knowledge? Something foul was in the air, something that reeked with the stench of deception. Miranda would never have agreed to go away without consulting him first. Who was taking care of the business, handling the household...controlling the money? The entire sordid affair had the shifty brothers Grimes written all over it, their lack of scruples commonly known, with the old man in on it too. Cranston was convinced that the three men were accomplices, involved in some treacherous scheme. Exactly what that scheme was, he didn't know, but was determined to find out.

In the meantime, Doctor Kessler returned to Trinity Court late that very afternoon, rearing to have a frank discussion with Colin and Landon. After all, they had a deal and it was incumbent upon them to keep it. He shouldn't ever have to look over his shoulder for fear of what they might do to him; and the money, of course, was not negotiable. They had already struck their deal days ago. If the boys couldn't play nice, then Doctor Kessler wouldn't play at all, gladly exposing the entire scheme to teach them a lesson. He wasn't going to allow them to intimidate or bully him any further. It was all of these things and more that he intended to say.

"Well, Doctor Kessler, you're back," said Colin, trying to look delighted in the old man's presence. "Mother all settled in, is she?"

"Yes, your mother is quite comfortable," began the doctor. "I've done everything that you and your brother have asked of me. I was able to get her into this facility without my motives being questioned. Her suite of rooms is beautiful and she'll be well-taken care of by the nurses and me. As far as anyone can tell, we've done nothing wrong, nothing…questionable."

"Well, that all sounds just fine," said Colin. "Is there anything else?"

"Yes, there is, Master Grimes," said the doctor. "There is the matter of the money."

"Ah, yes, the money," said Colin. "My brother and I have been talking it over and we don't feel that—"

"We should go back on our original agreement in any way," said Landon as he entered the room, finishing Colin's sentence in the nick of time. "After all, you did us a tremendous favor by getting Mother committed into this place."

"Without my motives being questioned," reminded the doctor, raising his pointer finger.

"Yes, yes, without your motives being questioned," repeated Landon. "So, my brother and I intend to do the honorable thing. We'll uphold our end of the bargain as long as you keep Mother out of our hair for a sufficient amount of time, perhaps a year or two."

"Then, I'll receive the money that was agreed upon?" asked the doctor, double-checking what Landon had just said.

"Yes, you *will* receive the money agreed upon and, perhaps, a bonus when the time is appropriate. Isn't that right, Colin?" Landon said, turning to his brother, who appeared to be confused. Hadn't they agreed that the old man would receive his usual retainer for now?

"Yes, that's correct," said Colin, following his brother's curious lead. "The money agreed upon and a bonus…when the time is appropriate," he bumbled along.

"That's fine, gentlemen," said the foolish old man. "Thank you for doing what is honorable." This was a most welcome and surprising turn of events for the doctor.

"After all, Doctor, we owe you," said Landon, lighting a cigarette. "Let's not discuss it any further. Consider the matter settled."

Doctor Kessler bowed slightly to the two brothers and quickly left the room. He had triumphed, having never experienced such compliant behavior toward him from either brother. Perhaps they were profoundly relieved that the misdeed was finally done or perhaps they were just grateful. One thing was for certain: they now held the purse strings to one of the greatest family fortunes in existence, making them extremely rich…young…men.

"Are you out of your mind?" Colin said to Landon, the doctor now out of earshot. "We're going to give the old man a raise *and* a bonus? Why would you make such a promise?"

"What's the difference?" laughed Landon. "We can promise him the world! It doesn't mean he's going to get it!"

"Then our plan remains the same?" asked Colin, finally understanding.

"It's the same exact plan that we discussed before," Landon assured him. "Nothing has changed. The doctor will pay for his sins…soon."

"And what about our sins?" asked Colin quietly.

"Haven't you been listening to me?" asked Landon, gently scolding his brother. "Our sins will languish in hell before I ever allow them to be revealed by *anyone*. Believe me, we'll pay for absolutely none of this. The family fortune will be ours for the taking…and ours alone…as soon as the doctor is out of our hair," Landon finished with a sinister stare, slamming his fist on a small side table. Colin looked at his brother with a tinge of fear. Had he finally become that depraved…that mercenary? Had they both? Only the dark days ahead would tell.

* * *

As Doctor Kessler slowly drove away from Trinity Court, he glanced apprehensively in the rearview mirror, his paranoia not yet completely gone. The brothers had assured him that he would receive his money and then some, but an ominous feeling of prickles and stings still gnawed at him. Could he be feeling guilty, a pang of conscience, as it were, or did he now know, deep down inside of himself, that he was a marked man whose complicity in the entire sordid affair would eventually have him hanging from the highest tree, probably at the hands of the Masters Grimes? There was far too much to think about, if one really wanted to think at all, but for now he must take the boys at their word. If only the butterflies in his stomach would stop fluttering and flitting about.

The old doctor felt relieved to finally pull into the drive of his house, pondering the situation for only a moment longer before slowly opening the car door. He looked forward to a long, hot bath and a cup of tea. Perhaps, then, his nerves would settle. What was he so worried about, anyway? After all, he was practically a member of the Grimes family, having been with them for so long…wasn't he?

"Good evening, Doctor," came a voice from behind the car. The startled old man flinched in terror, for the Masters Grimes must have come for him, just as he knew they would. He could feel it in the marrow of his old, rickety bones. "I've been waiting for you. We need to talk." Doctor Kessler, feet frozen to their spot, slowly peered over his shoulder.

"Oh…Cranston," the doctor managed to spit out in relief, his chest heaving uncontrollably. His pounding heart, audible within his ears, was unforgiving and relentless. "What is it that *you* want? I've already told you that, as Madam's physician, I have every right to treat her as I see fit." The old man took a white handkerchief from his coat pocket and wiped the beads of sweat from his brow as he climbed out of the car. All of this was an unbearable inconvenience far too much for him to tolerate.

"Something is quite wrong here," said Cranston in a low, measured voice, "isn't there, Doctor?"

"There most certainly *is not*, Mr. Cranston," said Doctor Kessler. "What right have you to follow me home, anyway? Is this a threat?" asked the old man, attempting to look incredulous and credible at the same time.

"I had every right to follow you home, especially considering that I think my client may be in danger," answered Cranston. "Where is she? Where have you brought her? Answer me, you silly old fool," said the annoyed attorney. "I won't move from this spot until you tell me where I can find Miranda Grimes."

"I'll tell you nothing," spat the doctor. "It's none of your business, I say."

"Then I shall call the police," threatened Cranston. "Perhaps they'll get you to tell me."

"I doubt that," countered the old man. "Every policeman is tucked neatly into the large pocket of Trinity Court, and you know that, Counselor. If you were to call the police," warned the doctor, pointing a bony finger in Cranston's face, "they would immediately call the Masters Grimes, who would, in turn, tell them that nothing was wrong and that Madam was fine…end of story. The police would never even attempt to investigate your inquiry, believe me," said the doctor confidently, "not to mention the fact that you'd certainly incur the wrath of the boys." The attorney looked at the doctor long and hard, knowing that the silly old man was probably correct. "I assume, Cranston, that you need your job just as much as I need mine," the doctor said slowly, inferring that things were better left unsaid. "Good night, Cranston," said Doctor Kessler as he slammed the car door and slowly walked towards the house stooped with the undeniable burden of treacherous complicity.

Cranston stood there and watched as the doctor entered the front door of his modest home and closed the door. He thought that he would have gotten much further with the old man, but, in the end, he knew that the doctor was absolutely right: anything that happened within the closely-guarded sphere of Trinity Court could be conveniently covered up if the brothers so wished it. Nevertheless, Cranston feared that time was running short for Miranda Grimes—wherever she was.

As he turned to leave the doctor's long drive, his car parked inconspicuously on the street, Cranston stopped short. He had a nagging feeling that something was not quite right…something in the way that Doctor Kessler had left his car and walked into the house. Quickly, he trotted over to the driver's side door of the car, keeping an eye on the old man's house at the same time. Peering into the car's window, Cranston immediately had his answer. Of course!

Slowly opening the unlocked car door, he grabbed the handle of a worn leather briefcase, the familiar accessory that Doctor Kessler carried at all times, and pulled it out of the car. After closing the door without slamming it, Cranston briskly walked down the long drive towards his own vehicle, all the while hugging the briefcase tightly to his chest. With any luck at all, a clue to Miranda Grimes' whereabouts would be discovered within the confines of the forgotten leather bag. Doctor Kessler, in the meantime, was inside making himself a hot cup of tea. He was unaware that his luck was just about to…run out.

Chapter 8
Bag of Tricks

If we command our wealth, we shall be rich and free. If our
wealth commands us, we are poor indeed.
-Edmund Burke

Cranston drove home as quickly as he could, actually speeding at times but only once running a red light. He knew, however, that he should avoid being pulled over if he didn't want to be found in possession of Doctor Kessler's old leather briefcase, a potential gold mine of information for which others would pay dearly. If the brothers Grimes were ever to become aware that probable evidence of their mother's whereabouts was no longer in the old man's hands, they would pursue any means to get it back, a potentially fatal affair in which Cranston wanted no part. Still, he couldn't help but feel giddy over his luck at having appropriated the briefcase from the unlocked car without getting caught. It was just like finding buried treasure, the pirate long gone…or preoccupied with his own guilt for the plundering of Miranda Grimes' life.

After looking over his shoulder for just a fleeting moment, Cranston promptly entered his dark house, again holding the old leather briefcase tightly to his chest. Immediately locking the door behind him, he turned on the kitchen light and sat down to open the case. His heart pounded with eager anticipation as a number of papers spilled out onto the table in front of him. *There must be something here, some type of clue that might indicate the whereabouts of Miranda Grimes,* he thought, an intense anxiety making him dizzy.

Cranston gathered up the papers on the table and placed them in a neat pile before beginning to sort through them.

There were a number of clothing and restaurant receipts that had no bearing on Miranda Grimes' whereabouts, along with paperwork from the doctor's mechanic and an old program from a theatre in town that was now closed. Far from discouraged, Cranston continued to look through the contents of the briefcase, setting aside two well-worn gloves and a pair of eyeglasses that had a slight crack in the left lens. He smirked briefly at these irrelevant things that the old man kept before spotting, what appeared to be, another receipt at the bottom of the case.

Fishing the wrinkled paper out from the very depth of the leather bag, Cranston could see that it was a prescription made out in Miranda Grimes' name for Valium. Had she been taking Valium? It wasn't an irregular or even surprising discovery, Miranda had been under an enormous amount of pressure lately and more high-strung than usual, given the abhorrent behavior of her two sons. Nevertheless, he placed the prescription carefully off to the side, the first piece of interesting information that he had found.

Cranston's heart sank, as he could see that only one more thin packet of papers remained at the bottom of the briefcase. If it proved to be of no consequence or value, then he must consider himself at an official dead-end, his efforts to find Miranda Grimes in need of redirection. If the papers somehow verified that he was on the right track in his search for the missing heiress, then his theft of the doctor's briefcase would most certainly merit a pardon, the offense having been committed for the higher good.

As he retrieved this last piece of potential evidence, Cranston closed his eyes, almost afraid to hope for the needed clue. He slowly brought the papers close to his face and held them there with two trembling hands before opening his eyes and focusing on the content. There was an official letterhead at the top of the first page and a couple of signatures at the bottom, with plenty of small print in between. Cranston needed to gather his thoughts and calm down, for there it was, exactly what he had been hoping to find.

Taken from the bottom of a leather briefcase left by accident in the unlocked car of an old fool, Miranda's faithful attorney had struck pay dirt. The large bold letters at the top of the first page read:

The Mountain Valley Sanatorium
For The
Addicted and Mentally Ill

Quickly scanning the page to the very bottom, he could read the clear signature of Doctor Kessler beside the unusually shaky signature of Miranda Grimes. Shuffling through the rest of the packet while hungrily scanning its contents, two other signatures jumped off of the last page, causing the attorney to gasp: Colin and Landon Grimes. Miranda had committed herself with the help of her physician and two sons, but did she sign under duress or perhaps in complete ignorance of what she was doing?

Cranston was dumbfounded as he placed the copy of Miranda Grimes' commitment papers on the kitchen table. He sat for several minutes in numb disbelief before gathering his scattered thoughts. How would he approach the situation? Did the prescription for Valium have anything to do with it? The attorney slowly began to realize the implication of what he had just found, which reeked to high heaven with the foul stench of treachery and deceit, two character traits highly attributable to the Masters Grimes.

* * *

In the meantime, Doctor Kessler had settled down to his hot cup of tea, completely unaware that he had left his briefcase in the car. He sank down in his old, overstuffed chair in front of the stone fireplace in the den, a blazing fire having already been lit by his loyal housekeeper, who was now gone for the evening. She was aware of his stress, for he confided many things in her, especially as they pertained to his dealings with the Masters Grimes. As the doctor's trusted confidant, even *she* knew of their guiling ways, their threatening and dangerous natures.

But it was here in this chair that the old man would try to forget about the duplicity in which he was involved and concentrate on clearing his mind. He would see Madam in the morning, but, until then, there was no sense in pondering the matter any further. After all, it was just business, just a part of being employed by one of the wealthiest families in the country. The Masters Grimes said that they would pay him, so it was best to just leave it at that. The old doctor was not afraid of Cranston either. The signatures on the commitment papers were perfectly legitimate; all four of them.

Doctor Kessler closed his eyes, his teacup now empty in his lap, as he tried to fall asleep in front of the fire. Something alarmed him, however, as he opened his eyes with a start. Something was wrong, strangely amiss. Where was *his* copy of the commitment papers, the thin packet that was handed to him after he deposited Miranda Grimes at the Mountain Valley Sanatorium? What did he do with it? He didn't indiscreetly leave it lying around somewhere…did he? The doctor thought about it carefully. Ah, yes…it was in his briefcase, and his briefcase was on the kitchen table…or was it? He didn't remember carrying it into the kitchen. Did he leave it at Trinity Court? Of course not! He remembered now. It was still in the car. A wave of relief came over him.

Just the same, the old man was aggravated at himself for having left the briefcase in the car. Just as he was getting comfortable, he now had to get up and go back outside to retrieve it from the front seat. How annoying. His nice hot cup of tea had relaxed him too, so much so that his legs felt like rubber. He actually had difficulty getting out of the chair. As soon as he stood up, he felt lightheaded, almost faint. The old doctor figured that he better make his way to the car quickly and then come right back in and go to bed. The day had been intolerably disquieting.

Doctor Kessler made his way out of the den and into the kitchen. He walked slowly, bracing himself against the walls and holding on to the table before reaching the back door. Turning the knob with great effort, the old doctor felt worse as he walked out onto the driveway, even though the night air was breezy and cool on his face. Shuffling with great effort toward the car, he intended to quickly grab the briefcase and get back into the house. How fatigued he felt…how drained. It was a strange feeling too. His muscles suddenly felt sore and it became difficult to breath. Struggling to inhale deeply, his chest got heavier and heavier.

Finally reaching the car, Doctor Kessler opened the driver's side door, knowing that he had left it unlocked; a bad habit. He was horrified as he stared down at the empty seat. The old leather briefcase was just not there…not on the front seat, the backseat, or even in the trunk. It was not in the car at all. What could have happened? The old man was now in a panic, sweating profusely and bewildered as to the whereabouts of his old leather bag. Then, it suddenly occurred to him.

"Cranston," the old doctor whispered to the night air. "He has the bag…and everything in it." Doctor Kessler just stood in the driveway frozen with fear, not quite sure of what to do before suddenly dropping to the ground. The silly old man would never have to worry about the Masters Grimes, Attorney Cranston, or his briefcase ever again, for, as it were, he was stone-cold dead.

Chapter 9
Dawn

*The real measure of your wealth is how much you'd be worth if
you lost all your money.*
-Unknown

Miranda Grimes opened her eyes after a dreamless night. She
stared at the stark white ceiling, hung over and foggy, as usual,
after having taken the pill. Where was this place? She looked
around the room and recognized nothing. Could this be Trinity
Court? She thought that she had been in every room, known the
décor of every nook and cranny. Miranda had completely
forgotten about signing the papers that had placed her here; she
had no memory of taking the pills given to her by Doctor
Kessler; and she didn't remember the conversations with her
two sons that ultimately pushed her into locking herself away.

"Good morning, Mrs. Grimes," said the nurse upon
entering the room. She was an old woman, quiet in her
demeanor, who knew exactly what to do. She had apparently
been given her orders, no doubt passed down by Doctor
Kessler.

Miranda couldn't yet speak, the mist in her head shrouding
her ability to function. Oh, she tried to say something, even
opening her mouth, but the words wouldn't pass her lips. Had
the words even left her brain? If they had, they were now lost
somewhere in the mist. Frozen to her sheets, Miranda was in a
stupor that she couldn't shake. Unable to talk or cry out, her
darting eyes conveyed her fright.

"There, there, Mrs. Grimes," said the nurse in a calming
voice, "don't be alarmed. You're safe here. Your family must
love you very much to have placed you with us. We give only

the best of care. Now, open your mouth, my dear, and take your pill."

Placed, thought Miranda. *I was placed here? Who placed me here…and why?*

The nurse lifted Miranda's head off of her pillow and deposited the familiar pill on her tongue. Providing small sips of water, she encouraged Miranda to swallow.

"That's right, my dear. You'll feel so much better now. Close your eyes and relax. Your doctor will be here soon…quite soon."

Placing Miranda's head back onto the pillow, the nurse quietly slipped out of the room. Miranda could feel herself gliding into a black hole. She desperately tried to hang on, wanting to speak to someone about all of this, but to whom could she speak? To…whom…could…she…speak? As if turning off a light, Miranda Grimes was back in the netherworld, floating in an existence of nothingness. There was no one to speak to, not today; even the nurses didn't yet know that Doctor Kessler would never return.

***

The Masters Grimes were triumphant, having disposed of their mother, and soon the meddlesome Doctor Kessler would be out of the picture too.

"It was really quite brilliant," Landon gloated, rubbing the whiskers on his cheek.

"What was brilliant?" asked Colin.

"The way our friend figured out a way to get rid of the doctor," Landon laughed.

"And just how is he going to do that?" Colin inquired.

"Are you ready for this?" said Landon, ready to tell a juicy story. "When I spoke to him—"

"You didn't speak to him on the phone, did you?" Colin interrupted, obviously overtaken by sudden panic. "Our entire cover would be blown if someone were to examine phone records. My God, we'd be finished before having even begun!"

"Would you calm down," Landon ordered his brother. "I didn't speak to him on the phone. As a matter of fact, I know that Tim doesn't even have a phone for that very reason."

"Well, how did you communicate with him then?" Colin asked, visibly relieved.

"Let me tell you," Landon said quietly, looking over his shoulder, for the servants tended to lurk. "We met over on Route 54 at a little-known rest stop and quickly wandered off into the nearby woods before anyone could see us. We had a nice little chat," Landon smiled, gloating over his cleverness. "Tim asked me all about the old man; his likes and dislikes…things like that."

"Why?" Colin whispered.

"Because he needed to figure out a way by which he could infiltrate the doctor's life with some sort of inconspicuous approach," Landon answered his brother.

"I don't get it," Colin said with a puzzled look.

"Think about it. No one would ever suspect foul play if the silly old man kicked off while eating his favorite food, drinking his favorite beverage, or smoking his favorite cigar."

"I suppose not," said Colin.

"So, I gave Tim a list of Doctor Kessler's indulgences, the ones I was aware of anyway: the blackberries that he likes to pick off of the bushes in his backyard every day; the glass of wine that he allows himself every Sunday afternoon; the cherry tobacco that he always smokes in his pipe—" Landon listed, only to be interrupted by his brother again.

"Hold on," said Colin, putting a hand up. "You've lost me again. Why would Tim need to know about berries, wine, and tobacco?"

"Let me finish my list before I explain," said Landon, continuing his item-by-item catalogue of the old man's indulgences. "He also likes to eat dried fruit and peanuts fresh from the shell. And oh, yeah, I almost forgot," said Landon, snapping his fingers. "He drinks a hot cup of loose tea every night before going to bed."

"How do you know all of this?" asked Colin. "I mean, you seem to know the old man more personally than I thought you did."

"I listen, little brother," Landon said shrewdly. "I eavesdrop, I pay attention. You'd be surprised at what you can learn if you just keep your ears cocked. Whenever the doctor spoke with Mother, the servants, Cranston, or even just talked to himself, I listened. You never know when you'll pick up useful information…remember that."

"I will, from now on," Colin said with a smirk.

"And the reason why Tim needed to know about things like berries, wine, tobacco, and all of the rest is because he has to find a way through which he can get the silly old man to ingest…you know." Landon didn't want to say it out loud.

"Ah, now I get it," said Colin, as though struck by an epiphany, "but how is he going to pull it off? How will he even get close enough to those things to, you know, poison them?" he whispered.

"That's *his* worry," said Landon with a grimace. "Believe me, he's being paid dearly to do this for us. Besides, I've known Tim to slip in and out of houses before without detection. He'll find a way of getting inside the doctor's house unnoticed, loading one of those items with poison, and then leaving the premises without being seen by a single soul. That's what makes him the consummate reprobate that he is."

"I guess you're right," said Colin, raising his eyebrows and exhaling loudly, "but I still think it's a crapshoot. Suppose the doctor doesn't want to eat peanuts, or smoke his pipe, or drink his wine?"

"Then he'll eat his dried fruit or drink his hot tea. Don't worry so much. Tim will figure it all out. It may not happen immediately, but I would say that within the next two or three—"

"Excuse me, sirs," said one of the servants upon entering the room. "There is someone here to see you."

"Oh, for Heaven's sake, who wants to see us this early in the morning?" asked Landon, decidedly annoyed.

"It is Doctor Kessler's housekeeper and she seems to be quite upset," said the servant.

The brothers exchanged quick glances. Colin felt a painful pit in his stomach, his thoughts running wild like a freight train. *Tim must have been caught,* he thought immediately, *and if he was caught, then we're caught too. The plan was far too sketchy to be carried out anyway. There were too many variables, too many possibilities in which it could easily go awry. We're in for it!* Colin felt as though he would be sick as he stood up from his chair.

"Thank you," said Landon to the servant as he looked at his distraught brother. "Give us five minutes, then show her in."

"Yes, sir," said the servant, not having noticed Colin's distress. She immediately left the two boys.

"Get that terrible look off your face. You're going to give us away if you're not careful," Landon warned his brother.

"I know," whined Colin, "but what the hell would she be doing here? Your friend must have been caught," he bemoaned, assuming why the housekeeper was there.

"You don't know that," Landon said, chastising his brother. "Lighten up, and keep your mouth shut. I'll take care of everything." Colin obediently sat back down and relaxed his facial features as best he could.

After exactly five minutes, the servant returned, this time with Doctor Kessler's housekeeper by her side.

"That will be all," Landon said to the servant, who promptly left the room, his eyes now intensely trained on the housekeeper.

"How can I help you?" Landon said to the obviously distraught woman.

"It's Doctor Kessler," she said, now beginning to sob.

"There, there, my dear lady," Landon said, patting her on the shoulder. "What about Doctor Kessler?" Colin apprehensively watched the exchange.

"I found him this morning, dead in the driveway," the woman broke down, her tears flowing freely.

"Oh, no!" Landon said loudly, feigning upset. "How did it happen?"

"I have no idea," she said, shaking her head while blowing her nose.

"I'm so sorry," Colin said, finally joining the conversation. "He always spoke kindly of you; the two of you must have been very close."

"I was devoted to him for almost 25 years," she bawled uncontrollably. The two boys looked at one another, never having thought that Tim could have pulled it off...so soon.

"We know how you must feel, because this is a tremendous loss for us too," Landon said, exhibiting false grief. "After all, the doctor was in our employ for many years." He extended his long arm around her shoulders. "We thought of him as a member of the family."

"I know that," acknowledged the housekeeper. "That's why I came to you first. I know he had no other family."

"That was smart of you," said Colin while nodding his head, looking to his brother for approval of his innocuous remark.

"I thought so," said the housekeeper, who, by now, had calmed down a bit.

"Where is the doctor's body now, my dear?" asked Landon softly.

"Oh, of course I called the proper authorities right away," she said with sweet innocence.

"Of course," Colin repeated.

"They took him away in an ambulance," she continued, blowing her nose again. "I was so distraught that I went into the house and began to make myself a hot cup of tea. I thought, perhaps, that it would calm me down." The two boys exchanged glances once again. "Curiously, I found *this* buried deep inside the doctor's tea caddy," she said, referring to something that she held gently in the palm of her partly-closed hand. "If it weren't for the one corner inadvertently sticking up out of the loose tea, I might have never even seen it," she said, suddenly quite collected and stony in her demeanor. Presenting Landon with an empty packet marked *potassium chloride,* she soberly said in measured words, "Someone made a very…stupid…mistake. Would you boys know anything about that?"

Chapter 10
Tail Him

Money is good for nothing unless you know the value of it by experience.

-P.T. Barnum

Cranston had made up his mind. He would go to the Mountain Valley Sanatorium to see Miranda Grimes. Perhaps she had committed herself voluntarily, but perhaps she hadn't. If Doctor Kessler and the boys had been keeping her drugged with Valium, then she may have signed the papers unknowingly…or against her will. Cranston didn't put it past either of the Masters Grimes to bully their mother into unwittingly signing her life away, especially if it were made easier by an incapacitating drug. If memory served, Miranda had never mentioned to him that she would be entering a sanatorium, and she told him everything. It was all too suspicious.

And what about this place? Cranston wasn't familiar with it, nor had he ever even heard of it. He picked up the phone and called several lawyer friends, inquiring about the facility…its whereabouts, operational procedures, specialties, and the like…but none of them knew anything about it and, like him, had never even heard of it. After several hours of fact-finding, Cranston concluded that Miranda Grimes' commitment to the Mountain Valley Sanatorium was probably ironclad; well beyond the reach of the law. His first instinct was to go back to Doctor Kessler's house and demand that the old man take him there. He knew, though, that he would only get a curt brush-off by doing that. If the doctor was working in tandem with the oily Masters Grimes, then he knew that he would receive no cooperation from him, or them, for that matter. Cranston rightly surmised that Miranda's vast wealth was the dangling carrot, the reason that they had her committed, and Kessler and the boys would chase it for as long as they had to, or until they got caught, in order to obtain control of the fortune that had eluded them thus far.

Now what? Cranston had hit a dead end. Where was this place? He had no way of knowing. Suddenly, the phone rang.

"Is this James Cranston the attorney?" asked the detective from the other end.

"Yes, it is," Cranston replied. "Who's this?"

"This is the police department in town. We're calling to inform you about a Doctor Horace Kessler. Do you know him?" asked the detective.

"I do. What's this all about?" asked Cranston.

"I regret to inform you, sir, that Doctor Kessler is dead," he said.

"Dead? What happened?" asked an appropriately stunned Cranston, immediately thinking that this bad news had the Masters Grimes written all over it.

"Apparently he had a heart attack," said the detective. "His housekeeper found him this morning in the driveway near his car."

"A heart attack?" asked Cranston curiously. He couldn't help but wonder if the old man had dropped dead while going out to his car to retrieve the old leather briefcase.

"So it seems," said the detective.

"That's too bad. How can I help you?" asked Cranston, a little puzzled as to why *he* was getting this phone call.

"Well, your name was found among the papers in the doctor's bedroom," said the detective. "Other than his housekeeper, you were the only other contact that we found. What was your relationship to the doctor?"

"I'm the lead attorney for the Trinity Court estate and all of its enterprises, and Doctor Kessler was the family doctor there," said Cranston. "I guess that made us co-workers."

"Oh, I beg your pardon, sir," said the detective, now realizing the importance of the person to whom he was speaking. "Trinity Court is well-known to the department."

"Yes, I'm sure it is," said Cranston, his voice tinged with sarcasm as he thought about what the doctor had said only the night before about how every policeman was tucked neatly into the large pocket of Trinity Court, all of them on the take.

"If I may ask, when was the last time you spoke with Doctor Kessler?" asked the detective.

"A few days ago," Cranston said quickly, confident that no one had seen him come or go from his encounter with Kessler last night, a meeting he was not yet ready to divulge to anyone. "Why do you ask?"

"Just routine, sir," he said. "Were you aware that the doctor had traveled into the hills yesterday?"

"No, I wasn't aware of that," said Cranston, his ears perked. *This could be the clue that he needed to locate the Mountain Valley Sanatorium.* "Where into the hills, Officer? The hills cover a lot of territory."

"We found a roadmap in the glove compartment of his car to the town of Cloudy Mountain with a piece of paper stapled to it," said the detective.

"A piece of paper?" asked Cranston. "What did it say?" He was jittery with anticipation.

"Nothing much," he said, "just yesterday's date…and something that looks like *Pebble Hill Pass* written underneath it. Hard to tell."

"Hmm, that's not ringing any bells for me," said Cranston as he grabbed a nearby pencil and quickly wrote down what the detective had just said with a shaking hand. *This was it. Pebble Hill Pass in the town of Cloudy Mountain. This was where he would find Miranda Grimes.*

"Is there anything else?" asked Cranston. "I have an urgent appointment that I must get to on time."

"No, that's all, sir," said the detective, having been cut short.

"If there's anything else that I can assist you with, please let me know," said Cranston, endeavoring to sound as cooperative as possible.

"We will, sir," said the detective. "Thank you for your time."

After hanging up the telephone, Cranston quickly threw a few belongings into a duffle bag and headed for his car. He would immediately head to Cloudy Mountain before it got dark, determined to find out what had happened to Miranda

Grimes. Come hell or high water, he would liberate her from that shadowy sanatorium, even if he had to do it surreptitiously. In the meantime, the chief of police gave his order to the detective who had just spoken to Cranston on the telephone: 'Tail him.'

* * *

"My dear Madam, whatever do you mean?" asked Landon, feigning incredulity. "Are you asking if we had something to do with Doctor Kessler's death? How dare you? He was like…one of the family," Landon repeated, cracking his voice with choked-up grief for effect. The wily housekeeper was unimpressed.

"I know about the two of you," she said, her voice deeply somber. "The doctor told me all about your bullying ways, your dangerous dealings…your threatening demeanors," she scowled, her eyes now reduced to slits.

"What reason could we possibly have for wanting to harm the doctor?" asked Colin while lighting a cigarette.

"I'm sure there were several reasons," she said, "all having to do with money."

"Tread lightly, dear woman," warned Landon.

"I'm not afraid of *you*," said the brazen housekeeper. "There is nothing you can say or do that could intimidate me," she declared.

"Why are you here?" asked Colin flat out. "Only to make awful and dangerous insinuations? What is it that you want from us?" Landon looked at his brother with a furrowed brow, afraid that he might say something to incriminate the both of them.

"Frankly, I don't give a damn what she wants," said Landon, standing up from his chair. "I would appreciate it if you would leave our house," he said, pointing to the door. "You've insulted and wounded us deeply."

"I have no intention of going anywhere," said the housekeeper, "except to the police. What do you have to say about that?"

"I have nothing to say about that," said Landon quickly. "We're sorry that the doctor is dead, but we had nothing to do with it; your threats mean nothing here, dear lady."

The housekeeper just stood there staring at the boys intently. She thought that they were playing their cards dangerously, a fact that she could almost admire. They certainly were every bit the formidable snakes about whom Doctor Kessler had often spoken. Could it possibly be that they were innocent of any wrongdoing? Who else would try to poison the doctor or want him dead? Only the Masters Grimes would have the resources to pull it off. Except for one thing, they didn't quite pull it off, not neatly anyways. No, she would stand her ground. She would ask, not demand, that they take her threat seriously. Then, perhaps, they would see their way clear to compensating her…for her sorrow.

Landon, in turn, stared back at the housekeeper just as intently while waiting for the other shoe to drop. Why else would she be there other than to blackmail them? He knew that if they gave in to any monetary demands, then that would be as good as an admission of guilt in a court of law. However, if she did, indeed, go to the police, they might very well trace the dirty exploit back to him and his brother with some good old-fashioned detective work, something that he had never thought possible…until now. He never thought it possible that Tim could make such a grave error either. What was he thinking? How could he make such a stupid mistake as to leave the empty packet of poison in the doctor's tea caddy? Landon's head now swirled with uncomfortable, paranoid thoughts.

"Well, perhaps my threats *should* mean something here," said the housekeeper ominously.

"What do you mean by that?" asked Landon, trying to buy some time as he mulled over some possible solutions to this mess in his head.

"I mean just this…" spat the housekeeper, quite confident in her blackmailing ability, "I want a million dollars to go away, to forget that I have ever met the two of you, to compensate me for my faithful service to the old doctor, and to deter me from going to the police. That is what I mean."

Colin took a good, long drag of his cigarette while Landon rubbed the whiskers on his cheek. She had them, in a way. Of course she would never see a penny, but Landon supposed that they had to play the game…for now.

"All right, my dear," said Landon, seemingly agreeable to her proposal. "I suppose that a million dollars is fair for, let's say, nothing more than many years of faithful service to our dear doctor." Colin, once again, was unable to infer his brother's true intention, sitting there with his mouth slightly agape.

"I'm glad that you finally see it my way," said the housekeeper, thinking that she had gotten away with something, just as Doctor Kessler had.

"Come back tomorrow," said Landon. "I'll have the money for you, in cash of course."

"Do you think I'd be stupid enough to come back here?" she asked with a laugh. "You could never guarantee my safety here. I want us to meet again in a public place," she demanded.

"What safer place is there than Trinity Court?" asked Colin, trying to allay the housekeeper's fears. "The house is filled with business people and servants all day along. We're never alone here."

"That's true enough," said the housekeeper, considering what Colin had just said.

"As a matter of fact," began Landon, "to show you that our only intention is to act in good faith, please join us tomorrow afternoon for luncheon at 2:00. There will be other guests present, and it will be then that we will give you your money. After that, we'll never have to see each other again…correct?"

"That's correct," said the delighted housekeeper.

Landon called out to his nearby valet, who entered the room immediately. "Jenson, this dear lady will be joining us for luncheon tomorrow. Please inform the cook to make something special."

"Yes, sir," Jenson nodded before leaving the room.

"Wait a minute," said the housekeeper, now having second thoughts. "Suppose you decide to poison me too?" she asked. "I'm not going to fall for *that*. Do you think that you're dealing with some kind of dolt?"

"We'll be surrounded by many witnesses, my dear lady, all eating the same food as you," laughed Landon. "Do you think that *I'm* the dolt here? Oh, no, I guarantee your safety on the strength that you'll never show your face around here again," he said with carefully measured words. "Besides, a million dollars means nothing to me, but a blackmailer who attempts to draw from the well more than once will arouse in me a dangerous displeasure. Do we understand each other?" he asked darkly.

"Perfectly," she said curtly before turning on her heels and leaving the room.

The brothers Grimes remained silent for a few minutes, both of them ruminating over what had just happened.

"The gall," Colin finally said. "A million dollars is a lot of money. How could you let her get away with that? And you invited her to luncheon too!"

"Believe me," said Landon with a sly smile, "she's gotten away with nothing."

"What are we going to do?" inquired the unimaginative Colin as Landon tapped his fingers on the table.

"Don't you worry about it," Landon said as he picked up the phone to make a call. "Don't you worry about it at all," he repeated in an ominous whisper while waiting for someone to pick up on the other end. His thoughts had obviously turned dark, once again.

Thunder suddenly wrapped the house in a tenacious grip. *A foreboding sign of what was to come,* Colin thought. The large house, suddenly enveloped in darkness, seemed to be at the mercy of a wicked force descended only to empower the Masters Grimes in their treachery. Something nefarious was about to happen—once again.

Chapter 11
Cloudy Mountain

Happiness is not in the mere possession of money; it lies in the joy of achievement, in the thrill of creative effort.
-Franklin D. Roosevelt

Cranston sped off toward Cloudy Mountain not at all certain that he would find the Mountain Valley Sanatorium when he got there; but he was determined to launch a thorough investigation into the whereabouts of the facility if he had to. He had never been to the area before, a three-hour drive from where he lived, but he could tell from the map that it was high up in the hills.

A place without distinction, Cloudy Mountain had a small population of third and fourth generation families that lived their quiet lives tucked into the gentle, wooded slopes. Cranston wondered whether or not anyone in that area ever questioned the existence of the sanatorium that he eagerly hoped to find on Pebble Hill Pass. Or perhaps they just looked the other way, like many people do when they don't want to get involved in a controversy, detrimental as it may be.

As he drove toward Cloudy Mountain, anxious anticipation making it difficult to concentrate on his driving, Cranston thought about Doctor Kessler. He was convinced that it was not just coincidence that the old fool had dropped dead right after committing Miranda Grimes to the mysterious sanatorium. Something didn't add up, and in the sphere of Trinity Court, when something didn't add up, it usually carried the stench of Landon and Colin Grimes.

Landon was the seedier of the two, the one most likely to do something heinous, but Colin was morally bankrupt as well.

Did they have the doctor killed and, if so, just how did they do it? Cranston was certain that the boys were in no way distraught over Doctor Kessler's death, neither of them having an ounce of sympathy in their nature. He felt badly, though. The old man must have gone back outside to retrieve the leather briefcase that had been inadvertently left on the front seat of his car; the briefcase that he had stolen. Briefcase or not, if the doctor was the targeted victim of the Masters Grimes, as Cranston believed he was, then his demise was inevitable, time and place to be determined by murderous fate.

Continuing to drive up into the hills, the air now filled with mist, Cranston was fixed on his mission. Small cabins could barely be seen from the road as his car snaked around and around into the vagueness of the mountain pass. He looked for a place to stop where he might find directions, but there was no such place. He really didn't want to just pull up to a cabin and knock on the door. Suppose strangers were unwelcome here. Secluded and quiet, Cloudy Mountain seemed quite capable of harboring secrets. Cranston would have to proceed with caution.

As luck would have it, a roadside bar and grill presented itself off to the right, a small establishment that held very little charm but might provide exactly what the lawyer needed. He could certainly go for a beer, but what he really wanted was some conversation. Someone might be willing to chat about Cloudy Mountain, its inhabitants, and the Mountain Valley Sanatorium for the Addicted and Mentally Ill. At the very least, he needed to find out how to get to Pebble Hill Pass.

Cranston entered the bar and grill to find two gentlemen sitting on bar stools. Both men were ragged and weary with character and age. They looked as though they could be lumberjacks or loggers, their tough and calloused hands gripping beer glasses filled with dark lager. Both men smoked, hanging a gray cloud over the room. Cranston sat on an empty stool at the end of the bar, not wanting to seem too eager to talk. Giving him a sideways glance, the two were decidedly unimpressed with the stranger and continued to drink their beers.

"What can I get you?" the bartender asked Cranston.

"I'll have what they're having," he said, pointing to his left at the only other patrons in the bar. That caused one of the men to look his way. This Cranston interpreted as an opening to introduce himself.

"Hello, fellas," he said, getting up and extending a hand. "My name is Jim Cranston. I'm just passing through here." Neither of the men, whose edges were obviously rough, said a word or offered their hands in return. The opening had been slammed shut and Cranston wisely withdrew his hand, but he would still fish for information.

"I'm looking for Pebble Hill Pass. Can either of you tell me where that is?" he asked. The bartender exchanged looks with the two scraggy men.

"What do you want with Pebble Hill Pass?" asked the bartender.

"I need to find a place that may possibly be located on that road," Cranston answered, grateful that someone, anyone, was willing to engage him in conversation.

"Oh, you must be thinking of a different road," the bartender said, shaking his head. "Pebble Hill Pass is desolate. You won't find anything up there. As a matter of fact, the drive along the pass can be dangerous, especially for strangers who aren't familiar with these parts," he said, placing a glass of dark lager in front of Cranston.

"No, I'm thinking of the correct road," said the attorney, contradicting the bartender. "As a matter of fact, I would appreciate it if you could point me in the right direction."

"Strangers ain't got no business on Pebble Hill Pass," said one of the men suddenly, his voice coarse, as though it had been raked through small pebbles. "Didn't you hear what he said?"

"I heard," said Cranston in a measured tone, "but I still need to get there. Is there some law against it?" he asked, staring straight in the eye of the cantankerous character.

"No, there ain't no law, but there ought to be," the man said, raising his voice. "Nothin' good ever happens on Pebble Hill Pass, so you might as well just turn yourself around and get off the mountain," he said in a threatening tone. Cranston took a sip of his beer and threw a five-dollar bill on the bar, feeling more unwelcome by the minute.

"I'm sorry if I upset you," Cranston said, making a general statement to the room. "I think it's probably best if I leave now."

"That's smart thinkin'," said the other man, who was just as cranky. "Strangers ain't too welcome around here, so the sooner you leave, the better."

As Cranston stood up to exit the bar, the bartender suddenly disappeared through a backdoor. The lawyer's interest in finding Pebble Hill Pass had now been peaked by the enigmatic words of the three men, finding the road suddenly an urgent quest. He carefully moved towards the door, nodding in the direction of the two ill-tempered men, who glared at him ominously, intent on getting out of there in one piece. Walking through the small gravel parking lot, he could see the bartender coming around from the side of the small building.

"Hey, wait up!" he shouted to Cranston, who stopped in his tracks. "Did I hear you say that your name is Jim Cranston?"

"That's right," said the lawyer.

"There was a man here looking for you earlier," said the bartender. "He grumbled that you took a different fork than he did coming up here, so he lost track of you."

"You mean I'm being followed?" asked Cranston.

"I suppose so," said the bartender. "He showed a badge. Who are you, Mister?" Cranston realized that it was time to trust someone with his story.

"My name is James Cranston and I'm an attorney looking for Pebble Hill Pass so that I can get to the Mountain Valley Sanatorium for the Addicted and Mentally Ill. I have a client whose commitment there is questionable and I'm looking to get her out. Now, can you help me find Pebble Hill Pass, young man…or not?" said the out-of-breath lawyer.

"We're not really supposed to talk about Pebble Hill Pass, *or* the sanatorium," said the bartender.

"Why not?" Cranston asked.

"It's just understood in these parts, that's all," he said.

"Would this help?" Cranston asked, pulling a 100-dollar bill out of his wallet. The young man looked at the bill and then at the determined lawyer, slowly taking the money from his hand while crumpling it into a closed fist. As though he were afraid that someone would overhear him, the bartender spoke softly under his breath, "Down the road, about 10 miles from here, take a right and then drive up the pass for as far as it will take you. I think you'll find what you're looking for."

"Thank you, young man," Cranston said. "You have two menacing gentlemen staring out of the front window of the bar, so I won't shake your hand."

With that, the lawyer and the bartender turned and slowly walked away from each other. At least Cranston now knew where he was headed. Pebble Hill Pass *did* exist, and the bartender seemed to know about the sanatorium. Hoping for his sake as well as the bartender's that the two rough men inside of the bar were unable to interpret what they had just witnessed in the parking lot, Cranston jumped into his car and sped off. With any luck, the police would never catch up to him.

After having driven 10 miles down the road, Cranston took a right, just as the bartender had directed. Following the pass for as far as it would take him, he could see a large building perched high on a hilltop in the near distance. Gothic in nature and shrouded in mist, the structure looked like it could have been a castle, or a prison. Wrought iron grates over every window accented the worn stone of the imposing edifice, and a long drive brought Cranston straight to the front entrance. It looked as though he had found his sanatorium.

Without delay, Cranston got out of the car and rang the bell that hung next to the impressive, albeit old, wooden door that was marked by many small cracks and crannies. Several minutes passed without anyone answering, causing him to ring the bell again. Another several minutes having gone by, Cranston now grew impatient. Ready to walk around the property to find another door or any sign of life at all, he walked down several stone steps before the door slowly creaked open.

"May I help you?" asked the woman who was dressed in a nurse's uniform. Cranston quickly turned around and bounded for the door in one leap, skipping several steps.

"Yes, you can. I'm looking for Miranda Grimes. Is she a patient here?" asked Cranston.

"Who are you?" asked the nurse.

"I'm her lawyer," said Cranston.

"I'm sorry. There is no Miranda Grimes here," said the nurse sweetly and calmly, as though trained to respond that way to any stranger.

"I beg to differ with you," said Cranston, presenting her with the commitment papers. "This is the Mountain Valley Sanatorium, isn't it?" the lawyer asked firmly.

"Why…yes it is," said the nurse, taken aback by Cranston's preparedness. "However, I cannot permit you to see her," said the stubborn nurse, changing her tone while admitting at the same time that Miranda was, indeed, there.

"On whose authority?" Cranston asked incredulously.

"On the authority of her physician, Doctor Kessler," said the nurse, who was now getting quite snippy.

"I'm here to tell you that Doctor Kessler is dead," said Cranston. "You'll never see or speak to him again. You must allow me to speak with Miranda Grimes," the attorney begged. "I have a hunch that she was placed here under shady circumstances." The nurse stared at him for a few moments before speaking.

"Can you prove that Doctor Kessler is dead?" she asked.

"No, not tonight," said Cranston. "I have no proof of that with me."

"Then I cannot help you," she said while slowly closing the large door. "I have my orders."

"I'll go to court," threatened Cranston, "and get an order from a judge!"

"All of her paperwork is in order," the nurse said calmly, peering through what little space was still left. "I cannot help you." And with that, the door was completely shut.

Cranston stood there in silence, having been turned away like a door-to-door salesman. Remembering that he had passed a small motel before ascending Cloudy Mountain, he decided to backtrack and try again in the morning. He would have to come up with a plan, though, that would allow him to infiltrate the sanatorium. The good thing was that he had found Miranda Grimes. The question was: how would he get her out of there in one piece and without the knowledge…of the Masters Grimes?

Chapter 12
Luncheon

Never spend your money before you have earned it.
-Thomas Jefferson

Landon made frequent trips to the kitchen before the luncheon, speaking to the head chef of Trinity Court more than he ever had in the past.

"We've a special guest coming today, a good friend. I ask that you prepare luncheon as though we were expecting royalty," he ordered.

"Yes, sir. Everything is in order and luncheon will be sumptuous," replied the proud chef, the delicious aromas from his cooking pleasantly wafting through the warm air of the kitchen.

"May I see the menu?" asked the unscrupulous brother.

"Of course, sir," he said, nodding compliantly. "I believe you will be pleased."

Walking over to his small desk in the corner of the kitchen, the chef picked up a freshly-printed menu and handed it to Landon. It was certainly impressive:

Wines
Sherry, Champagne, Merlot, Sauvignon Blanc
Soups
Asparagus Cream Soup, Chowder Françoise
Main Courses

Shrimp Scampi, Chicken Francaise, Beef Bourguignon Tarts, Trout a Aleman, Fillet of Duck Marsala, Mutton Chops with Garden Fresh Mint, Fresh Peas, Asparagus with Hollandaise

Sauce
Desserts
Cold Peaches, Sorbet, Crème Brule, French Pastries
After Dinner on the Private Patio
Coffee, Digestifs, Chocolate

"You're correct, I'm quite pleased," Landon concurred with a slight smile on his face. "This is a luncheon fit for a king." If nothing else, the scandalous brother was quite adept at being complimentary. Whether it was sincere or not, no one knew, including Colin.

"Will there be the usual number of people attending luncheon, sir?" asked the chef.

"Yes, the usual number…a dozen or so," said Landon in a matter-of-fact tone. He wanted everything to seem typical; absolutely nothing was to appear out of the ordinary.

"If I may say so, your guest must be quite special, sir," the chef sincerely commented.

"Oh, quite special indeed," Landon repeated deceptively. "I look forward to hosting her and I'm sure the other guests will take delight in her as well. Carry on then," he ordered the head chef, the spider leaving the kitchen with nothing left to do but wait patiently for his fly…or so it seemed.

Distinguished people, including captains of industry, bankers, and operating officers of the estate, descended upon the large dining room at 2 o'clock sharp. There were three sizeable round tables carefully situated in one corner of the capacious room, set beautifully with the finest of English bone china and sterling silver. Flowers from the hothouses rested perfectly in the center of each table, emanating a sweet fragrance that only they could, the envy of several prominent French perfumeries. Landon and Colin sat at one such table with Mr. Gilliard, liaison for the European Association of Textile Trade, a group currently in negotiations with the estate.

"Please leave that fourth chair for my special guest," directed Landon to no one in particular. "She should be here presently."

"Alright," said Mr. Gilliard softly, a classy gentleman, who then pulled out his chair from the table and sat down quietly. "I will make sure that no one sits here," he said as he unfolded his napkin with the gold brocade and placed it on his lap. Colin just nodded at his smiling brother, not sure what was going to happen here today.

Landon stood and gently clinked his crystal glass with a fork, invoking prompt silence. "I welcome you to this grand luncheon at Trinity Court," he said in a commanding boom. "I've invited all of you here as my special guests to say thank you for all of your hard work and to introduce each one of you to someone new. Together, we'll invigorate our business and increase its great relevance in the high world of finance. I encourage you to speak to the guests seated at your table and, after we've eaten, mingle with those who were not seated with you. Talk things over, make agreements, come to understandings, and initiate plans," he said flamboyantly, waving his hands, "all to strengthen our position, here and abroad!" Landon's comments were greeted with cheers and applause. He smiled as he raised his champagne flute in a brief toast: "Long live Trinity Court!"

The guests toasted exuberantly and immediately began to engage in lively conversation as they drank their champagne in anticipation of a lavish meal. Landon waved the wine stewards into the room to pour the select wines that were chosen specially by him from the wine cellars of the estate. Out came the extravagant soups and sorbets, meats and cheeses, vegetables and fruits, and breads and pastries. It was a meal fit for a king, just as Landon had said. The guests ate, drank, laughed heartily, and engrossed themselves in high discourse. It was a fine gathering of brilliant minds, and Landon made certain to get up from his seat several times throughout the meal to visit the other two tables. Each time he sat back down, he made it a point to comment to Mr. Gilliard that the special guest he was waiting for still had not yet arrived. "I wonder what could be keeping her?" he mused each time. Colin just shrugged, not having been let in on his brother's plan. He figured that the less he knew, the better. Landon figured the same thing, preferring lately to keep his nervous brother in the dark.

After gorging themselves, the guests got up and mingled, just as Landon had told them to. Retreating to the private patio for coffee, digestifs, chocolates, and cigars like everyone else,

Colin found himself deep in conversation with Mr. Gilliard discussing the European economy and the willingness of foreign associations, such as his, to work with large American companies. The conversation would have been interesting enough to someone else, but Colin couldn't care less about the European economy and whether or not Trinity Court could impose itself on the sagging European textile industry. Such things bored him. Thankfully for Colin, Landon once again interrupted the conversation by gently clinking his coffee cup.

"Ladies and gentlemen, it bears mentioning that a guest who I had been expecting never arrived at our luncheon. I don't know what kept her, but it must have been something important, I'm sure. Since I don't believe that she'll be joining us, given the lateness of the hour, I want to say a few words of thanks to this dear lady for all that she's done. I'm sure that you've all heard by now of the death of our dear Doctor Kessler. He was a fixture here at Trinity Court and was in our employ for many, many years before recently succumbing to a heart attack. Well, this kind woman served as his faithful housekeeper for almost 25 years. She was devoted to him and saw to his every need. That's why I pay tribute to her today for taking such good care of our fine doctor, which in turn allowed him to serve my family well here at Trinity Court for so many years. Therefore, it is to her that my brother Colin and I are eternally grateful and, of course, may God bestow His bountiful blessings on Doctor Kessler."

"Amen!" shouted everyone on the patio, raising coffee cups in one final toast.

Soon afterwards, all of the guests departed, thanking Landon and Colin for their hospitality. Some would go back to their offices in the great mansion, while others returned to their respective banks. Mr. Gilliard would board a boat the very next day for Europe. Colin didn't know if their conversation would reap any benefit for Trinity Court, but he was grateful to be done with it. He felt the entire luncheon tedious and found himself on pins and needles after it was over, wondering what had really happened to the blackmailing housekeeper.

"You sure poured it on thick," said Colin to Landon after everyone, including the servants, had left the private patio.

"What did you expect?" asked Landon with a smirk. "No one must ever *really* know how we feel about that damn housekeeper. That would give everything away…which I will not allow," he growled through his Cuban cigar.

"Give what away?" asked Colin. "Where's the housekeeper? What's happened to her?"

Landon drew deeply from the rich tobacco of his lit cigar, loath to answer his brother for fear that someone would walk back onto the patio from the house. Besides, Colin was beginning to annoy him, especially the way he was getting so nervous about everything lately.

"I have no idea what happened to her," said Landon, smirking as he flicked his cigar ashes onto the symmetrical tiles of the patio floor. "Something must have held her up, but I'll be damned if I know what it was."

"You'll be damned, alright…straight to hell," Colin said to his brother, not believing him one bit. "Of course you know. You never had any intention of paying her off, so where is she?" he repeated. "What have you done to her?" Colin's skin crawled with anxiety. He was dying to know what had happened to the blackmailing housekeeper. Why wouldn't his brother tell him?

"I told you not to worry about it and I meant it," said Landon, taking another long draw on his cigar. "Things always have a way of working themselves out."

"What do you mean by that?" asked Colin.

"This conversation is becoming irksome," Landon snipped. "I told you that—"

"Excuse me, sir," interrupted Jenson, causing both brothers to flinch as he quietly walked onto the patio.

"Yes, what is it, Jenson," snapped Landon. "We're having a private conversation here."

"I thought you might like to know, sir, that the guest you were expecting for luncheon has been found."

"Found?" repeated Landon. "Found where?"

"In a ravine, sir. There are news reports that she accidentally drove her car off of the road, causing it to flip over several times into a deep ravine. When the police arrived, the car was lying on its roof, the tires still spinning, and the woman inside the car dead."

"What a shame," Landon uttered in a well-rehearsed tone of grief, shaking his head somberly. "That will be all, Jenson, thank you," he said, quietly dismissing the servant. Saying nothing further, Jenson nodded respectfully and left the patio. Blowing smoke rings into the air, Landon gloated as he looked at his brother.

Colin was drawn in by Landon's darkly ominous eyes. What had really happened? How did his brother do it? Colin took a deep breath before deciding not to question Landon any further, simply looking at him in steely silence.

Landon smiled at his brother coldly while flicking off the ash of his cigar one last time. Standing up from his chair, he turned his back and slowly walked across the patio towards the French doors of the house, mumbling in a barely audible voice, "I told you not to worry about it, didn't I?" Colin had to admit, that was *exactly* what he had told him.

Chapter 13
The Plan

Many folks think they aren't good at earning money, when what they don't know is how to use it.

-Frank A. Clark

Cranston returned to the base of Cloudy Mountain and checked into the dilapidated, seedy motel, which was situated far off the road. As he lay on the bed, nibbling on a large crisp apple that he had thrown into his duffle bag, he ruminated over and over again the potential options that might facilitate the successful rescue of Miranda Grimes. He could brazenly storm the place, locate her quickly within the confines of the facility without permission of the personnel, and then run her the hell out of there before anyone could catch them. *How silly,* he thought. That would never work; after all, this wasn't a movie. What were the chances, really, that he could get in there, locate her quickly, and flee, the both of them, without being seen or stopped? Not a chance.

His second and more reasonable option was to go to court and legally press for her release, but that could take days, maybe even weeks. Besides, even though he knew a few judges, he also knew that they, too, were deep in the pocket of Trinity Court, just like the police. They would quickly notify the Masters Grimes and then all hell would break loose. No, he needed to get Miranda out of there quickly, preferably tomorrow. If only he could get in there…

Cranston tossed and turned as he tried to sleep, unable to stop mulling over and over again in his mind the various plans that he had conjured up, only to dismiss them all as improbable and ill-conceived. The circumstances that brought him to

Cloudy Mountain were certainly far-fetched and dangerous, and he wasn't even aware yet of the further tragedy of Doctor Kessler's housekeeper. The bodies were piling up fast, but Cranston had no intention of getting caught in the inescapable, sticky web so broadly cast by the Masters Grimes; this their means of intimidation and treachery. No, he wouldn't allow himself to fall victim to that, and he made a vow to himself, right then and there, that once he freed Miranda from the sanatorium, never again would she ever fall victim to it either.

Suddenly, Cranston sat straight up in his bed, an epiphany of sorts having struck him with an idea that just might work. Perhaps he wouldn't have to approach this thing alone; perhaps there was someone out there who might be willing to help…for a price. He would get up early the next day and return to the bar and grill on Cloudy Mountain, certain that it was there where he would find his accomplice, despite the two cantankerous characters who blatantly concealed the existence of the sanatorium. Having made up his mind to give the idea a try, Cranston fell fast asleep.

Returning to the bar and grill early the next day, Cranston parked his car in the small gravel parking lot and waited for the place to open. He would sit in his car for as long as he had to, but, as it so happened, he didn't have to sit for long. As though he knew that the determined lawyer would be there awaiting his arrival, the young bartender sped into the lot and parked his typical mid-size car, distinguished only by its dull paint and numerous dents, under a large oak tree. Either he had no money to drive something better or he didn't care what his vehicle looked like, and Cranston was hoping for the former.

"Excuse me, young man," Cranston said as he got out of his car.

"Oh, it's you again," said the bartender as he walked up to the door of the small building and unlocked it. Cranston followed closely behind as they entered the bar.

"You know, those two guys grilled me after you left here yesterday," said the young man. "They wanted to know exactly what we had talked about in the parking lot, even though they had already figured out it had something to do with Pebble Hill Pass. If they catch me here talking to you again, they'll beat the crap out of me…and you."

"Would you be willing to help me get a client of mine out of the Mountain Valley Sanatorium…for a price, of course?" asked Cranston, cutting to the quick of the matter.

"Boy, Mr. Cranston, you sure have a way of getting me involved in things that are none my business," said the young man.

"I figure you know the area and might be willing to help me out if it paid well," said the lawyer. "You look like you could use the money…you certainly took it yesterday without hesitation."

"That was different. You weren't asking me to go up there with you. Maybe there are a couple of things that you ought to know," said the bartender, finally deciding to come clean. "You see, my mother works up there as a laundress, and anyone who works up there is sworn to secrecy, or else they can be run off the mountain…or worse."

"What do you mean, *or worse*?" Cranston asked.

"Those two men that you met here in the bar and grill yesterday, well, they're my uncles," said the young man with a bit of a quiver in his voice, "and they've been known to rough up anyone who comes sniffing around Cloudy Mountain uninvited, especially if they mention the Mountain Valley Sanatorium."

"Is that a fact?" commented Cranston, nodding his head. "Why would they do that?" he asked. "What are they trying to hide?"

"The place isn't exactly legit, if you know what I mean," said the bartender. "Being the ruffians that they are, they were hired by people in high places at the sanatorium to fend off anyone who attempts to get too close to the truth about the place."

"So, it's a real family affair, is it? Your mother works up there and your uncles play the bouncers. How cozy," said Cranston sarcastically, shaking his head. "Why haven't the police ever been able to figure out what's going on up there? All those people locked up against their will."

"Oh, they know," said the young man. "They're paid well to stay away. You see, all of the patients up there are extremely wealthy, and their money helps to sustain the mountain and its people in a lot of ways…except that," the young man said in a low voice, hanging his head in what appeared to be shame, "they've all been committed there under less than justifiable circumstances by greedy relatives who want them gone."

"Power and money do all the talking, a lot of people get paid off, and everybody is happy, is that it?" smirked Cranston.

"That's it," said the bartender, "and, in exchange, the only thing we're expected to do is steer inquisitive strangers clear off the mountain."

"So, the sanatorium pays your bills," said Cranston, "for just keeping quiet."

"In a way," said the young man. "It isn't lucrative, but it helps.

"Making what you did yesterday an extraordinary thing," Cranston said as a compliment, hoping that this would be his opening. If the bartender could be bought once, then he could be bought again. "I'll give you 500 dollars if you'll help me," he said in a low voice, placing a hand on the young man's shoulder.

"You don't seem to understand, Mr. Cranston. That could be dangerous for my mother…and for me," he said.

"It's all I have left in my wallet," said the lawyer. "If I had more, I'd give it to you. Besides, the police from my town are tailing me…you said so yourself. They may be just as crooked when it comes to being bought off, but they're not vested in this depraved, God-forsaken mountain. They might just get a little too curious about what really goes on up here and blow the top right off of this massive heap of rock you call home. And, guess what?" Cranston asked, impulsively grabbing the young man's arm, "You and your entire family would blow with it."

The bartender retreated into deep reflection and remained there for several minutes, pacing back and forth in front of Cranston while kicking the gravel in the small parking lot. He felt conflicted, thanks to all the years of conditioning that he should never speak to anyone about the sanatorium, but he also felt trapped by the lies and deceptions with which he grew up. The hairs on his arms were suddenly raised, now that he was being given the opportunity to finally break out of the repressive mold of Cloudy Mountain and its secrets. He finally decided that the offer was generous enough to persuade him. If they could make their move in such a way that it would cause no harm to his mother—or alert his boorish, bullying uncles—then he would do it. The young man stopped pacing and decisively walked back to Cranston.

"Okay, I'll do it," he said. "I hope I never regret it."

"You won't be sorry," said Cranston, slightly smiling as he pressed the 500 dollars, finely rolled up, into the bartender's hand. "This is what we have to do."

* * *

As the two men sat in Cranston's car, the lawyer realized the importance of the bartender's collusion immediately. Not only did he know the layout of the sanatorium, but he also knew the wing in which most of the patients lived and how to get there without being detected.

"My mom has been working there for many years," said the young man. "She comes home every night, we sit down to dinner, and she talks about her day."

"What do you talk about?" asked Cranston.

"All kinds of things," he said. "We talk about the place itself, the patients, the daily routine…things like that."

"Has she ever spoken about my client?" asked Cranston.

"She may have. She speaks about the patients all the time, but the people who work in the laundry are never told their names or the circumstances under which they've been committed," he said. "It doesn't matter, though; you can be sure that they all come from money, and their families are rich and powerful enough to dump them there without interference from anyone, not even the courts."

"I suppose you can't get any more clandestine than that," said Cranston.

"I suppose not, but I can get us in there, alright. You just have to trust me," said the bartender. "They've known me up there since I was a kid and they'll never suspect a thing if I show up."

"I have no choice *but* to trust you," said Cranston seriously. "There's one thing, young man. I don't know your name."

"It's Eric…Eric Weaver, Mr. Cranston," he said, extending his hand.

"Please, call me Jim," said the lawyer, shaking the young man's hand warmly. "But how are you going to explain *my* being there, Eric? Remember that one nurse has already seen me…she shut the door in my face."

"Don't worry, I won't have to explain *your* being there at all, because no one will actually see you," said the bartender. "Let me clarify. I thought that maybe we could drive up there and then…"

A loud tapping on the car window suddenly interrupted the conversation, causing both men to jump.

"It's that detective who was looking for you yesterday," said Eric, sinking a little in his seat.

"Don't worry, we haven't done anything wrong…yet," said Cranston, slowly lowering the car window. "Is there anything I can do for you?" he asked in an annoyed tone of voice.

"Excuse me, Mr. Cranston," said the detective, showing a badge. "May I speak with you?"

Cranston got out of the car and slammed the door.

"What about? Remember that I'm an attorney, Detective, and I want to know why you're following me," Cranston demanded, pulling his identification out of his wallet.

"I'm well aware that you're an attorney, sir. I spoke with you on the phone the other day regarding the death of Doctor Kessler," he said.

"What about it?" Cranston asked. "I already told you everything I know."

"Yes, sir, but do you know a Margaret Housner?" asked the detective.

"The name sounds vaguely familiar," said Cranston, squinting his eyes, trying to place it.

"She was Doctor Kessler's housekeeper," said the detective. "State police found her dead inside of her car, which was found off of Route 139 flipped over in a deep ravine. Would you have any idea, sir, why the doctor and his housekeeper might have both turned up dead within a day and a half of one another?"

Cranston intently looked at the detective, debating in his mind whether or not to tell him the suspicions he had concerning the Masters Grimes: that they had their mother committed to an illegal sanatorium under dubious circumstances and then had Doctor Kessler killed as well. Now, the fact that the old man's housekeeper was dead too only confirmed those suspicions. Only Landon and Colin had the money and the power to dispose of 3 people within 48 hours. But the detective, who Cranston had never met until today, could also be in the deep pocket of Trinity Court and the treacherous brothers. The savvy lawyer decided to play it safe.

"I'm sorry, Detective. I know nothing about it. I simply can't help you," said Cranston.

"Well, thank you, Mr. Cranston. If you can think of anything, please give me a call," said the detective, slipping the lawyer a card.

"I'll do that," said Cranston. And, with that, the detective was gone.

Cranston got back in his car. Undeterred, he and the young bartender continued to discuss how they would gain entry into the sanatorium in order to rescue Miranda Grimes. The young man's knowledge of the large building's layout would prove invaluable and his mother, without her knowledge, would be the linchpin of the entire scheme. It would work. It had to. In the meantime, the detective would continue his plan as well: to tail Cranston.

Chapter 14
Inside

When I have money, I get rid of it quickly, lest it find a way into my heart.

-John Wesley

Cranston and Eric drove up Cloudy Mountain and onto Pebble Hill Pass in separate cars, both advancing around the winding pass in the same destination. Would the plan work? Cranston thought that it looked plausible on paper but remained skeptical as to whether they could really pull it off.

"Keep in mind, young man, that we're not play-acting in a movie," Cranston warned. "These people are dangerous. There's enough money up there to make you and me disappear without a trace...forever." Eric, on the other hand, was much more optimistic. *Perhaps because of his youth,* Cranston thought.

"Don't worry," he said, smiling broadly. "I know my way around up there. Nothing will go wrong. I promise." As he had acknowledged earlier, Cranston had no other choice but to trust the young bartender. His priority was to find Miranda Grimes and get her out of there, and this was the only way to do that right now. Even though he could hardly believe that he was actually going through with this, Cranston knew that he had better become a believer quickly. They had finally arrived at their destination...and there was no turning back.

Cranston pulled his car around the back of the building, just as Eric had instructed.

'There's never anyone back there,' he had said. 'We'll park our cars in a secluded spot where no one will notice, and then we'll make our move.' And so they did.

Following the young man to a hidden area behind a wall of thick brush, the two parked their cars and got out, their adrenaline pumping. Seeing no one, they quickly ran to a service door that Eric knew was always unlocked and cautiously walked into the facility, scanning the hallways with darting eyes before proceeding to the laundry room. Here were the uniforms and scrubs worn by many of the personnel at the facility.

"Put this on," said Eric, handing Cranston a complete set of medical garb, including a mask. "No one will question you if you're wearing this."

"What about you?" Cranston asked. "Won't they question you?" he whispered.

"They know me, remember?" Eric whispered back. Cranston was nervous and had to keep reminding himself to trust the young man, just as they had discussed. "Now, take this gurney and push it in front of you," Eric ordered, grabbing the rolling table from against the wall and passing it over to Cranston. "Remember to walk slowly, never panic, and keep your head down. I'll be walking a safe distance in front of you." Cranston felt as though he would be sick.

The two men vigilantly walked the long corridor—its walls and floor made of cold, damp stone—with Eric ahead of Cranston by about 15 feet. They snaked their way around the chilly basement of the facility and, thankfully, saw no one. Getting on a large service elevator, they said nothing further, remaining silent throughout the ride. The cables of the elevator creaking and vibrating as it went, it brought the two men up to the main floor of the sanatorium where a few nurses and several maintenance men walked about, tending to their business. Nothing appeared to be out of the ordinary as Eric exited first, followed by Cranston pushing the gurney.

Taking a sharp left, the men headed towards the area of the facility where the patients lived. As Eric expected would happen, he ran into someone he knew, someone who was a friend of his mother's.

"Eric, what are you doing here?" said the housekeeper with a smile. "Are you here to see your mother?"

"As a matter of fact, I am," Eric said in a friendly manner, kissing the woman on the cheek. No indication of why he was really there ever slipped out or became apparent. His demeanor was as smooth as glass.

"Well, she just so happens to be right down this way," indicated the housekeeper with a pointing finger, "changing the bed linens for a new patient. Follow me."

Cranston overheard everything they said. *New patient? Could it be Miranda Grimes?* He slowly followed at a respectable distance with his gurney as Eric and the housekeeper made their way towards the first suite of rooms. Poking her head inside of the door, the housekeeper called out, exclaiming cheerfully, "Guess who's here! Come and see!" Eric's mother quickly came to the door and smiled brightly when she saw her son. "What are you doing here?"

"Hi Mom," he said, placing his arm around her shoulder. "I have something to show you." Walking with her down the long corridor, he pulled the roll of money that Cranston had given him out of his pocket. "It's 500 dollars, Mom," he said happily, placing the money in her hand, which was more than she had ever held in her life. Her friend and coworker peered over their shoulders jealously.

"Where did *you* get 500 dollars?" she asked suspiciously.

"Well, I know you won't like my answer, but I'll tell you anyway," he said, still smiling. "I won it in a poker game last night," he blurted out quickly, "and before you start yelling, just let me say that Lady Luck was on my side all evening, so I hung in there…just for you."

"For me?" she shot back. "You know I don't like you gambling," she said with a stern look on her face.

"I know, Mom, but I also know that you've been doing an awful lot of complaining lately about the bills. This money will help. Come on, Mom. Let me help."

As mother and son gently squabbled back and forth over the money, the jealous friend still peering over their shoulders, Cranston was still a respectable distance behind, watching them carefully as he lingered around the suite of rooms from which Eric's mom had appeared. It was time to make his move, and Eric shot him a quick glance over his shoulder as if to confirm that.

Without further hesitation, Cranston ducked into the suite, pulling the gurney behind him. He looked around the first room, seeing nothing but a configuration of couches and chairs. Leaving the gurney there, he walked with a speedy gait into the second room, immediately noticing a bed in the corner, its patient covered over with a blanket. He quickly headed in that direction, looking forward to finally rescuing Miranda Grimes from her virtual imprisonment. After quietly approaching the bed, Cranston gently pulled the soft blanket down, revealing the pasty face of a sleeping patient. To his disappointment, it wasn't Miranda Grimes.

Finding himself in a panic, Cranston ran from the second room back into the first. Grabbing the gurney, he left the suite of rooms quickly, knowing he had to catch up with Eric and his mother. As it so happened, they were still standing in the same place in the corridor, Eric making good on his promise not to leave Cranston to his own devices until he knew Miranda Grimes was safely away from the Mountain Valley Sanatorium. The nervous lawyer slowed down considerably and took a deep breath, once again maintaining a safe distance behind the threesome still engaged in conversation as he leisurely pushed the gurney.

Seeing that Cranston had come out of the suite of rooms without Miranda, Eric began to walk again as well, causing the two women to follow him. As they continued to discuss the 500 dollars, the bartender's mother became far more amenable to accepting the money to pay her bills. As they rounded a corner, the three stopped again.

"Wait here," ordered Eric's mother. "I need to pick up some dirty towels from this suite." She proceeded to enter into another suite of rooms while Eric and her friend waited outside in the corridor. *Another suite of rooms coming up,* Cranston thought to himself as he stopped once again, many feet behind them. Could this be it? He couldn't help but be amazed that his presence in the corridor hadn't aroused any suspicion in either of the two women. Eric must have been doing a great job of keeping them distracted.

His mother having walked back out into the corridor with an armful of dirty towels, Eric and the two women proceeded again, talking and laughing quietly as they sauntered. Once more, Cranston followed at a respectable distance. When he came upon the suite of rooms that Eric's mom had just left, he quickly entered with the gurney to find the luxury that he was so accustomed to seeing…at Trinity Court. His heart raced as he ran over to the bed to find Miranda Grimes laying there, her eyes closed.

"Miranda," Cranston whispered, shaking her shoulder. "Wake up…it's me, Cranston. I've come for you…wake up," he repeated, shaking her shoulder a little harder. Miranda Grimes opened her eyes and stared at the lawyer.

"Cranston?" she said in a barely audible whisper. "Is that you? I feel so sleepy…so tired."

"I've come for you, Miranda," Cranston repeated as he picked her up in his arms and gently placed her on the gurney. Covering her from head to toe with a blanket, he quickly pushed her out of the room and back into the long corridor, where a slight nod at Eric, who stood about 10 feet down the hall with his mother and her friend, told him that Cranston had found his client. It was now time to flee.

Cranston hastily pushed the gurney in the opposite direction, back towards the service elevator. He was absolutely frantic, his heart pounding out of his chest. He could never have imagined in his wildest dreams that one day he would actually kidnap a client from a sanatorium. He had told Eric that they were not play-acting in a movie, but where else would such a plot unfold? It was all so unreal…until reality came crashing in once again.

Eric subtly watched Cranston and the gurney speed down the hallway without letting on to his mother and her friend the hijinks unfolding behind their backs. *Slow down,* he thought as Cranston was clearly making a break for it. This was the plan, but Eric was now anxious to walk back towards the service elevator himself to witness what, he hoped, would be a clean escape for Cranston and his client. After all, he took the 500 dollars, so, naturally, he wanted the plan to work, lest he be considered a phony *and* a cheat.

"Well, Mom, I need to get back to town and open the bar and grill. It was good seeing the both of you," Eric smiled, putting his arm around his mother's shoulders.

"I suppose I should be grateful for this money," his mother said humbly, "even if I don't like the way you got it."

"I'm just glad I could help you out, Mom. Now, I really need to get back to town," Eric said, trying not to appear anxious.

"Let me walk you out," she said.

"No, no," said Eric. "I can see myself out. You just continue with what you're doing and I'll see you at home tonight."

"All right, my good son," his mother barely had a chance to say before Eric began walking in the opposite direction. When he rounded a curve in the corridor, his mother and her friend completely out of sight, he began to run. Reaching the service elevator, he promptly pressed the button. *Cranston must have gotten into the elevator undetected*, he thought. He couldn't wait to get back down to the cold basement where he hoped to witness an unobstructed getaway, but as Eric slowly descended, the usual creaking of the elevator cables was suddenly interrupted by the piercing sound of an alarm. Something had gone wrong.

The opening of the elevator was painfully slow, but Eric ran out as quickly as he could, squeezing his body through the mechanically lethargic doors. He looked up and down the corridor, frantically hoping to spot Cranston and his gurney, but he saw no one. Running past the laundry room where they had gotten the medical garb and gurney, Eric ran out of the service door and into the parking lot. It was there that he saw Cranston pushing the gurney in a frenzied manner towards his car. Eric couldn't help but smile, especially because no one appeared to be following in pursuit.

Suddenly, a security thug emerged from the basement, pushing past Eric towards the running Cranston. Eric ran after him and wrestled him to the ground, the two tussling in punches and kicks just long enough for Cranston to load Miranda Grimes from the gurney into his car and hastily pull away from the secluded spot, tires screeching. Still on the ground, Eric watched with glee as Cranston's speeding car flew through the back parking lot of the Mountain Valley Sanatorium and headed for Pebble Hill Pass. The plan had worked…almost.

The interloping thug, seething with anger after having been bested by the young man, abruptly sprang to his feet and pulled a gun from his pants pocket, firing numerous shots at Cranston's car as it rapidly made its departure. Two bullets struck the vehicle on its way out, one hitting the passenger side door and the other hitting a tail light, neither shot causing the car to stop. As if to answer this hail of bullets, gunfire came from an unknown direction, whizzing closely over Eric's head as he still lay on the ground, afraid to move. Having been shot in the leg, the security thug went down quickly, his gun leaving his hand and landing several feet off to his right. Crawling over to it, the thug picked up the gun and aimed—at what, Eric didn't know. It was in that instant that he was shot again, this time the bullet killing him.

Eric watched in horror as the detective who had been tailing Cranston walked over to the body, his gun still cautiously drawn.

"Are you all right?" he asked Eric.

"I think I wet my pants," the young man answered, trying to be funny, "but I'm all right. Is it okay to stand up now?" The detective pushed his gun back into its holster and walked over to Eric, lending him a hand as he pulled him to his feet.

"I'm sure you have some things to tell me," said the detective, still a little out of breath. "Fill in some gaps for me," he ordered. "What the hell was that all about?"

"Beats me," said Eric with a shrug. "Beats me."

Chapter 15
On the Outside Once Again

Never stand begging for that which you have the power to earn.
-Miguel de Cervantes

Cranston sped down Pebble Hill Pass as quickly as his car would take them, Miranda Grimes laying across the backseat, unaware of what had just occurred. Still in a drug-induced haze, her words made little sense as she slipped in and out of consciousness. No matter, for Cranston would quickly get her to his deceased grandmother's beach house, a small cottage that he had inherited only one year ago. No one would look for them there, not even the police.

The cottage was situated on a high cliff overlooking a small bay; Cranston had never mentioned his inheritance, not even to anyone at Trinity Court. He always figured, and rightfully so, that if he ever needed to get away from the daily complexities of the vast estate, then he would go there, and no one would ever know where to find him. Now, it would be their refuge, somewhere he could detoxify the abused heiress and bring her back to her senses, which had been decidedly dulled by the drugs. It would also be there that he would plan his next move.

As Cranston drove off of Cloudy Mountain, vowing never to return, he wondered about Eric, who had been so instrumental in the rescue of his client. Hoping for his safety, almost certain that he was being questioned by all kinds of people from the notorious facility and, perhaps, even by the police, Cranston's mind was presently trained on the young man as Miranda Grimes slept in the backseat of his car. He couldn't help himself from asking a few questions too. Was Eric left unscathed by the shooter who had emerged from the basement of the sanatorium? Would his mother ever find out about his role in the kidnapping of a patient and, if so, would she be forced by the crusty uncles to sever her relationship with her beloved son?

The young man had been so certain of the successful rescue of Miranda Grimes that Cranston hadn't given much thought to the aftermath...until now. There just hadn't been enough time to think about every angle or anticipate every potential consequence. Cranston felt a little guilty about leaving Eric with a messy situation to clean up on his own, and he couldn't help but wonder if the 500 dollars he had given him would be enough to buy his silence if someone really backed him into a corner. The tired lawyer blinked hard as he drove, as if to put Eric and Cloudy Mountain out of his mind. It was now time to concentrate on his client and to get her as far away from the detriment of her sons as possible.

Cranston's car was now well away from the ominous mountain and he was nearing the dirt road that would take him down to the rocky coast and his beach house. Checking the rearview mirror frequently, he concluded that they had not only successfully escaped from the Mountain Valley Sanatorium, but they were not being followed either. Turning onto the narrow dirt road, he followed it down and then around and around as it led up to the cliff where the beach house was perched. Cranston had not been there for many months, but he remembered, gratefully, that he had left a plentiful supply of canned goods in the pantry. Once they got there, perhaps he could concentrate on nursing Miranda Grimes back to health without having to leave the house. He would park his car in the small garage and illuminate each room only when necessary. Mulling over several options, a plan was beginning to formulate in his head.

Cranston pulled into the long gravel drive of the beach house and parked his car near the back entrance. It was an older cottage that had suffered the ravages of salty air and blustery winds, but it had a quaint charm that presented itself above all else. No neighbors nearby, it was the perfect hideaway. Cranston had always intended to eventually spruce the place up, but for now he was content to take refuge within the old walls that were held together by a weather-worn frame of nails and clapboard.

Oh so carefully, he lifted the fragile Miranda Grimes out of the backseat of his car and gently carried her through the backdoor of the house. The restorative smell of salt air permeating the small cottage, Cranston couldn't help but to breathe in deeply, sparking happy boyhood memories of summer days spent with his grandmother. He carried Miranda into the small back bedroom and gently placed her on the bed, covering her with the blanket that he had taken from the sanatorium. Stirring only slightly, she quietly moaned before falling back into a deep sleep. This was good. It gave Cranston time to think…and to move the car.

Driving the bullet-damaged car into the small garage, Cranston figured that he could do the repairs himself when the time was right. He knew he had an extra tail light somewhere in the basement of his house in town, and perhaps he could cover up the small hole in the passenger-side door with putty and paint. He decided to forget about the car for now, though. Miranda Grimes had to be his first priority.

As darkness fell, Cranston became more confident that they had not been followed and his nerves began to settle down a bit. Not knowing when his client would wake up, he fixed himself some hot soup and sat at the small kitchen table, deep in thought. There was a judge that he knew, someone with whom he had gone to law school many years ago; in fact, someone with whom he had been romantically involved as a second-year law student. Perhaps he could go to *her* and relay the entire story. Being a woman, she might have greater compassion for the heiress and less tolerance for her questionable sons than other judges, but he hadn't seen her in a long time and, ever aware of the long reach of Trinity Court, the question had to be asked…was she now in the deep pocket of the Masters Grimes as well?

Cranston understood that many in the courts and other law enforcement agencies made their *real* money from Trinity Court, but, nevertheless, he would keep his old friend in mind as he formulated his plan. Interrupting his thoughts, however, came a weak cry from the bedroom. Cranston jumped to his feet and immediately went to Miranda. Perhaps now they could talk and she could begin her journey on the road to recovery.

"Miranda," he whispered gently, taking her hand as he sat on the bed. "It's Cranston. You have nothing to fear…you're safe with me."

"Cranston?" she said weakly. "Where am I?"

"You're at my beach house, Miranda. I took you away from the sanatorium and brought you here."

"Sanatorium?" she said softly. "What sanatorium?"

"Where Doctor Kessler had left you," Cranston replied. His answers short and clipped, he had decided not to give Miranda too much information all at once. She simply wasn't up for it…not yet.

"Where is Doctor Kessler?" she asked, her voice still weak. Ignoring her question, Cranston offered her something to eat.

"Are you hungry, Miranda? I've made some soup. It's really quite good and you should try to eat something," he encouraged with a gentle voice.

"I'm not hungry right now," she said. "I just want to go back to sleep."

"You go right ahead," said Cranston softly, patting her hand as he stood up. "I'll be here when you wake up."

"Cranston?" said Miranda.

"Yes, dear," he answered softly.

"Where are my boys? Where are Landon and Colin?" she managed to ask in a breathless voice.

"I don't know the answer to that, Miranda," said Cranston, slowly shaking his head.

"Do you think they know that I'm here?" she questioned pathetically, still unaware of their role in the scheme to dispose of her.

"No, dear, they don't know that you're here," the faithful lawyer confirmed, smiling sadly. And with that, Miranda Grimes closed her eyes and, once again, fell into a deep sleep. *Tomorrow then,* Cranston thought. *Tomorrow*.

* * *

Miranda awoke to a full complement of tea and sympathy from Cranston. Her head was sufficiently cleared to hear the entire story: how Doctor Kessler and her sons had kept her drugged, and tricked her into thinking that she was gravely ill, so that they could control her money; how they deceitfully had her sign herself into a strange and questionable sanatorium, where they planned on leaving her indefinitely; how Doctor Kessler and his housekeeper were now dead, perhaps the victims of foul play perpetrated by Landon and Colin; and how Cranston took it upon himself to liberate her from the illicit facility, a dicey and dangerous scheme that ultimately paid off with her successful rescue.

Unable to conceal her wide-eyed amazement, Miranda was incensed, the betrayal of her sons especially grievous. Nevertheless, she hungrily ate the plateful of noodles that Cranston had placed in front of her, the only item in the pantry that he felt was somewhat acceptable as a breakfast food. Today, she was feeling much better and even stronger, a sure sign that her medication was wearing off.

"We're not out of the woods just yet," warned Cranston. "You need more rest, and then, when you're strong enough, we'll go to court and have all of your rights, and your fortune, reinstated.

"Do you think that will be a problem?" she asked, almost nonchalantly.

"It could be, but I'll prepare myself thoroughly," said the lawyer. "I know some people who might be able to help."

"You know, I always wondered what it would be like to be unaffiliated with Trinity Court, to have a normal life, and to possess only an average amount of money," Miranda mused. "Did you know, Cranston, I had made up my mind a long time ago to cut Landon and Colin out of the family fortune because the money had so ruined them? I never followed through, though…couldn't get up the nerve. And, now, to think that they would dispose of their own mother like an old dish rag…I find that…beyond appalling," she said haltingly, the volume of her words trailing off as she stared off into the distance.

"They must have known somehow that you intended to disinherit them, Miranda," Cranston commented.

"Not to mention all of their other depravities," Miranda continued, as though she had never even heard Cranston's comment. "Only the devil incarnate would commit murder," she stated as though in a trance. Cranston placed his hand on her shoulder. "Not only will they never see another dime of my money," she said with spiteful resolve, "but they'll woefully regret the day they put me away."

"I'm sure, Miranda, that I can take care of all of that for you…legally," Cranston said, raising a reminder finger. After all, he was an officer of the court.

"And, Cranston," Miranda began quietly, "as my lawyer, I want you to figure out a way to cut me loose too, and I mean quickly." Her instruction was clear, but Cranston questioned it anyway.

"Excuse me," said Cranston, "what do you mean by that? Cut you loose from what?"

"From everything—the estate, the business, the money…everything," Miranda said, her strength and resolve returning.

"How do you expect me to do that?" he asked. "Where do you want all of your money to go, if not to your sons?"

"I leave it to you to come up with that plan," she said standing up, always her signal that a conversation was over.

Miranda returned to the bedroom to lay down once again, still feeling physically weak but clear of thought. It appeared that she had made up her mind regarding the matter of her fortune, but Cranston knew that he had a lot of legal untangling to do first; something that could take a long time. How does one dispose of almost a billion dollars anyway, and quickly at that?

The ever-faithful attorney would have to eventually deal with Miranda's instruction…and with the Masters Grimes as well.

Chapter 16
On the Mend

Empty pockets never held anyone back. Only empty heads and empty hearts can do that.
-Norman Vincent Peale

Miranda continued to recover at the remote hideaway, remaining there for six days. She grew stronger in mind and body daily, her anger towards Landon and Colin bubbling and boiling over too as the clock ticked away the hours of her seclusion. Her deep resentment served a most useful and more general purpose in hastening her recuperation. At first, after having regained some strength, she irately paced the floors of the small, quaint cottage, apparently thinking about the predicament in which she was now embroiled, thanks to her own flesh and blood. If she could get her hands on them now, she would strangle them both without regret…the devil be damned.

After a few days had passed, Cranston encouraged Miranda to step outside, not only to breathe in the fresh, salty air of the sea but to gather the small rocks and stones that littered the ground as well. Together, they placed them in a large basket and, when she was back to her old self again, Miranda stood near the edge of the cliff upon which the weathered beach house rested and threw the small rocks and stones into the bay, one by one. This was somehow cathartic, allowing her to be physical and contemplative at the same time. *If Cranston hadn't been on the ball, I'd still be hidden away in the sanatorium, a place where I didn't belong,* she angrily ruminated over this repugnant thought as she threw each successive rock with more force into the bay. Even though she was angered and repulsed by the situation, she couldn't help but feel a bit melancholy over the death of Doctor Kessler, especially after having known him since childhood. This caused painful conflict in her heart, for Miranda secretly hoped that the old man was burning in hell right now.

"What shall I do, Cranston?" she asked desperately. "Where shall I go from here?"

"I've been in contact with several lawyers and a judge who, I'm pleased to say, is not on the take," said Cranston with a reassuring smile, "and they all say that if I can prove that you're of sound mind and body and were committed under false pretenses, then your rights and fortune will be reinstated under the law."

"How do we go about proving those things?" she asked curiously.

"First of all, I've arranged for you to see a doctor. As soon as you've been examined, it will be painstakingly obvious that you're, well…cantankerous, but well. Secondly, I'll show the judge, who also happens to be an old friend of mine, all of the papers and prescriptions that I discovered inside of Doctor Kessler's old leather briefcase. She seems to think that this paperwork alone will obviously indicate a chronicle of deceit. Last, but not least, an investigation will be launched into the pernicious dealings of your sons and the Mountain Valley Sanatorium. Together, these will prove, beyond a shadow of a doubt, that you're perfectly well."

"Why must I fight for what's already mine?" she asked angrily.

"I understand why you're so furious, Miranda," Cranston said softly, "but remember that you signed your name to the commitment papers too, which turns the situation into a complicated legal web. Don't worry yourself too much, because, in the end, you *will* prevail…I promise."

"Are you sure?" asked Miranda.

"I'm positive," replied Cranston confidently, "but I fear that when everything is said and done, I'll probably be disbarred." The lawyer smirked and shook his head. "But, it will have all been worth it," he said, placing a hand on her arm. "Seeing you here…safe…is more important than anything else, I assure you."

"Cranston, I can't thank you enough for all you've done," said Miranda softly. "I can't imagine what you went through to get me out of there, but I'll never forget it, and you'll be well taken care of." Cranston modestly lowered his eyes. "But remember," she continued, "that as soon as I get my fortune back, I leave it to you to figure out a way to dispose of it…quickly."

"One thing at a time," Cranston replied with a smile. "One thing at a time."

* * *

The next morning, Cranston and Miranda left the seclusion of the quaint, little cottage perched on the cliff overlooking the bay. They drove down and around, sorry to leave the hideaway, while, at the same time, anxious to remove the false cloak of illness and incompetence that wrongly disguised the real Miranda Grimes.

"I saw the bullet hole in the passenger-side door," she commented as they drove along.

"You didn't think I was lying, did you?" asked Cranston with a smile.

The day was bright and sunny, and their first stop would be at the office of a top-notch doctor who Cranston had previously consulted and come to know well during a lengthy court trial several years before. He would determine Miranda's mental state and do a quick physical exam.

"He's well-respected," Cranston assured Miranda, "the kind of doctor you can trust with your life. Try not to worry."

When the two arrived in town, Cranston parked the car on the street, undeterred by what people might think of the bullet-hole in the passenger-side door or the broken tail light in the back. He hoped that they could settle all of Miranda's legal difficulties before that nosy detective showed up again, for it was only a matter of time before he would have to answer for his actions at the sanatorium. For now, though, Cranston left the past behind him as he and Miranda got on an elevator in the large medical building. It was time to declare her fit, mentally and physically.

Cranston and Miranda sat in the large waiting room for 20 minutes before someone called out her name in a loud voice.

"Miranda? Miranda Grimes?"

The heiress quickly left with the friendly nurse, petrified of being recognized by the other patients in the waiting room. Cranston gave her an encouraging smile but, out of habit, he, too, cautiously scanned the waiting room at regular intervals, not yet able to shake the feeling that he was being followed. Knowing that he was behaving in a paranoid manner, Cranston stood up to stretch and casually walked over to the magazine rack. Scanning the assorted periodicals, a sports magazine caught his eye first and he plucked it off the rack, quickly flipping through its pages.

Football. Soccer. Basketball. Lacrosse. The articles were endless, giving Cranston plenty of reading material. He figured that Miranda would be in there for quite a while, so he decided to start with the football article and not stop until he had finished reading the lacrosse article. He loved sports, having lettered in both high school and college football. Those days were long gone, but he had fond memories.

Suddenly, an ad in the front of the magazine caught Cranston's eye. At first, he didn't know why, but he soon came to realize that behind the web of legal entanglements caused by Doctor Kessler and the Masters Grimes loomed Miranda's instruction that he figure out a way to cut her loose from the estate, the business, and the money. *Dispose of it quickly*, she had said. Cranston carefully ripped the ad out of the magazine, folded it neatly, and stuffed it into his pocket. No longer interested in reading the sports articles, he would just sit there and wait for Miranda, his mind now focused on the ad. Perhaps he could figure out a way…after all.

After two hours, Miranda emerged from her examination, the doctor following closely behind her. Cranston jumped to his feet in anticipation. This was the first hurdle, the first hoop through which Miranda Grimes would have to jump. Only with the doctor's cooperation would he be able to take her to a judge and have her rights restored…and the sooner the better. After all, Miranda could now be considered a missing person. Cranston had her holed up at that remote beach house for six days, but now that they were back in town, the Masters Grimes would certainly be looking for her. His heart was pounding uncontrollably. This had to work…it had to.

"Jim, may I speak with you privately," the doctor beckoned. "Miranda, you may come back to my office too," he said, smiling. Cranston was encouraged as he followed the two of them down a short corridor and into the doctor's office.

"Please, sit down," he said in a friendly manner, directing Cranston and Miranda to the two overstuffed leather chairs that sat in front of his imposing desk. "It's all good news," he said as he shuffled through his papers. "I find Mrs. Grimes to be quite fit, both mentally and physically, no small feat given what she's been through. I would suggest, however, that she attend several sessions with a therapist to deal with any post-traumatic stress from which she may very well suffer." Cranston and Miranda both listened intently. "Finally, as part of her therapy, she should receive treatment for the drug abuse she endured as well. It appears that she was given high doses of Valium to keep her sedated."

"She was," said Cranston, "but in the six days that she stayed with me at the beach house, she showed no signs of wanting more."

"Well, she said she was agitated, angry," said the doctor, looking at his notes.

"Wouldn't you be?" asked Cranston. "What her family doctor and two sons did to her was…beyond…horrible," he stuttered, indignant every time he thought about it.

"Granted," said the doctor, "but these precautionary measures will alleviate any possible desire that she may feel for the drug in the future. Someone doesn't go through what Mrs. Grimes has and then suddenly be okay. It's going to take a little time."

"How much time?" Cranston asked. "We really don't have the luxury of time. I was hoping that you would sign the papers today, allowing me to take the next steps in having her full rights restored."

"I already have," said the doctor gently. "I can see that Mrs. Grimes is a very sane and competent woman, and the suggestion of therapy doesn't negate that fact. It will all be in my report," he said, closing the folder in front of him and clasping his hands together on the desk. "Now, are there any further questions?"

"Not from me," said a relieved Cranston, who then looked to Miranda, her cue to speak.

"My only question is this," said Miranda, her voice clear and strong. "How soon may we get in to see that judge?" She looked at both Cranston and the doctor, but Cranston immediately deferred to his friend for an answer.

"I can have your papers all prepared for the court by 2 o'clock tomorrow afternoon," he affirmed. Both Cranston and Miranda appeared to breathe a sigh of relief. The first hurdle had been successfully overcome.

As the two got into the car with the bullet hole in the passenger-side door, Cranston and Miranda chatted excitedly. "This first step turned out wonderfully," he said, smiling with grateful satisfaction.

"It did, but where to now, Cranston?" asked Miranda. "I can't go back to Trinity Court."

"That's true," confirmed Cranston, "and for that very reason, I've decided that we must return to the beach house until tomorrow…for our own safety," he added, knowing that Miranda was not going to be happy about the long trip back there. She was starting to show her fatigue and, frankly, he could use a nap as well. "We'll return to town tomorrow, pick up the doctor's report at 2 o'clock, and take it straight to the judge. She's awaiting my call right now. Yes, everything is falling right into place."

"But the beach house is so far away," Miranda pouted.

"No matter," said Cranston. "The long ride will give us a good opportunity to talk. I think I've come up with a way to dispose of your money…quickly."

Chapter 17
Panic

If you want to know what a man is really like, take notice of how he acts when he loses money.
-Simone Weil

Landon and Colin paced the floor anxiously smoking their cigarettes. Landon emanated his customary darkness, staring with a piercing glare out of the large window of the sitting room each time his long strides took him there. As though waiting for someone to come crashing through the glass, his eyes sporadically darted about, frantically searching the grounds for any kind of clue that might pertain to the predicament in which he and his brother found themselves. He was livid, his brain on the boil every time he thought about it. He could very easily put his hands through the windowpane in anger and not feel a thing. His mind told him to calm himself and come up with a plan, but his cold and ruthless heart told him to murder the person responsible. Throwing his cigarette butt to the floor, he extinguished it with his foot before lighting another, and with characteristic anger he cleared some precious porcelain off of the mantle of the fireplace with a sweeping hand before ordering Jenson to sweep it up.

Colin, on the other hand, shook with the fright of a small child as his endless perseveration on the disturbing turn of events drove him to maddening distraction, this apparent when he tried to light another cigarette but couldn't. He rung his hands and then slipped them in and out of his pockets, as though they must somehow remain occupied. Jingling his change with one trembling hand while trying to raise his cup with the other, he spilled hot coffee all over his starched white shirt. He most certainly got on his brother's nerves as he whined and lamented, spouting *I told you so* over and over again along with other various platitudes.

"Shut up!" Landon shouted. "Will you just shut up and let me think?"

The two boys hadn't slept in several days, neither had they changed their clothes nor even ate much. Every time the phone rang, they jumped, frightened of whom their servant might say had called or whether there was some news…any kind of news that would tell them what was happening. How could the Mountain Valley Sanatorium for the Addicted and Mentally Ill allow their mother to get away…and where the hell was she?

"This is the worse mess we've ever been in," said Landon, the anger seething through his teeth. "Where the hell is Mother? How could she have gotten out of there…and who helped her? That's what I want to know," he said, kicking the leg of a table. "She certainly didn't escape on her own if she was as doped up as she was supposed to be."

"Who knows where she is…I don't know how she could have gotten out of there…anybody could have helped her…I don't know, I don't know," Colin prattled on endlessly. "She could be anywhere by now, telling people how we sent her there…and now Doctor Kessler is dead…his housekeeper is dead," he rambled on. "Someone is going to put it all together…figure it all out…and come after us."

"I told you to shut up," said Landon, picking up the telephone. "I've been trying to get a hold of Cranston ever since we found out, but he's not answering his phone," he said, dialing with an angry finger. "He'll know what to do."

Landon listened to the phone ring a number of times before slamming it back into its cradle. Resuming his pacing back and forth, he cursed and spat, damning his mother, Cranston, and the Mountain Valley Sanatorium for the Addicted and Mentally Ill. "Damn it," he said under his breath. "Where the hell is Cranston?"

Without much notice, Jenson walked silently into the room until he made his presence known. "Excuse me, sirs," he said with a slight bow of his head.

"Damn it, Jenson, what the devil do you want?" asked Landon. "Can't you see that we're occupied with an important matter?"

"I have some news, sir," Jenson said stoically.

"Well, spit it out and leave us," Landon commanded.

"It seems, sir, that Cranston was spotted in town yesterday by one of the other servants," he began, "accompanied by a woman…who appeared to be…your mother." Jenson looked straight ahead as Colin laughed nervously.

"What are you talking about?" Colin asked with a chuckle. "Cranston and Mother? Impossible. I don't believe it. Are you trying to tell us that it was Cranston who took Mother out of the sanatorium?" He looked at his brother and chuckled some more, but Landon found the news sobering, slamming both fists on the table.

"Be quiet," Landon said to Colin through clenched teeth. Turning to Jenson, he spoke with a low, measured voice. "Is that what you're trying to tell us, Jenson? That it was Cranston who took Mother out of the sanatorium?"

"It appears so, sir," said the servant, still staring straight ahead.

"No wonder I haven't been able to get a hold of him," Landon muttered, now aware of what Cranston had been up to in the last week. "Is there anything else, Jenson?"

"No, sir, nothing else," said the servant, bowing his head ever so slightly before leaving the room.

"Well, well," said Landon, rubbing the whisker stubble on his face, "it's good old Cranston who has our mother. I'm sure he wouldn't be stupid enough to keep her at his house. They must be at a hotel somewhere," Landon figured, talking more to himself than to his brother.

"What is our mother doing with Cranston?" Colin asked.

"No, dear brother, the question should be: what is Cranston doing with our mother?"

"Okay—what is Cranston doing with our mother?" Colin immediately repeated.

"It's my guess that he's fixing her situation…legally, that is. And do you know what that means for us?" Landon asked, looking at his brother with dark foreboding.

"It can't be anything good," said Colin with a squeamish look on his face.

"It's not good at all," said Landon, his low voice, having been controlled and measured up until now, beginning to rise in anger. "It means that we'll lose control of everything," he said, pounding his fist on the table once again. "It means that the money and the estate will no longer be in our hands!" he bellowed. "It means that we can go to jail for what we've done if Cranston can prove that we had the doctor and his housekeeper killed and Mother fallaciously committed to the sanatorium."

Landon's eyes were now wild, darting about the room in desperation like an animal that had been cornered. He lit another cigarette and began to pace again, knowing it would be difficult to get out of this predicament. He had no idea where Cranston and his mother were and, even if he could locate them, he knew that his scheme could no longer withstand Cranston's legal interference. No doubt he had been to court, the entire intrigue now exposed. There was only one thing left to do.

"We have to get the hell out of here," said Landon desperately.

"Where will we go?" asked Colin like a small child.

"I don't know...maybe South America," his brother answered.

"South America? Will we have to stay down there for long?" asked Colin.

"I suppose we will," answered Landon in an irritated voice. "Now, let me get things straight in my head," he snapped. "If you stand there and ask too many questions, then I won't be able to..."

Suddenly, Jenson walked back into the room. "Excuse me, sirs," he said in his usual monotone.

"Oh, what the hell is it *now*, Jenson?" Landon snapped again. "Can't you see that I'm busy?"

"Yes, sir, but there are people here...to see the two of you," he said haltingly.

"What people?" Landon asked cautiously.

"Hello, my sons," said Miranda as she emerged from behind Jenson along with Cranston and the detective who had been tailing him.

"Mother," Landon said breathlessly. "Thank goodness you're all right. Colin and I have been worried sick about you. Where have you been?"

"It's no use, Landon," said Miranda. "I know what the two of you did, not only to me, but to Doctor Kessler and his housekeeper as well."

"We just came from the judge who reinstated your mother's rights and control of her money," interrupted Cranston triumphantly, flaunting the court order in the faces of the Masters Grimes. "The two of you have been cut off."

"More than that," the detective chimed in. "Both of you are under arrest for being accessories in the murders of both Doctor Kessler and his housekeeper, and there will be more charges forthcoming…I'm sure." The two brothers looked at one another with uncharacteristic resignation as three more officers of the law walked into the room. After Jenson excused himself with his customary bow and quietly slinked out of the room, Landon and Colin were both placed in handcuffs and led out of the stately mansion by the persistent detective and the three other officers. Miranda Grimes' nightmare was finally over.

"Well, Cranston," she said resolutely, "when can we start on that plan of yours to dispose of my money?" The reluctant heiress was unmistakably ready to move on.

"Right away," he said, smiling.

"Explain it all just one more time," she requested excitedly as she sat in the large, overstuffed chair that Landon had just vacated.

"Okay," said Cranston, happy to see his client on the mend, as he sat across from her. "The advertisement that I ripped out of the magazine yesterday announced the date for the much-anticipated maiden voyage of a brand-new luxury liner destined to take passengers on an around-the-world cruise. It will stop at ports of call all over the globe, which will take approximately eight months, plenty of time for the implementation of my plan."

"How exciting," said Miranda, rubbing her hands together with childlike anticipation? "Please…continue," she smiled, getting comfortable in her chair.

"Well, I thought that you could take this cruise. It's really quite exclusive," he assured her, "and your privacy will be well-protected."

"Get to the part about how I'll be able to dispose of my money," Miranda ordered Cranston gleefully.

"At each port of call, you'll have time to disembark and travel extensively within that particular country, all the while looking for a good cause or charity to which you'll donate a considerable amount of money. If you do that at every port of call, your fortune will be substantially depleted by the time you return home."

"Suppose I can't find any good causes or charities?" she asked naively.

"Oh, don't worry, you will," Cranston promised. "Every country has its poor, its orphans, and its other disadvantaged souls. And while you're getting rid of your fortune," he continued, "I'll be here at home selling the property and the business. Upon your return, you'll keep as much of the proceeds as you wish, in order to live a comfortable life, and then dispose of the rest by donating to good causes and charities right here in our own country. Your philanthropy will still be remembered all over the world long after you're gone."

Miranda Grimes sat back in her chair with the deep satisfaction that comes with a redemption warmed by a thousand suns. Now, her life would take on a whole new meaning, affording her the opportunity to make good in a way that she never could before. She would mourn the loss of her sons, of that she was certain. But even though she would always blame herself for their greed and lack of morality, she would find it in her soul to gratefully rejoice in this new venture, one that would allow her to make amends. Miranda's life was about to change, launching her into a world of love and affection that she had never known before, her past already…a lifetime ago.

Part Two

"It doesn't matter about money; having it, not having it. Or having clothes, or not having them. You're still left alone with yourself in the end."

Billy Idol

Chapter 18
Bon Voyage

A wise person should have money in their head, but not in their heart.

-Jonathan Swift

Cranston drove Miranda down to the pier where the imposing luxury liner awaited her passengers. Deck after deck of majestic elegance, the ostentatious *Cavalier* was a floating city of opulence, her epicurean delights there to gratify all who came aboard. It was an exclusive group of passengers too, for not everyone could afford her passage. Miranda smiled as she observed the grandeur of the ship and those who were embarking upon the same journey.

"This was a marvelous idea, Cranston," she said, placing her hand on his. "I can't thank you enough."

"You're most welcome," he said gently, "but we still have much to do over the next eight months." He hardly had to remind her of that.

"Yes…find a good cause in every country. Don't you worry; I'm entirely up to the challenge. Unloading the oppressive weight of my fortune will be a blessing that I've craved for a very long time."

"And I'll be here at home, selling the business and the property. I've already had several offers to discuss merger possibilities, and one company made an overture to buy Trinity Court Enterprises outright. Believe me, there are plenty of other companies that would like to see you out of business."

"Well, they'll finally get their wish," Miranda stated in no uncertain terms. "The timing couldn't be better."

"Don't forget to contact me every day with your thoughts and questions," said Cranston. "As soon as you give me the name of a charity, no matter where it is in the world, I'll immediately research it thoroughly and dispense the funds as soon as it's legally possible. And, Miranda, don't forget to have some fun too," Cranston reminded his beaming client.

"Don't you worry, I will, Cranston," Miranda assured her lawyer, embracing him one last time in a show of gratitude. She promptly ascended the footway and turned to him one last time before entering the belly of the capacious ship. "So long, Cranston!" she shouted, waving her hands. "The liberation of Miranda Grimes is at hand!"

Upon entering the ship, Miranda knew that she was in a special place, never before having seen such grandeur beyond the walls of Trinity Court. Now, on her own with a mission to divest herself from her wealth, the rescued heiress couldn't help but to revel in the magnificence of this palace on the sea, a cradle of splendor in which she would live for the next eight months. Overwhelming in its scope, it was almost too much to take in all at once; she was having to make a conscious effort not to become overwhelmed. As she was graciously led to the penthouse suite by her assigned cruise staff, a group of three women and two men who would see to her every whim and necessity throughout the duration of the cruise, Miranda's eyes flitted about delightedly as she became enraptured by the sumptuousness of her temporary home. She couldn't wait to explore her new surroundings, for whereas the thought of Trinity Court suggested vulgarity, this place was a veritable feast for the eyes.

Her delightful walk to the penthouse suite took Miranda through many magnificent halls and up several grand staircases. She slowly turned her head back and forth, drinking in the magnificence of the mahogany panels and enormous crystal chandeliers. The floors were carpeted with deep piles of burgundy and emerald silk, while large fireplaces burned brightly in every hall, some of them having two or three fireplaces to accommodate their size. Masterpieces on loan from museums all over the world, including the Hermitage and the Louvre, hung on the walls of the great ship. Champagne fountains flowed everywhere, passengers only having to fill their glasses whenever they desired. String quartets and orchestras played on every deck, while an exotic animal menagerie delighted onlookers. Tropical fruit in crystal bowls and unusual flowers from faraway places sat on tables everywhere, which were beckoning people to sit and indulge themselves with gourmet platefuls of lobster, caviar, and steaks taken from the lavish buffets set up in every corner of each deck. Passengers delighted as they ate off of the antique porcelain plates and silverware manufactured long ago by the House of Faberge. And, finally, as though it were a present meant just for her, Miranda spotted a museum of fine arts located directly across from her suite of rooms, the first place she would visit after settling in.

Entering her impressive suite of eight rooms, no less opulent than the rest of the ship, Miranda sat down in the first room, having been poured a drink by one of her staff. She took off her shoes and allowed her feet to sink into the deep carpet of Turkish silk, decorated in royal patterns of red and gold, as she beheld her luxurious surroundings. Rare paintings by Renaissance masters and antique furniture from the 17th century made her feel right at home.

"Is there anything else we can do for you, Mrs. Grimes?" asked one of her appointed staff.

"Not right now," Miranda replied. "I'd like to be left alone…until dinner, perhaps?"

"Of course, ma'am," said one of the young men. "Someone will be back at 7 o'clock to escort you to dinner. Will that be all right?"

"Certainly, thank you," she said, lighting her own cigarette as her staff quickly left the suite.

Still holding her drink, Miranda stood up and walked over to the fireplace, already lit, and gratefully warmed her cold hands. Starting to feel warm all over, as much from the drink as from the fire, she began to wander leisurely from room to room, marveling at the classy elegance of each one.

The master bedroom, decorated with blue and green Chinese silks, had a large brass bed generously blanketed with downy comforters along with an excessive number of overstuffed pillows. She placed her drink down on the nightstand and threw herself onto the plush bed, sinking into its soft indulgence. She felt safe here and well cared for, yet she couldn't deny that she was very much alone.

Not wanting to fall asleep or think about her solitary life any longer, Miranda forced herself to get off of the comfortable bed, which was no easy task. As if holding her in a billowy embrace, it wouldn't let her go easily, as she had to twist and turn to free herself from the abundance of blankets and pillows.

Picking her drink back up from the nightstand, she walked down a short hallway, her feet sinking once again into the deep carpet, and into a sprawling bathroom of marble. This grand room was outfitted with a sauna, a hot tub, and a small swimming pool filled with warm, bubbling water dyed a royal blue. Quickly finishing her drink, Miranda sat on the edge of the pool and immersed her feet into the bubbling elixir. Now relaxed and feeling a bit heady from the drink, she couldn't help but ruminate over the recent events that she actually longed to forget. Where were her sons and would she ever see them again? A large part of her had already disowned them, but, as their mother, a smaller part longed for them as the sons she once knew all those years ago. If only they could be as innocent as they once were before money had corrupted them beyond remedy. Miranda immediately shook off her longing for the past, knowing that things would never be the same again…her sons would never be the same again.

Taking her feet out of the water, Miranda walked back through her bedroom and explored the rest of the suite. Two more sitting rooms and several smaller bedrooms rounded out the penthouse of the *Cavalier*, a most impressive display of floating wealth. She could certainly entertain a large number of guests, something that she would be expected to do…eventually. For now, she would live in only several of the rooms, all that was necessary for an alone woman who was looking to free herself from the life in which she was now embroiled. The sudden ringing of the suite doorbell, however, would eventually shatter her lonely reality.

Slipping on a pair of sandals, Miranda headed for the main door of the suite wondering who could be looking for her so soon. Perhaps it was the purser, there to inform her that her money and jewelry were now securely stored in the ship's safe. Or maybe it was the ship's captain, paying a personal call to invite her to dine at his table this evening. She quickly concluded that it was probably one of her staff who had forgotten to tell her something significant or give her something to sign. She couldn't remember a day in her life when she didn't have something to sign.

Arriving at the door, Miranda peered through the small peephole, a little taken aback that she didn't recognize her visitor as an officer from the ship or one of her staff. Pleasantly surprised, she spied a distinguished-looking older gentlemen, perhaps one her age, wearing a black cowboy hat and a bright smile. *Now, who would wear a cowboy hat on a ship?* Miranda wondered. *And why would this good-looking gentleman be ringing my doorbell?* She continued to peer at her visitor through the small peep hole in the door when, suddenly, he waved a hand as though he knew she was staring at him. Startled and embarrassed, the lonely heiress decided to take a chance and open the door. After all, he had a great smile and a friendly wave.

"My apologies, ma'am, for disturbing you," he said, tipping his Stetson the way only a real gentleman would. "My name is Cosborn T. Dakota, but my friends call me Tom. I'm staying in the suite one deck below yours, and it appears that one of your bags got mixed up with mine. I found it sitting right on top of the pile between my trunk of boots and box of hats," he said, clearing his throat nervously. "Well, anyway, rather than wait for someone to come pick it up and bring it to you, I thought I'd deliver it myself…just in case it contained something important." Miranda was smitten.

"Please, come in, Mr. Dakota," she gestured with a reserved smile, which belied her racing heart.

"Call me Tom," he smiled, putting up a reminder finger as he stepped into the suite, "and don't mind if I do." Miranda closed the door and took in a deep breath.

"Would you like a drink?" she asked, taking her small cosmetics bag out of his hand.

"Oh no, ma'am, I never drink before 12 o'clock," he said decidedly as he looked around the lavish suite. "Not anymore, that is. Oh, I could down a few whiskies back in the day when I was a young cattle-herding cowboy, but all that has changed now," he said, a soft chuckle escaping his throat. He was smitten too.

"What has changed?" asked Miranda with a coy smile. "You look as though you can still down a few whiskies and not be any worse for wear."

"Aren't you sweet," said Tom, "but when I became the head rancher on the Dakota Fetch, I realized that I had to have my wits about me at all times."

"The Dakota Fetch? Is that the name of your ranch?" asked Miranda. "What an interesting name. How did you come to call it that?" she asked, gesturing for Tom to sit down.

"Well, it was my father who named it that," he said, sitting on the chair nearest the door. "You see, before he bought this 500 acres of pasture about 50 years ago, he would say, 'Son, I'm gonna go fetch me that land,' and that's exactly what he did, hence the name Dakota Fetch. When he died, about 20 years ago, the ranch passed on to me."

"That's a wonderful story," said Miranda, making sure to appear interested. She was clearly attracted to the rancher.

"Well, thank you," he said modestly, "but I'm afraid I've been doing all the talking. What is it that you do...Mrs....?"

"Grimes, Miranda Grimes. Perhaps you've heard of Trinity Court Enterprises and my manufacturing business," she said stoically.

"I can't say that I have, Miranda, but you must be pretty well off to be staying in a suite like this. It's much nicer than mine," said Tom, looking around, "and that's going some...my place is pretty swanky too," he affirmed. "Well, I suppose I should leave you to your unpacking. It was awfully nice meeting you," said the handsome cowboy as he tipped his hat and stood up to leave. Miranda had to think quickly on her feet. There was really no other way to put it.

"If you don't mind my asking," she began, "is there a Mrs. Dakota?"

"No, ma'am," he said, his voice tinged with a bit of sadness. "My wife passed on about seven years ago. And you? Is there a Mr. Grimes?"

"Mr. Grimes died many years ago," said Miranda, slowly shaking her head. The two had this in common...along with an obvious attraction. "I hope you don't think me forward if I ask you to join me for dinner tonight," she said, not sure if she had crossed some boundary line of propriety. It had been many years since she'd flirted with anyone.

"I'd be delighted," said Tom, looking quite pleased. "I'll come back to call on you at 7 o' clock this evening. We'll head on over to the dining room and sit down to a nice dinner together where we can get to know each other. After all, we'll be neighbors on this ship for the next eight months," he reasoned, tipping his hat one more time before leaving the suite.

The loud sound that bellowed from the towering smokestacks of the ship brashly signaled that the massive ocean liner had finally pulled away from her pier. Miranda immediately rushed over to the ship's telephone to call her staff.

"Don't come for me at 7 o' clock," she ordered. "My plans have suddenly…changed."

Chapter 19
Getting to Know You

Money has never made a man happy yet, nor will it. There is nothing in its nature to produce happiness. The more a man has, the more he wants. Instead of filling a vacuum, it makes one.

-Benjamin Franklin

Miranda and Tom went to dinner that night, a strikingly handsome couple that looked as though it had always been together. She felt more comfortable with him than she had in years, even more so than she remembered feeling with her own husband. The conversation was light and airy, and the two talked and laughed all evening long over a number of topics. She told him all about Trinity Court Enterprises while he described to her, in great detail, the daily operations of a cattle ranch; their conversation soft and low, as though they were the only two in the grand dining room. Their worlds couldn't be farther apart, but the attraction between the two of them was unmistakable, and their bright and effortless way with one another signaled early on that they could probably remain a couple with charming ease.

Miranda instinctively knew, even before they sat down at their table, that she would eventually tell Tom that evening all about what had happened to her; about how her own flesh and blood had conspired against her; about how her trusted friend and lawyer had rescued her from the mysterious sanatorium to which they had committed her; and about how, as a result, she was finally ready to shed her immense wealth in exchange for the peace of mind that she had so desperately craved for such a long time. It was a lot to swallow, to say the least, but Miranda recognized that, if she wanted to cultivate an honest relationship with this man, she had to come clean…about everything. And so she did, right before the orchestra began to play at 11 o'clock.

"Well, that's quite a story, Miranda," said Tom, visibly startled. He cast his eyes down at the table for a minute as he nervously broke apart the toothpick that had been in his mouth, while Miranda searched his face for some kind of clue as to how he felt about the matter. He finally looked at her and slapped the table with his hand. "It's a shame what money does to some people…a damn shame. I'm sorry that your sons put you through all that, Miranda, and I admire you for wanting to rid yourself of your fortune," he said decidedly. "I sometimes wish that I could unload my money too. The more you have, the more people demand of you. Yes sir, it's a damn shame what money does to some people," he repeated. Miranda was relieved, because he had listened and understood…everything.

"There's only one thing left to do," said Tom as he stood up from the table, extending a hand to Miranda.

"What's that?" she asked, feeling like a nervous teenager as she reached out and gently clasped his hand in hers.

"Will you dance with me?" he invited her charmingly.

"I would love to," she said, smiling back as she stood up from her chair. She was sure that she must have been blushing.

Miranda and Tom danced until 2 o'clock in the morning. He held her tightly as they continued to talk and laugh throughout almost every number, sitting down only occasionally to sip champagne and catch their breath. After dancing, they took a long stroll on the deck of the ship, silently walking arm-in-arm, for they knew that they had already said enough. As the warm breeze blew through their hair, they turned to one another and embraced, then gently kissed. Miranda hadn't experienced such an enchanted evening in quite some time, feeling butterflies in her stomach whenever Tom held or looked at her. He brought her back to her suite and, after a prolonged goodbye, the two reluctantly parted, not wanting to cheapen the evening by staying together…not yet.

Over the next seven glorious days, Miranda and Tom spent every waking moment together, enjoying all of the amenities that the *Cavalier* had to offer while, at the same time, falling head over heels in love. They first visited the museum of fine arts located directly across from Miranda's suite of rooms. It was a treasure trove of antique oil paintings, porcelain, and jewelry from all over the world. Tom bought her a small piece of 16th century Chinese jade that she immediately slipped into her pocket for good luck, and it would remain there for the rest of the cruise. That was only the beginning.

They would visit other places on the ship too, participating in the many fun and interesting events that would allow them to enjoy each other's company. They attended a fashion show where elegant models, dressed in the latest haute couture from Paris, sashayed down a long catwalk to the applause of the audience. They listened with keen interest to a lecture given by the crown prince of a tiny kingdom in the Himalayas and, with rapture, during a moving performance of Beethoven's Fifth Symphony, both held in the ship's elegant theatre, which was outfitted with red velvet seats and gold bunting. They gambled, went on a scavenger hunt, and attended cooking and painting classes; they played deck games like shuffleboard and sat in hot tubs where they talked endlessly about this and that; Tom taught Miranda how to Skeet shoot; and, of course, they dined and danced together every evening. Life had never been more wonderful for either of them and—although it was entirely too soon to tell, especially since life on a cruise ship was sometimes known to tend toward the romantic—it appeared that Miranda and Tom were a perfect match; two people who could conceivably consider a future together. Just the previous week, Miranda could never have expected such an enchanting turn of events.

"You would just love the Fetch, Miranda," said Tom. "It's my pride and joy. Nothing would give me more pleasure than to show it off to you."

"I would love to see the Fetch," Miranda mused. "Perhaps *you* would like to see Trinity Court, before it gets sold, that is."

"That would be real nice," Tom smiled. "Real nice. But where will you go after you sell Trinity Court?"

"Oh, I'm not sure," said Miranda, appearing to be unconcerned about it. "I haven't thought that far ahead." The two let it go at that, for soon they would dock at their first port.

126

***

After the *Cavalier* had docked in the beautiful port city of Marseilles, Miranda and Tom disembarked together. It was a balmy 88 degrees and the streets around the port bustled with both natives and tourists. The, now inseparable, couple immediately noticed that there was plenty to do and see as they studied a map of the city while planning their itinerary for the day.

"I'd like to see as many museums as possible," said Miranda, reading the long list of sights in the pamphlet she had gotten from the ship's activities director. "There's the Musee du Vieux Marseille, which is housed in the 16th century Maison Diamantee," she said in perfect French. "It describes everyday life in Marseille from the 18th century onwards. How fascinating," she said with wide-eyed interest. "There's also the Musee d'Histoire de Marseille, which is devoted to the history of the town. It displays remains from the Greek and Roman history of Marseille, along with a preserved hull from a 6th century boat. The Jardin des Vestiges is an adjacent archeological garden that displays ancient remains from the Hellenic port. Oh, there's just so much to see," Miranda said breathlessly.

"Now hold on there, little lady," said Tom. "The first thing we ought to do is grab a bite to eat. I'm starved, and I would just love to try the snails in butter. What are they called?" he asked, squinting his eyes.

"You mean escargot?" Miranda smiled.

"That's right…escargot," said Tom, snapping his fingers in recognition of the word. "They'll surely be a far cry from the big steaks I'm used to eating," he said with that big cowboy smile of his, "but I bet they'll be mighty tasty."

"Well, I *could* go for some bouillabaisse," Miranda thought out loud. She definitely had the more discerning palate of the two.

"What in the world is that?" asked Tom, wrinkling his nose.

"It's a wonderful fish stew," said Miranda with a chuckle, "really quite good."

"If you say so," said the beef-eating rancher. "I never went in for fish, but I guess I can give it a try…along with the snails, that is," he decided, not *really* looking forward to the prospect.

"That's the spirit," said Miranda, throwing her arms around his neck and kissing him gently on the cheek. "No wonder I love you." Tom smiled adoringly as she took his hand, and together they began to explore Marseilles.

The culture of the city was unique, and Miranda immediately surmised that the people who lived and worked here were proud of their heritage, which was distinctly different from that of the rest of the country. The busy cultural center abounded with museums, art galleries, cinemas, theatres, and a beautiful opera house. However, it was on the waterfront, lined with its many cafes, restaurants, and chocolatiers, where Miranda and Tom gorged on escargot, bouillabaisse, and truffles.

"Not bad," said Tom, discreetly using a toothpick after his first meal of escargot and bouillabaisse. "It couldn't compare to prime rib and a baked potato, but it wasn't bad," he repeated.

Guarded by Fort Saint-Nicolas and Fort Saint-Jean, the Vieux-Port of Marseilles was a most welcoming entryway into the city, a feast for the senses, and a marvelous introduction to this unique city and its people. Miranda and Tom walked about the waterfront hand-in-hand, taking in the beautiful sites of the ancient harbor as they digested their food. They could have stayed there for hours, lured in by the charm of their very first port of call, but, regrettably, they had to move on if they were to see more of the city.

"There just isn't enough time," beamed Miranda as she squeezed Tom's hand. "Isn't this all just absolutely delicious?" He was delighted by her blissful countenance, this previously trapped heiress was now free to move about as she pleased.

Tom and Miranda's stay in Marseilles would be a short one, only several days in duration, but, besides the museums, they would also visit the 17th century baroque Hotel de Ville; the Porte d'Aix triumphal arch; a baroque chapel situated in a courtyard lined with arcaded galleries known as La Vieille Charite; and the Cathedral of Sainte-Marie-Majeure, originally founded in the 19th century.

"Well, darlin'," began Tom, "it has surely been a full three days. Are you ready to move on to Barcelona?" he asked, his arm around her shoulders as they walked again through their favorite part of Marseilles: the waterfront.

"I am," said Miranda, who hadn't stopped smiling since they had docked. "Tom, tell me something," she said thoughtfully. "Do you notice anything here…on just about every street?"

"What do you mean?" he asked, quickly looking around him as they continued their stroll on the waterfront.

"I mean…what's the one thing that's been a fixture on just about every street?" she asked again.

"Well, I've never seen so many sidewalk cafes," said Tom, shrugging his shoulders. "Hell, I never even knew what a sidewalk café *was* until I came here."

"No, I mean besides the cafes and museums, besides *all* of the tourist places," Miranda corrected him.

"Gee, I don't know, honey," Tom said before a young boy nearly knocked him off his feet trying to catch a ball. "I can tell you this," he said in an exasperated tone, dusting off his shirt, "I've been wrangled more than once by a cow-punchin' street urchin. They're *all over* the place…on just about…"

"Every street," Miranda chimed in, nodding her head.

"Well, I'll be," said Tom, suddenly realizing what Miranda had been referring to. "I never really thought about it much until you just mentioned it. The streets are crawling with them…big and small."

"Children don't seem to have any place to go," Miranda observed. "The older ones should be working, while the younger ones should have a place where they can participate in activities that would get them off the streets. I can have it built right here on the waterfront," she said excitedly.

"That's quite an undertaking," said Tom, his eyes darting about the long boardwalk. "Now there's a pretty piece of acreage way down there," he pointed out in jest, never thinking for one moment that Miranda was speaking in earnest. "That would be a great place to build," he smiled.

"I'm serious, Tom," she said, shading her eyes as she looked towards the far end of the marina. "The older children can work there, run the activities, look after the younger ones," she thought out loud. "And if it can't be built on the waterfront, then it can surely be built elsewhere in Marseilles."

"How would you pull that off?" asked Tom. "You're talking about a lot of planning…years of planning, as a matter of fact…not to mention the construction itself. It was a nice thought, honey, but you have to be realistic."

"Tom, you seem to forget," Miranda said in her most professional, business-like, Trinity Court voice, "I'm one of the richest women in the world. When I want something done, people fall all over themselves to do it…just to please me. If I want a youth center built here, then a youth center will be built here." Tom looked at her, his mouth slightly agape, never before having heard Miranda use such an imperious tone. He felt a mix of admiration and fear. She was one tough lady.

"The first step I need to take is to get to the telegraph office," she said, abruptly turning around and lively stepping in the other direction.

"What for?" asked Tom when he caught up to her.

"I must get in touch with Cranston," she said. "He'll know exactly what to do and who to call. I believe he knows the French president," she said off-handedly.

"You really want to do this, don't you?" said Tom seriously.

"You bet I do," said Miranda. "It'll be the first step…in disposing off my fortune."

Chapter 20
I Can Wipe My Own Nose

*Don't tell me what your priorities are. Show me where you
spend your money and I'll tell you what they are.*
-James W. Frick

The illustrious *Cavalier* glided smoothly over the
Mediterranean with the ease of skates on ice, carrying its
passengers to Barcelona, a familiar and welcoming city for the,
now quickly recovering, heiress, who had already been there
numerous times in her life. The manufacturing sector of
Barcelona had always played a consistently important role in
the economy of the city, and, to this day, one of its leading
businesses was still the textiles trade. Miranda could fondly
recall traveling to Barcelona a number of times on behalf of her
father, who sent her there to make partnership deals with many
of the other textile companies.

"Papa loved Barcelona," she told Tom. "The textile
industry was as important there as it was back home, maybe
even more so. I had some appreciable contacts there too, I still
do, and they helped Trinity Court make a lot of money."
Miranda smiled as she reminisced about Barcelona. Traveling
there was her foray into the family business, and her father was
always pleased by the lucrative deals that she was able to make
there.

After disembarking once again, Miranda and Tom visited
the Minor Basilica de la Sagrada Familia and the Palau Reial
Major before attending a champagne reception and symphony
concert at the National Museum of Art of Catalonia. It was a
formal affair, all gentlemen wore black tie and tails, while the
women wore fancy floor-length gowns, not an uncommon

occurrence in this major fashion center of the world. It was the first time that Miranda had seen Tom this formally dressed and she was enthralled by his savoir fair. From the top of his black cowboy hat to the bottom of his black spit-polish shoes, he was as sexy a man as she had ever seen, and she was beginning to absolutely adore him. *The trip*, Miranda thought, *would have never been as cathartic if the two had never met, and even though she sometimes tried to envision a future without him…she simply could not.* As it were, her recent past was already dimmed by memory, thanks to Tom. His head turned at the sight of Miranda in her jewels and sequined gown. It was obvious that he was spellbound, like a schoolboy for the very first time.

"You look beautiful," Tom said, taking her hand and kissing it as they sipped champagne waiting for the symphony to begin.

"I was thinking the same thing about you," Miranda said, breathless in her attraction. "You look ravishing in your tuxedo." Her eyes locked with his for what seemed an eternity before the symphony started. Quickly taking their seats in a private box, the two would hold hands until the music stopped. And that night, for the first time, he would stay until the morning light.

The next day, Miranda and Tom visited the Parc de la Ciutadella located at the site of an old military citadel. There, they strolled the grounds, visiting the Parliament building and the Barcelona Zoo. The next day, before getting back on the ship in the late afternoon, they would go to La Playa de San Sebastian. Miranda, however, had an important visit to make first.

"Darling, before we go to the beach tomorrow, there's something I must do," she said with a determined edge to her voice.

"All right," said Tom. "Just tell me what it is and we'll do it."

"It's something I need to do alone, sweetheart," she said, squeezing his hand. "I have to pay a call to an old friend. It shouldn't take long."

"An old friend? Who do you know in Barcelona?" Tom asked curiously.

"When my father first sent me here many years ago to make partnership deals, my first friend in Barcelona was a man by the name of Señor Alphonso. He owned a sprawling textiles company, the largest in all of Spain. He taught me more about running a textiles business in one week than my father had taught me during his entire lifetime. He took me on a tour of his factories and shared the intricate details of his many contracts within the industry, which extended across the entire continent of Europe. He became like a second father to me, hosting my stay here in Barcelona whenever my father sent me back to conduct business. Later on, he opened up a fashion house called Casa Bourbon and made me a lucrative offer to stay in Spain and run the business. Of course I couldn't leave Trinity Court, but I always appreciated everything that Señor Alphonso had ever taught me. He's now 80 years old and in poor health, so I need to see him...before it's too late." Miranda's eyes filled with tears as she remembered her old mentor with great affection.

"Alright, darlin', if that's what you need to do, then you go right ahead," Tom encouraged her. "I'll be here waiting for you when you get back." Miranda appreciated his support, something that she hadn't had from anyone in a very long time.

The next morning, Miranda left Tom sleeping peacefully when she departed from their hotel, taking the private limousine that Señor Alphonso had sent for her to the Plaza del Sol. There, his ornate townhouse sat between the Escalada Hotel and the Castilla Infanta. Miranda was led through the sprawling reception room by a kindly old butler into a private study where Señor Alphonso, frail and aged, welcomed her with open arms and the heartfelt smile that was already so familiar to her.

"Querida," he said softly, "it is wonderful to see you again. It has been far too long." His delicate frame and quiet demeanor startled Miranda. He was merely a shadow of his former self, hardly the man she once knew. This indestructible mogul, who had once ruled the textile industry in Spain and much of Europe, was now a sick and vulnerable old man, dependent upon those around him for just about everything.

"I can wipe my own nose," he told her in an attempt to be funny, "but I can do nothing else. My servants keep me alive and, if they so desired, they could just as easily kill me. I have no strength...no fight left in me, Querida. My days are coming to an end."

"I was told that you have a rare degenerative disease," said Miranda softly, taking his hand.

"I have had it for five years," he said, shaking his head. "They were never able to cure it or treat it successfully...I cannot even pronounce it."

"Are you comfortable?" she asked.

"As comfortable as can be expected," he shrugged. "But seeing you makes me feel wonderful...young again," he smiled. "What about you? I hear that Trinity Court now owns the most powerful textiles conglomerate in the entire world. You have been a busy lady," he said, slowly shaking a weak finger at her.

"You taught me well," said Miranda, squeezing his hand. She had decided long before she got there that she would keep the conversation light, not telling her old friend what had happened to her back home, the very reason for being in Barcelona in the first place. What purpose would it serve? Besides, she didn't need to spread this kind of news internationally; it was sure to spread quickly enough on its own.

"Those were the days, were they not?" he asked weakly.

"They certainly were," answered Miranda with a sad smile. She stared at him intently. "Is there anything I can do for you?"

"Cure me," he said at once, faintly chuckling at his own absurd request. "Buy me another 20 years with my family," he said, this time a little more sedately. "They will miss me." His small granddaughter suddenly ran into the room, laughing and singing as she took her grandfather's hand and kissed it.

"*Te amo, abuelo*," she giggled. "*Te amo, te amo, te amo!*"

"*Te amo, nieta*," he answered feebly as she ran out of the room just as quickly as she had come in, far too young to understand the gravity of her grandfather's illness.

"Do you see what I mean?" he asked. "My family will miss me terribly, and I will not be here to see my *nieta pequeña* grow up. If only the *Institut d' Investigacions Biomediques* could have found a cure."

"Perhaps they will," Miranda whispered.

"Not for me…not in time," said Señor Alphonso as he closed his eyes and nodded off to sleep before saying goodbye. His kindly old butler entered the room as though he knew exactly when the old mogul would drowse.

"This is his time for a short siesta," he said, slowly wheeling Señor Alphonso out of the room while escorting Miranda to the front door at the same time.

It was difficult for Miranda to leave her old mentor, knowing as she did that she would never see him again, but perhaps she could somehow pay him tribute. On her ride back to the hotel, in the comfortable limousine that Señor Alphonso had graciously placed at her disposal, Miranda fixed herself a drink and thought about all of the things they had discussed. Could she, somehow, turn the sad experience into a positive one? She pondered endlessly, lighting a cigarette as the limousine made its way, block by block, towards the elaborate hotel where Tom was waiting for her.

"Hello, darling," she said, wrapping him in a bear hug upon entering the room.

"Well, hello," he answered, surprised at Miranda's strength. "How's your friend?"

"Old and dying," sighed Miranda. "I'll miss him terribly."

"I'm sorry," said Tom. "Is there anything I can do?"

"No, not really," she answered, biting her lip, "except that maybe you can give me your opinion about something."

"Sure, I'd be happy to," said Tom. "What are you thinking?"

"Well, I know that it's far too late for Señor Alphonso, but if I could arrange to build another research wing into the Institut d' Investigacions Biomediques in his honor—a wing specifically dedicated to finding a cure for his particular disease—then perhaps I would have found a way not only to thank my dear friend for all that he taught me, but to help other people at the same time," Miranda stated eloquently.

"Did you just come up with that plan on the way home?" Tom asked with surprise.

"Don't you like it?" she asked.

"It's a pretty tall order," Tom commented, underestimating Miranda's ability to get things done…big things.

"No research hospital would ever turn its nose up at a lot money," she said confidently. "Besides, the idea fits nicely into my plan."

"First, a youth center in Marseilles, and now this. You're bound and determined to get rid of your fortune and, at this rate, you'll be dead broke real soon," Tom declared.

"I hope so," Miranda smiled as she picked up the telephone and had another telegram wired to Cranston immediately.

Miranda and Tom left their hotel and went to La Playa de San Sebastian. The day was bright and sunny and the beach was full of sunbathing tourists who all had the same idea they did. Frolicking in the waves like two teenagers, the couple laughed and splashed, Miranda feeling the weight of her money lessen on her shoulders, confident that Cranston could put her plans into action in both Marseilles and Barcelona.

Even though she was no stranger to philanthropy, she felt a giddy gratification by what she was doing, as though it were her first time promoting the human good, all the while falling more deeply in love. And there were many more countries to visit…and much more money of which to dispose.

Miranda and Tom boarded the docked *Cavalier* late that afternoon and readied themselves for a few days in Funchal, Portugal, after which they would cruise across the Atlantic and into the Caribbean. Everything was going as smoothly as she had hoped it would, and she would wait patiently for Cranston's replies to her telegrams. She found it ironic, though, that it took her family generations to build such a fortune, while with the flair of a pen she could dispose of it in seconds. She wondered if her father was looking down on her now, furious at what she was doing. Hoping to heaven that he would understand, Miranda knew that she had no choice but to continue unburdening herself of her vast fortune as Tom took her in his arms and kissed her gently. Life, as she knew it, would never be the same again.

Chapter 21
Calm Blue Waters

If money is your hope for independence, you will never have it.
The only real security that a man will have in this world is a
reserve of knowledge, experience, and ability.
-Henry Ford

Spending a few days on the Madeira archipelago was exactly what Miranda needed after having seen her dear friend Señor Alphonso for the last time. The beautiful hills of Funchal accentuated the scenic harbor as well as the many manicured gardens found throughout the capital city. Miranda and Tom walked around the 17th century Sao Tiago Fortress and visited the Contemporary Art Museum, where they sipped Madeira wine, cherished not only in Portugal but around the world. After visiting the centuries old Funchal Cathedral, known for its beautifully carved wooden ceiling and an architectural style interwoven with both Gothic and Romanesque influence, they boarded the *Cavalier* and headed across the Atlantic towards the Caribbean Islands.

On board, they would bask in each other's company for an entire week before reaching their destination, once again enjoying all of the amenities that the opulent ship had to offer.

"If I'm not careful," said Miranda, "I'll gain a 100 pounds."

"That'll just give me more of you to love!" said Tom with a laugh. "My broke, overweight heiress!"

"Very funny," said Miranda, playfully hitting his arm. "Perhaps tonight I'll eat the lobster without the steak."

The *Cavalier* cruised into the calm blue waters of the welcoming Caribbean, easily Miranda's favorite part of the trip thus far. Passengers only had to stand on the deck of the ship to behold the miles of paradise that unfolded right before their eyes, but Miranda and Tom would experience the beauty and charm of each island, disembarking at every port, if only for a day. Dressed in their fine white linens, they would bask in perfect loveliness, something that all of the islands had in common. They would also take pleasure in the rich history and distinct characteristics of each place, immersing themselves in the many cultural aspects that extended well beyond the magnificent sandy beaches. The sun offered a different kind of warmth too, and—mixed with the delicious scents of cocoa butter, pineapple, and coconut—dazzled the senses. Miranda was simply euphoric.

In Puerto Rico, Miranda and Tom took in all the sites of this most popular island, quickly learning why it was dubbed the Island of Enchantment. Miranda bought many souvenirs there and enjoyed the local culture. In the Dominican Republic, they visited one of the highest peaks in the region, while on the island of St. Martin they indulged in quiet ambience and charming mountainside scenery. How peaceful and uplifting it was.

When they later arrived on Curacao, Miranda and Tom immediately boarded a bus to the Hato Caves, where they saw the elaborate network of stalactites and stalagmites, a different experience from the Bahamas, where they simply chose to relax on a white sandy beach, remaining there until they had to return to the ship. In Jamaica, Miranda bird-watched for the first time, after which the couple visited a banana grove where they dined on freshly-caught seafood and fruits picked right in front of them from trees in the grove. The dining was fine on St. Barthelemy too, and the serene trails of the Cayman Brac made Miranda grateful for her sturdy walking shoes. She had no trouble falling right to sleep that night.

Upon arrival in the U.S. Virgin Islands, the couple visited many historic colonial buildings and hidden coves, prompting Tom to rent a sailboat that took them lazily around the coast of St. Croix. The sugar plantations on St. Kitts and the beautiful vistas of Aruba continued to provide them with unbridled pleasure; the oldest brand of rum distilled in Barbados quickly became Tom's new blissful indulgence, prompting him to buy three cases to have at his disposal during the rest of the cruise.

Miranda's cultural side simply adored the historical sites of Antigua, along with the 25 historic landmarks of Martinique, including the birthplace of Napoleon's empress Josephine. Later, after picking up several volcanic rocks from the island of Montserrat before visiting its ruins, they went on to bathe in the rejuvenating waters of the sulfur springs on St. Lucia. Miranda didn't like the smell of the sulfur, but she loved the way it made her skin feel afterwards.

The lush hills of Trinidad and the beauty of Grace Bay in Turks and Caicos accentuated the abounding beauty of the Caribbean as though they were diamonds on a royal necklace, while the black sand beaches of Dominica and the breathtaking Guadeloupe National Park of Basse-Terre were a reminder of nature's diversity. There were more ruins to visit in Tortola and many exotic spices to buy in Grenada, where Tom graciously declined to dive with the sharks, although swimming with the dolphins in Anguilla was something they both enjoyed. The powder-white sandy beaches of the Grenadines rounded out their tour; Miranda and Tom had spent an entire month in the Caribbean before heading to Colombia and Brazil. She gave away 5000 dollars in petty cash to local natives, but her largest endowments would go to a school for the deaf in Jamaica and an orphanage in Haiti. Cranston was once again instructed by telegram, this time telling him to wire the money directly to these two worthy institutions.

To Miranda's relief, her trusted lawyer finally sent her a telegram in return, informing her about the status of her charitable contributions thus far:

Offer to build youth center in Marseilles accepted **STOP** Architectural plans underway **STOP** Estimated at one-hundred-seventy-eight-million **STOP** Offer to build new wing onto research hospital in Barcelona accepted **STOP** Will meet with officials in Barcelona next month **STOP** Estimated at two-hundred-million **STOP** One-million sent to school for the deaf in Jamaica **STOP** One-million sent to orphanage in Haiti **STOP** Keep going **STOP**

The *Cavalier* moved on to the northern tip of South America as Miranda and Tom were still reveling in their Caribbean memories.

"Are you happy, darlin'?" Tom asked Miranda.

"I'm happier now than I've ever been," she answered, her light brown hair being gently blown back by warm tropical breezes as she and Tom stood on the top deck of the *Cavalier* watching as the immense cruise ship entered the port of Cartagena. "I'm certainly happy that I've met you, sweetheart," she smiled at Tom, taking his hand, "but I'm also happy to be helping other people. It's funny. For years, I worked to make money for myself, for the company, for the estate. Money had always been my sole reason for living, and I realize now just how badly it had blinded me. My sons, however, have been more than just blinded…they've been absolutely ruined," Miranda said softly with obvious regret, the thought bringing about the usual emotional pause that occurred whenever she thought of Landon and Colin, despite what they did to her…or perhaps because of it.

She regained her composure quickly, though, vowing that she wouldn't dwell on her sons any longer. What was done was done. "As for me, I never gave too much consideration to other people's needs if it meant that I had to think about something other than the almighty dollar. Does that make sense?"

"It makes perfect sense, darlin'," said Tom. "I don't have as much money as you do, but I'm comfortable enough. Every once in a while, I have to take stock of myself and re-evaluate what I do with all the money that the ranch hauls in. Whenever things get a little too unwieldy for me, like when large companies try to pressure me to sell off my cattle or when other ranchers propose a merger deal, I just step back and remember how proud my daddy had always been of the Fetch and what he had to go through to get it. I want it to remain the ranch that he had always cherished—no bigger, unencumbered, and without interference from other businessmen—the same old Fetch that he had started when I was a boy. That kind of thinking has always kept me grounded. You know what I mean, darlin?"

"Perfectly," Miranda answered with a sigh. "I wish I had thought that way. My life has been anything but grounded." She looked around the port of Cartagena from the deck, once again revitalized by her pretty surroundings. "There is no use in having regrets, is there? The important thing is that I'm making up for all of those years now, awakening in me the person who wants nothing more out of life than to love, and be loved, while helping other people. Is that too much to ask after all these years?"

"No, darlin'," said Tom softly, shaking his head. "And you don't need to ask any longer. You're already loved…by me," he said, taking her in his arms and kissing her passionately as the smokestacks of the great cruise ship blew their signal. They had arrived in Colombia.

Sitting on the northern tip of South America, Colombia was marked by its many coffee plantations and a divergent topography comprised mainly of the Andes Mountains, the mighty Amazon River, many rainforests and cloud forests, and a vast tropical grassland. These various ecosystems made Colombia the second most bio-diverse country in the world, containing thousands of plant and animal species.

Unfortunately, acres of forest were cleared every year, many of them illegally, for agriculture, mining, logging, construction, and other activities, causing many animals to lose their habitats and entire species of plants to be destroyed…not to mention the resulting pollution. The couple was about to bear witness to the natural beauty of Colombia, and the modern development…that always threatened it.

After docking in Cartagena, Miranda and Tom would visit the walled colonial Old Town and a castle built in the 16th century before heading over to Leticia. There, they boarded a smaller boat that took them down the Amazon River, granting them passage through this most vulnerable of ecosystems placed in constant danger by man's so-called progress.

Enthralled by the rainforest and mesmerized by its many plant and animal species, Miranda and Tom glided down the smooth waters of the Amazon, pink dolphins their escort the entire way. They pulled over to its banks numerous times to spy on the caiman, piranha fish, and, at one point, visit the local mestizos that crowded near the edge of the dark waters to catch the coins, balloons, and bubblegum thrown to them by the tourists.

After graciously presenting the captain of the boat with a wooden bowl of freshly-picked papaya, the mostly-naked treehouse dwellers melted back into the forest, waving goodbye to their gawking visitors. Civilization would come knocking with every new boatload of tourists, prompting the Indians to run back down to the banks of the river each time, lured by the sight of fully-clothed, funny-looking white people.

Further on down the river, Miranda held a tiny monkey in her hand and picked a plantain off of a small tree that she had spotted on the bank. They watched as several burnt-out logs were fashioned into canoes by the locals; they looked up as colorful toucans flew through the trees; and lunched mainly on rice and beets, which was much more satisfying to Miranda than she thought it would be. This vast ecosystem, so intricate by nature yet so simple at the same time, was a treasure trove to be protected. Miranda left the rainforest with a determined air.

"I sense something in you," said Tom, having gotten to know her pretty well.

"Wasn't the rainforest beautiful, Tom?" she asked him. "It's a pity that it's so disregarded by modern expansion…just a pity." Miranda was silent on their short ride to the local airport, where a small plane would take them to the beaches of Ipanema in Brazil.

Staring out of the window of the plane as its engines roared, Miranda thought about the rainforest and everything that lived within its vastly unprotected boundaries as they noisily took off from Colombia. She would always remember the pink dolphins and the caiman; the local mestizos and the tiny monkey; the plantain and the burnt-out logs fashioned into canoes; and the colorful toucans and the rice and beets. Miranda appreciated how enchanting it all was and just how important. She should do something…she must do something. It was time, once again, to send a telegram to Cranston. Only he would know exactly what to do.

Chapter 22
Other Side of the World

Money cannot buy peace of mind. It cannot heal ruptured relationships, or build meaning into a life that has none.
                                                        -Richard M. DeVos

It took the *Cavalier* only 6 hours and 37 minutes to get from one end of the 48-mile long Panama Canal to the other.

Initially, cruising through the Pacific Ocean towards Bora Bora was just as calm as the Caribbean Sea had been, lacking the dipping and rocking that came with some of the stormy swells they had experienced in the Atlantic Ocean. The boat was certainly large enough to absorb the impact of sizeable waves such as those, but Tom could always tell when the *Cavalier* was experiencing a bit of instability, having cut himself several times while shaving.

Before reaching the small South Pacific island of Bora Bora, northwest of Tahiti, however, a monsoon that had cut a path many miles away caused large swells through which no cruise ship captain ever wants to travel, lest every passenger turn green with mal-de-mer. Tom was able to handle it all right, as he was more than used to the jarring up-and-down motion, given his lifetime of horseback riding, but Miranda took to her bed, the ship's doctor prescribing a mild sedative to stem her dizziness and nausea. Within a day, though, the ocean was calm once more and she looked forward to a short stay on Bora Bora.

The French Polynesian Island was luxurious and sundrenched, much like the islands of the Caribbean, a welcome change from the tiring humidity and basic living of the rainforest. The surrounding sand-fringed islets were picturesque spots that arose from the clear waters, while the sparkling turquoise lagoon, protected as it were by a coral reef, beckoned scuba divers and snorkelers. Their bungalow, perched on stilts over bejeweled water shared graciously by the lagoon, gave Miranda and Tom a bird's-eye-view of the extinct two-peaked volcano in the center of the island, Mount Otemanu being the higher of the two peaks. Finally, the fresh seafood and plentiful coconut provided a constant tropical feast. Life just kept getting better and better.

Tom couldn't wait to scuba dive, but Miranda decided not to join him and waited on the beach. A hired boat took him out into the lagoon, where, perched on his haunches, he tumbled backwards into the crystal-blue waters. The fish were a dazzling array of colors no less in number than the contents of a colossal box of crayons. The blues, greens, and purples were unsurpassed in their vibrancy, while the reds, yellows, and oranges rounded out the lagoon's rainbow, a kaleidoscope of colors that Tom had never seen in nature all at once, not even in the wildflower meadow of his ranch. After a while, his experienced guide tapped him on the shoulder and gave him a thumbs-up sign, the signal to surface. As they slowly ascended through the magical turquoise waters, Tom looked over his shoulder to see a slowly moving black tip reef shark and, below it, closer to the bed, a lemon shark. He was told that it was highly likely that he would see these types of sharks in the lagoon and that they were not aggressive or the man-eating type, but he still chuckled to himself wondering how in the world he would convince Miranda of that!

Sun-burned and tired, but having the time of their lives, the couple watched the brilliant sunset that night over drinks and dinner in their bungalow.

"I saw two sharks," Tom told Miranda cautiously, for she always seemed to worry about such things.

"You did not," she challenged him lightheartedly. Tom figured the time was right for a little sarcastic levity.

"I most certainly did," he asserted, "and one of them came right at me, jaws wide open, ready to swallow me whole."

"That never happened…did it?" Miranda said, smiling coyly.

"Sure it did!" Tom shot back with a twinkle in his eye. "The bastard swallowed me right up, but I guess he didn't like the taste, because he spit me right back out!" The two laughed out loud as they ate their Poisson Cru, a favorite Polynesian dish of tuna marinated in lime and coconut, while drinking ginger margaritas. Miranda had encouraged Tom to leave the rum that he had purchased in Barbados back on the *Cavalier*, surmising that the cocktails on Bora Bora would be as exotic and colorful as the fish in the lagoon. She was so right.

After a couple of days on the island, the *Cavalier* left for Fiji, an archipelago of more than 300 islands in the South Pacific. The rugged landscapes of Fiji took Miranda by surprise, having just been surrounded by the pristine waters of the turquoise lagoon that had even run under their stilted bungalow, but the palm-lined beaches, coral reefs, and clear lagoons fell right into line with her expectations. For two days, they stayed on the island of Viti Levu, where the capital of Suva proudly displayed its many buildings in the architectural style of the British colonial era. They found much to see while visiting several of those buildings in the charming port city, along with the Fiji Museum located in the Victorian-era Thurston Gardens. There, they enjoyed the museum's exceptional collection of archaeological and cultural objects before they, once again, romped uninhibitedly on the white sandy beach of their exclusive resort.

While on the beach, they were invited to experience a Fijian lovo, where all the meats, fish, vegetables, and other local delicacies were cooked for several hours in a hot rock oven under the ground. This style of cooking went back thousands of years in Fiji, the smoked-style meal always enjoyable, surpassed only by the colorful celebration of the natives who brought the food back up from the blistering hot pit. It was quite a show. Miranda and Tom snapped pictures while watching, intermittently sipping on yaqona, an earthy-tasting drink made from the root of the pepper plant.

"Remind me to ask you something important when we get to New Zealand," he said, smiling at Miranda as he held her hand.

"Ask me now," she said softly, instinctively fingering the small piece of 16th century Chinese jade that he had bought for her on the ship, keeping it in her pocket at all times for good luck.

"I can't," Tom said sheepishly. "I have to get up my nerve first." His face flushed red, even through his tan. Miranda had goose bumps.

"And you figure you won't have the nerve until we get to New Zealand?" she asked.

"I figure that the boat ride between here and Auckland ought to be time enough to make a man out of me," he said shyly. "This lonesome cowboy has had just about enough of being alone." Tom took Miranda in his arms and kissed her gently, ignoring the presence of the others at the lovo. She gently touched his warm cheek with the fingertips of one hand while continuing to hold the jade in her pocket with the other. Fiji was a charming place, but New Zealand now promised to be…magical.

The arrival of the *Cavalier* in New Zealand signaled a new adventure for Miranda and Tom, both of them particularly interested in familiarizing themselves with the Maori, the indigenous Polynesian people of New Zealand. Originating with settlers from eastern Polynesia, the Maori arrived in New Zealand by way of canoe centuries ago, developing their own culture over several hundred years of disconnect from other peoples, along with their own distinct language. The early Maori organized themselves into tribal groups based on the social customs of eastern Polynesia and later on developed an illustrious warrior culture, still an outstanding facet of the Maori mystique of the present day.

In Auckland, Miranda and Tom were invited to visit a *Marae*, the tribal meeting grounds of the local Maori, greeting them with the traditional pressing of noses. They listened to Maori speeches and watched them perform; they saw carved meeting houses and enjoyed a *Hangi* feast, which was much like the lovo in Fiji. They also learned that, even today, an extensive number of Maori face critical obstacles that affect the way they live and interact in New Zealand. Their life expectancy and income are lower than those of other ethnic groups in the country, and they endure higher levels of health crises and, most disconcerting to Miranda, educational failure. Could she, somehow, contribute to an ongoing initiative designed to improve education for Maori children?

"Tom, do you know that, compared to other ethnic groups, Maori children are less likely to graduate from secondary school and that the chances of attending a university are even far less likely?" she asked.

"I heard the tour guide say that," he answered, shaking his head.

"Those dear, sweet children," Miranda said sadly. "If there's anything that I ever did right with my two sons, it was to insist that they get a good education and graduate from college." Miranda never had any doubts as to the value of that.

"I'm sorry, darlin', but it didn't seem to get them too far, did it?" Tom commented delicately.

"They never channeled their talents in a positive direction," she said regretfully. "They were smart, but they didn't act smartly. All of the education in the world can't force you to do the right thing if your heart is held hostage by greed."

"And you think that you can make up for their shortcomings, and yours, by spreading your money around the world?" Tom asked, able to discern Miranda's motives and way of thinking more and more every day.

"Money is all I know, Tom," she said. "If I can put it towards the common good of others, then yes, I believe that I'll have sufficiently atoned for the shortcomings of my sons…and me."

"In my eyes, you *have* no shortcomings," he said softly, placing both of his hands on her shoulders. "You're the most magnificent person I've ever known, and I think that what you're doing is not only admirable, but above and beyond what any human being can be expected to do, especially after what you've been through. I'm proud to know you, and I mean that from the bottom of my heart." Tom's words were genuinely sincere, and it was obvious just how deeply in love he had fallen.

"Then, will you go with me to meet the Maori Council on Education in Rotorua, tomorrow?" she asked. "I'd like you to be by my side when I make my proposal."

"What proposal is that?" he asked, waiting to hear about Miranda's next project.

"I'd like to build a school for Maori children," she said, "that would take them right up through university."

"That's a *huge* undertaking," said Tom, "but it seems that this Cranston of yours has a talent for working anything out."

"He has so far," said Miranda, smiling as she answered a knock on her hotel room door. Finally catching up to her, was the latest telegram from the trusted lawyer.

"Well, speak of the devil," she said, tearing open the communication:

Ten-million deposited into the bank account of the World Foundation for the Preservation of Rainforests through their lawyer **STOP** Eternally grateful for your contribution **STOP** Small acreage of forest in Colombia named in your honor **STOP** Keep going **STOP**

Miranda smiled, stuffing the telegram into her pocket on top of the ever-present jade good luck piece. Rotorua would be their last stop in New Zealand before getting back on the *Cavalier,* now docked in the Bay of Plenty, and heading over to Australia. She certainly hoped that it would be a watershed experience…in more ways than one.

The plane ride from Auckland to Rotorua took only 45 minutes, offering the couple a short respite before meeting with the Maori Council on Education. What Miranda and Tom immediately noticed, as all tourists and other outsiders do, was the smell of sulfur that permeated the air.

"Oh, what a horrible odor," Miranda declared, waving a hand in front of her nose.

"You'll get used to it," said their driver, who heard that same comment every day. He carefully placed their baggage into the trunk of a limousine before taking them to a government building in the city proper. Miranda lit a cigarette.

"Are you nervous, darlin'?" Tom asked.

"A little," said Miranda, puffing away. "I always get nervous before negotiating a deal."

"Are you sure you don't want Cranston to handle the whole thing for you?" he asked, putting an arm around her.

"I'd like to initiate this one," she said, "and get a better feel for what they need. You *will* come in with me…won't you?" she reminded Tom.

"Yes, darlin'," he replied. "I'll be right there by your side…and thank you for asking." Tom smiled reassuringly as they arrived at the government building. Miranda had negotiated many deals in her day, but this, perhaps, would stand alone as the most significant deal ever.

Miranda and Tom were escorted into the office of the Maori Council on Education, where three Maori gentlemen in suits sat at a long conference table. They stood and introduced themselves cordially, shaking hands with Miranda and Tom before the five of them sat down to talk.

"This is my associate, Mr. Cosborn Dakota," she said, referring to Tom. Taking control of the meeting, Miranda got right to the point. "I'm honored that you gentlemen have agreed to meet with me, because I know that you're extremely busy with the daily affairs of this all-important council. Therefore, I don't want to take up any more of your time than is necessary, but I sincerely hope that we can come to some type of agreement today. The bottom line is that I want to build a state-of-the-art school for Maori children here in New Zealand. Is that a proposal in which you might be interested?" Tom thought that she was masterful in her confident approach, while the three councilmen could hardly speak.

"Of course, we would welcome that," said one, clearing his throat.

"Tell me what you need," said Miranda, immediately reaching for a notepad and pen from her briefcase. The three councilmen were shocked, no one ever having asked them that question directly, especially a foreigner.

After regaining their composure, they overwhelmed Miranda with a barrage of information about the Maori education system in New Zealand. Taking copious notes, she was armed with enough credible data to come back with a lucrative offer, if only on paper at the moment, that would fulfill the needs of many Maori children. Through the development of a new school, built on Maori land and funded completely by her, now dwindling, fortune, Miranda was certain that she could make a difference with a facility governed by the newest ideas and up-to-date features.

After the two-hour-long meeting, the councilmen gratefully shook hands with both Miranda and Tom before they got up from the table.

"As I said before, I have many business concerns on this side of the globe," Miranda reminded them, once again emphasizing her vast wealth. "I have no doubt that we can get this project off the ground soon."

"Your generosity will not go unrewarded," they said to her.

"My reward will be the opening of the school, for which I will gladly return. I'll immediately wire my lawyer, instructing him to dispatch a team of American attorneys that I employ in Japan. They'll come to see you soon to work out the financial and legal details. Thank you, gentlemen," Miranda said as she got up from the table. "It's been a privilege." Miranda would send a telegram to Cranston that night, but this time she had brokered the deal herself, pleasantly surprised at not having lost her touch.

That evening, after dinner, Miranda and Tom visited a restorative hot spring where they completely undressed and slipped into the bubbling water, just as the spa owner had instructed them to do. Miranda privately contemplated the events of her day thus far, which were a complete success, but would she ever attain her most fervent desire? Did she dare remind Tom to pop the question? After all, he had practically told her to do so when they were at the lovo in Fiji. It was getting late, and they would return to the *Cavalier* early the next morning to depart for Australia. Had he forgotten? Where was her good luck jade when she needed it?

"You were a smash today," said Tom, reveling in the bubbles.

"Thank you for coming, sweetheart. It gave me a real boost of confidence," said Miranda.

"I don't see how," Tom said. "I didn't say a word."

"Just your being there," she said, swimming over to him. "We make quite a team…don't you think?" She hoped that Tom would take the hint, but how could he propose now? He was buck-naked and couldn't possibly have a…

"Would you take a look at my pinky finger, darlin'," asked Tom. "Something is pinching it badly." Miranda twisted her face in curiosity as she lifted his hand from the hot water. "Oh, there's the problem," Tom said in a matter-of-fact tone before Miranda could even comment. He closed several fingers from his other hand around the engagement ring that he had surreptitiously placed on his pinky finger before they had even gotten into the water. Gently twisting the gold band, set with a sparkling marquise diamond that he had concealed in his palm, Tom removed the ring from his finger and smiled, holding it up in front of Miranda. "There's the problem," he said again. "That ring was on the wrong finger. It should be on *your* finger," he smiled. Holding up her left hand, he slowly put it on her ring finger and proposed marriage.

"Miranda, would you do me the honor of being my wife?" Tom asked, right in the middle of the sulfur-smelling hot spring, buck-naked and all. She replied with a resounding yes, astonished that he had figured out a way to have a ring with him under the circumstances. Her most fervent desire now satiated, Miranda knew that she had been right. New Zealand, for her, would forever remain…magical.

Chapter 23
Crikey

Money won't create success, the freedom to make it will.
-Nelson Mandela

After already having spent more than several months at sea, Miranda and Tom were now seasoned travelers, accustomed to getting on and off the *Cavalier* for both long and short stays on dry land.

Miranda had already pledged three-hundred-and-ninety-million dollars to various good works around the world, Cranston encouraging her with each telegram to 'keep going'. While awaiting word from her trusted lawyer about the Maori school that she had promised to build, Miranda would enjoy a few weeks' stay in Australia with her beloved cowboy, a welcome respite of fine cuisine and five-star hotels. Finally engaged to be married, their illustrious trip around the world would take on a whole new meaning. Each port of call brought them a step closer to establishing a married life together, not on the *Cavalier,* but on the Dakota Fetch.

"Let's get married on the Fetch," Miranda suggested to Tom, cozying up to him in the dimly-lit, romantic restaurant before their dinner arrived. "That's where I want to begin my new life with you."

"If that's what you want, darlin'," he agreed readily. "I'd be honored to marry you on the Fetch."

"It just seems like the perfect place. I want to live there for the rest of our days together," she said, gazing at Tom lovingly.

"I used to *think* that it was the perfect place," Tom began, "until I met you. Then, I realized what the Fetch was missing…what I was missing."

"And what was that?" Miranda asked, hoping she already knew the answer.

"The tender, loving care of a good woman," he said with a lump in his throat while squeezing her hand. "Someone who would not only love the Fetch as I do, but also bring me the joy and happiness that I've been without for all these years. Now that you're coming home with me, the Fetch *will* be the perfect place…in every way."

"I hope I can live up to your expectations," Miranda said, trolling for validation the way a giddy teenager would.

"I have no doubt that you'll fulfill my every wish," Tom said, giving her the only answer that a newly-engaged man could give. He kissed her tenderly over the platter of tantalizing seafood discreetly placed before them.

The stars seemed to sparkle more brightly that night as the two planned their life together while strolling the pier. Heaven was finally smiling down upon Miranda Grimes, and no one would ever be able to take that away from her…ever again.

Miranda and Tom enjoyed many of the places for which Australia was well-known, taking advantage of every excursion along the way as they traveled the coast of the island continent, sojourning inland only to pay special visits to Canberra and a wildlife sanctuary.

They attended a performance of La Boheme at the Sydney Opera House; relaxed at sidewalk cafes and sat on white sandy beaches to lick their ice-cream cones and watch the surfers; marveled at the cockatiels that covered the grounds of the Parliament House in Canberra; visited animal reserves where they excitedly snapped photos of kangaroos and wallabies, fox bats, duck-billed platypus, Tasmanian devils, and the koalas that climbed the eucalyptus trees lazily munching on their leaves—Miranda even got to hold a baby koala in her arms, a surprisingly heavy animal that attempted to take a gentle bite out of her cheek; watched a sheep shearing on a ranch, an event of particular interest to Tom, where the ranchers bragged that the Aussies did it better and faster than the Kiwis; Tom snorkeled at the Great Barrier Reef in Cairns, Miranda agreeing this time to go down in a submarine to see the beautifully-colored reef fish; and, finally, they ate…and ate.

"I don't think I can eat another lamb chop," said Miranda, when they were in their hotel room.

"I can't get over the way they serve it up for breakfast, just like bacon," Tom mused.

"Well, I've had enough," she repeated, jokingly rubbing her belly.

"I hope you never feel that way about beef," Tom smiled. "That's what the Fetch is all about."

"Do you ever eat fruits, vegetables, chicken, or fish on the ranch?" Miranda asked, already knowing what the answer would be. "Now *that* is healthy eating."

"Chicken on a cattle ranch! Hell, no!" Tom exclaimed, adamantly shaking his head. "As for fish, can you see me offering poached salmon to a hungry hand? He'd head for the hills faster than a jackrabbit!" Miranda laughed out loud.

"Don't you ever worry about high cholesterol?" she asked.

"Darlin', the day I worry about high cholesterol is the day I hang up my 10-gallon hat," said the cowboy, stubbornly unwilling to bow to the pressures of medical science.

"All right, sweetheart," said Miranda gently. "We don't need to talk about your dietary habits on the Fetch right now. We have plenty of time before I get you home and start introducing you to salads."

"Oh no you don't," Tom chortled, playfully shaking a scolding finger at his fiancé. "You'll never catch *me* eating a salad," he emphasized as Miranda grabbed his finger and pulled him close, planting a passionate kiss on his lips before a knock on the hotel room door interrupted them. Miranda thought that this would be a steward from the ship with an itinerary that outlined the next week or so, as they would be boarding the awaiting *Cavalier* at the Cairns Cruise Liner Terminal the next morning and departing for Port Kelang in Kuala Lumpur. To her delight, it was a telegram from Cranston instead:

Favorable outcome at Barcelona meeting **STOP** Building of medical research wing to begin within the next four months **STOP** Digging has already begun in Marseilles **STOP** Financial and legal details of Maori school successfully ironed out **STOP** Approximate cost one-hundred-fifty-million with plans underway **STOP** Received a generous offer for Trinity

Court mansion and property **STOP** Think you should accept **STOP** Boys to go to trial in three months **STOP** Get back to me on sale of Trinity Court **STOP** Keep going **STOP**

Miranda read the telegram, her mouth slightly agape. There was a great deal of information to absorb from this solitary communication, which was more than Cranston had sent in previous missives. She hadn't expected an offer for Trinity Court this soon and, although she knew that her two sons would eventually go to trial, she still recoiled after reading the actual words to that effect in the telegram, causing her world to stand still for just a few moments. Although extremely happy with her new fiancé, Miranda's recent past was still a sore spot, nonetheless, its intrusion by way of telegram a grim reminder that she still had matters to settle at home. Tom could see the faraway look in her eyes.

"Is there something wrong, darlin'?" he asked, putting an arm around her shoulder.

"Good news, for the most part," said Miranda, handing the telegram over to Tom, who read it carefully.

"Well, it seems as though matters are moving right along," he said cautiously, knowing that the line about the trial seized Miranda's heart.

"I suppose they are," she said, taking the telegram back.

"That's great news about Trinity Court," Tom said in an attempt to take the spotlight off of Miranda's two sons. "You wanted to sell it, and now it looks as though you have a buyer. Cranston sure is crackerjack…you're lucky to have him."

"I certainly am," Miranda said softly, still holding the telegram in her hand. Always a straight shooter, Tom decided to address her most distressing issue, the crux of her pain.

"Look, darlin'," he said tenderly, "you knew that, sooner or later, your boys would have to answer for what they did, not only to you but to other people too. I know they're still your boys, but you owe them nothing, not even a thought," he said, pointing to his head. "They tried to get rid of you and they had people killed, all because of a sick greed that's beyond fixing. I'll do everything in my power to help you forget the pain and move on with me to a life that is rapturous beyond your wildest dreams. I promise that I'll make you the happiest woman in the world." Miranda threw her arms around him and wept.

"I know you will, sweetheart," she whispered, "I know you will." The two stood silently for a few minutes until Miranda could regain her composure. Taking her hand, Tom led her into the bedroom, where they kissed and caressed, making sweet, tender love until they both fell asleep in the amber glow of the comfortable bedroom. Miranda would answer Cranston tomorrow, but for tonight, her sad thoughts would melt away quickly and her placid dreams would go undisturbed as she lay in Tom's arms.

Sending Cranston a telegram first thing the next morning, Miranda instructed him to sell the estate at a price that he thought was fair and thanked him for all that he was doing. She also wired him a bonus check, something that she felt he deserved as the point person back home making possible all of her philanthropic deeds around the globe. Tom was absolutely right: Cranston *was* crackerjack and Miranda knew that she was beholden to him in more ways than one.

A five-day stay in Kuala Lumpur would, once again, allow Miranda to put Trinity Court and her two sons in the far back of her mind.

Staying in the Hotel Majestic, Miranda and Tom enjoyed the cultural diversity of Kuala Lumpur along with its many different types of foods and shopping opportunities.

They were able to accomplish a great deal in their five short days, visiting the Petronas Twin Towers, Chinatown, the Bukit Bintang shopping district, the House of Parliament, the National Museum, and the National Palace, among other places. Particularly captivated by the Sultan Abdul Samad Jamek Mosque, they also attended the Thaipusam procession at the Sri Mahamariamman Temple, a popular cultural festival that wound its way through the city, ending up at the Batu Caves in Selangor. Enjoying their last night in an upscale nightclub, Miranda and Tom would get back on the *Cavalier* the next morning and head out for the islands of the Maldives, but not before Miranda wired Cranston again, instructing him to send a bank check for five-million dollars to the Malaysian School for Orphaned Girls. It was at this point that she also informed him of her engagement.

"Cranston will be delighted for me," she told Tom, "and I'm sure that once the two of you meet, you'll become fast friends."

The comfortable *Cavalier* carried the couple over 1900 miles to their next destination: the beautiful islands of the Maldives. There, on the island of Veligandu, they enjoyed their privacy while excitedly talking about their upcoming three-month stay in Asia.

"I can't wait to see China," Miranda said excitedly. "The Chinese culture is something that I've always wanted to learn more about. Can you imagine being able to see the Great Wall from space? And in just a short while we'll be standing right on top of it!" She was absolutely giddy with anticipation.

"I'll enjoy China all right," Tom commented, "because I'll be with you, but *I'm* looking forward to India. I want to ride on top of an elephant and see the great Taj Mahal. Little did they know of the impact it would have on their hearts, and their very souls. It gives me chills just thinking about it." Until now, Miranda had never seen Tom so stirred by an impending visit. She was finally getting to know him on a deeper level, admiring everything she saw in the man…and loving him for it.

Besides anticipating the next great leg of their journey, Miranda and Tom reveled in their seclusion on the island and took the bare-foot policy to heart, leaving their shoes behind no matter where they strolled, especially on the luxuriant white sandy beaches. Splashing about in the crystal-clear lagoon, they took the utmost pleasure in this warm and relaxing paradise, their love more intense with the dawn of each passing day. They would both be sorry when it came time to leave their villa on the beach, but it was Miranda, especially, who had a special affinity for the Maldive Island, the place where she was able to clear her mind of the news contained in her last communication with Cranston. But, for all of their beauty, the islands had their problems.

When they returned to the ship, Miranda sent Cranston another telegram, this time instructing him to wire a bank check for one-million dollars to the International Federation of the Red Cross to be earmarked for the Maldives. A donation to be specifically allocated toward the building of new housing and schools on several of the islands that had fallen victim to a devastating tsunami, Miranda hoped that this money would alleviate the suffering of many Maldivian people. It was a small gesture that she hoped would go a long way. Little did she know, however, of the further hardships that she would encounter during their three-month stay in Asia. Miranda would have no difficulty…depleting her bank account.

Chapter 24
Party Before Asia

Money is only a tool. It will take you wherever you wish, but it will not replace you as the driver.

-Ayn Rand

Their days at sea slipping idly by, Miranda felt that it was time to throw a party on the *Cavalier*, knowing that her wealth and status as a global businesswoman obligated her to do so. Although too many rich people in one room, all flaunting and preening like peacocks, was never her idea of an enjoyable affair, Miranda thought that it would be a good place to announce her engagement. Vast fortunes aside, the other passengers on the *Cavalier* were pleasant enough, so perhaps it was time to be gracious and let them into the private lives that she and Tom had created for themselves, if only for one evening. Besides, Tom was crazy about the idea.

"Party? Now you're talking!" he exclaimed. "I can't wait for people to know that we're engaged!" Tom was radiant as he sunbathed on the balcony of Miranda's suite.

"I can't either," Miranda beamed, although she felt she should caution him about something. "All I ask, darling, is that you refrain from mentioning to anyone what I've been doing with my money. I prefer that my business dealings remain our secret, especially on the ship. Speaking prematurely can put them in jeopardy, especially in a room full of powerful people."

"If that's what you want, darlin', then I won't breathe a word of it. It's just that I'm so proud of what you're doing," Tom beamed.

"I know," Miranda said sweetly, "but I don't want anyone to start questioning *why* I'm doing it. If people get a whiff of the recent discord at Trinity Court, it can put my business in danger of a hostile takeover before I'm ready to sell it on my own terms. Besides, I don't want anyone to inadvertently find out about my two boys just yet; word will spread about them soon enough," she said, feeling more angry now than upset. "You can be sure that, beyond the painted-on smiles of this crowd, there will be the instinct to take advantage of any opportunity to make a blessed buck with no regard for propriety. Building a fortune is a dirty business," Miranda said, raising an eyebrow while shaking her head. "I'm sure you know what I'm talking about."

"I sure do, darlin', so we'll just have ourselves a good time *without* talking business," said Tom, hugging her tightly. "Won't people be so surprised when we tell them that we're engaged?" He had goose bumps just thinking about it, so enraptured that he was now Miranda's fiancé.

"I'm sure that some of the women will be jealous," she said sincerely.

"You always flatter me, little lady. That's why I love you!" Tom proudly exclaimed, covering Miranda with kisses.

"I'll get the preparations underway," she giggled, gently pushing him away. "I would like to do this before we dock in Japan." Miranda knew that there would be much to do and little time in which to do it all. The nature of these soirees was always the same, whether on land or sea.

That afternoon, Miranda personally went to the ship's captain and asked for permission to have the party. The gathering would be sizable and she wanted his approval. Of course he would be invited as well. Then, she summoned her staff of three women and two men for a meeting, delegating various jobs to each one of them. With pad and pencil in hand, notes were written with feverish urgency as Miranda emphasized the importance of making arrangements quickly but with seamless perfection. This party must be one of the most memorable events of the cruise. She would accept nothing less.

As invitations to the formal affair were being sent out to some of the wealthiest and most influential people onboard, the kitchens were receiving their instructions to prepare Miranda's favorite delicacies, which were to be complemented by the appropriate wines and champagnes. One of the ship's jazz bands was hired to play and the waiters and waitresses were carefully chosen from the ship's staff. The party, to take place in Miranda's penthouse suite, was becoming the talk of the *Cavalier*, many people angling for an invitation to the exclusive event if they hadn't already received one.

The evening in which the party would be held had finally arrived. This gathering of the rich and famous was a stellar and elegant affair yet intimate at the same time, by virtue of its exclusivity. All of the gentlemen wore black tie and tails while the ladies wore long gowns especially designed by the greatest fashion houses of Europe and adorned with exquisite jewels.

The group of 40 or so couples snacked on Beluga caviar, drank French champagne, and danced to the cool sounds of Bayou Road, a jazz band from New Orleans. Miranda danced with the captain twice while Tom danced with a Mrs. Van Kissel only once, finding her tedious talk of fractional shares and blue-chip stocks dull and tiresome. Some couples strolled arm-in-arm out onto the balcony, while others comfortably nestled themselves into private corners to discuss business, the waiters and waitresses circulating, all the while, with champagne, lobster, shrimp, escargot, and, at Tom's insistence, beef sirloin tips on a skewer for 'the real men in the room'.

By the time Miranda and Tom had announced their engagement, it was already 2 o'clock in the morning, the party still going strong. Hearty congratulations were shouted, toasts were made, hands were shaken, and cheeks were kissed, for the guests, by this time, were relaxed and jovial, having had all the champagne they could possibly want. The captain even offered to marry them on the spot, an offer graciously declined by the couple, as they still planned to be married at the Fetch.

Miranda was correct in saying that some of the women would be jealous, their pouty faces painfully indicative of that. Several of them gathered in a small group, staring on enviously as Miranda and Tom danced cheek to cheek, holding each other tightly. The only guests who refused to clap upon seeing the happy couple twirl around the floor, they abruptly left the party after a hurried round of curt goodbyes. Miranda couldn't help but smile, Tom giving her a knowing wink.

It was 4 o'clock in the morning before the party broke up, the guests discreetly reminded by one of the stewards that the *Cavalier* would be arriving at the Port of Kobe in less than three hours. Miranda's party had been a complete success, for she and Tom had to recuperate until midday before leaving the ship. She would look forward to this leg of their journey, an immersion into the continent's ancient world of beauty and culture. Many of the sites in Asia would inspire a reverence in Miranda she had experienced nowhere else, but there were many societal issues that immediately grabbed her attention, reminders that they were not in the West.

The island nation of Japan delivered an interesting mix of ancient and modern cultures, Miranda and Tom taking advantage of the many excursions offered to them by the cruise line. This was Miranda's first time in the Land of the Rising Sun, even though Trinity Court Enterprises had been doing business there for years. To protect her interests, she had long ago retained a set of lawyers who permanently resided in Japan, the same legal minds that had ironed out the pertinent details regarding the Maori school to be built in New Zealand. Miranda had been correct in assuming that it would be beneficial to have a legal team on this side of the world, a tribute to her business acumen, and she would pay them a surprise visit before leaving the country to thank them for a job well done.

But, for now, it would be pleasure before business, as Miranda and Tom visited as many sites as they could all over the Japanese nation, enjoying good food and shopping, while learning about the rich history of the imperial palaces and the religious significance of the temples. They rode a bullet train to Honshu, where they remained in Tokyo for a couple of days, and went on to visit the Hiroshima Peace Memorial, a moving sight. They stood in front of historic monuments, toured Himeji Castle, and drove to Mount Fuji, crisscrossing the country over an 11-day stretch in an attempt to see as much as possible, for these places represented the essence of Japanese culture. They even climbed together into a hot spring once again, this time up on a mountain where the air was fresh and crisp, no smell of sulfur there, unlike in the town of Rotorua. Miranda was taken by the loveliness of the Japanese people, especially the children, and she would long remember her visit with warm affection.

"Tomorrow, we cruise to China," said Tom, raising his eyebrows.

"Aren't you looking forward to it?" Miranda asked.

"Sure I am, but it scares me a bit," he said, slowly shaking his head. "They're hard-core communists, something that offends the capitalist businessman in me, I suppose."

"You realize that their economy has just about topped our own," Miranda informed him.

"Well, I suppose that's true, but Daddy never had a good word to say about them. He fought in Korea, you know. He used to tell me about this reoccurring dream that he would have long after the war was over and he was home. Chinese soldiers, wearing slippers, would silently sneak up on him in the middle of the night and kill him in his bed. He could somehow see them coming in his sleep, but there was never anything he could do to save himself, no matter how many times he had that dream. He would always wake up in a cold sweat and Mama would have to remind him that he was home, safe and sound."

"I appreciate your sharing that memory with me, Tom," Miranda said, placing a gentle hand on his arm. "We stand to learn much about the history of China, which I'm sure we'll do once we get there. Much of it will be wonderful and fascinating, but, unfortunately, some of it will be riddled with uncivilized acts…not unlike our own history," she reminded him.

"Our own history? What do you mean?" he asked.

"Don't forget about slavery, for one thing," she said, "and the lynching that went on for years after it had been abolished. Tom, if there's one important thing that I've learned on this cruise so far, it's that people all over the world have this in common: they love their family, country, and god, no matter where they live, what their government, or what their history. Rest assured that the first thing you'll notice about the Chinese people will be their humanity."

"I suppose you're right, darlin'," he said sheepishly, having been gently scolded without even realizing it at the time, "but will you hold my hand while we're there and rock me to sleep in your arms if I get scared?" Tom was being facetious now, although, deep-down inside, he longed for an affirmative answer to the question.

The couple would dock at the Shanghai Port International Cruise Terminal in a couple of days, Miranda hoping that Tom would change his mind set by then. They had been away from home now for over four months and he was somewhat fatigued…they both were.

Before their arrival in Shanghai they would rest on the luxuriant *Cavalier,* their elegant party still the topic of conversation among the guests. Although grateful for the respite, Miranda looked forward to their three-week stay in China, which promised to be a learning experience no less than…spectacular.

Chapter 25
China

If you want to know what God thinks of money, just look at the people he gave it to.

-Dorothy Parker

The *Cavalier* docked at the Shanghai Port International Cruise Terminal as expected, passengers disembarking for a three-week tour of China beginning in the city of Shanghai at the mouth of the Yangtze River. Miranda and Tom joined the throngs of people that jammed the sidewalks in this modern, bustling city that displayed its wealth and economic achievements with pride, especially on the Bund.

"I've never seen so many people in my life," Tom commented with amazement as he held on tightly to Miranda's hand. "Don't let go," he cautioned. "You may get swept away and I'll never see you again!"

"Don't worry," Miranda laughed, "I have no intention of letting go!"

"Besides, I don't hear a single soul speaking English," he stated.

"Well, we are in *their* country," Miranda reminded him. "*We're* the foreigners, Tom."

"My point is that if we get separated, there won't be anyone to ask for help," he said, seriously intimidated by the multitude of non-English speaking Shanghainese, hustling up and down the city streets, shoulder-to-shoulder, slightly grazing each other as they hurriedly passed. "No one will be able to understand us," he surmised. Tom was only slightly exasperated, but his voice was elevated enough so that Miranda could hear him over the chatter of the crowd and the noise of the traffic.

"Does this make you feel better," Miranda said as she tightly linked her arm into his, their two bodies now close together like an impenetrable wall.

"That's much better," said Tom, feeling more secure. They would continue their walk on the Bund, arms tightly linked, gazing at the many buildings distinctly European in architectural style.

One of the most distinguished skylines anywhere in the world, the Bund was known for its colonial European buildings, wherein Shanghai's internationally-known business district lay. An already prosperous area in the late 18th and early 19th centuries, the first British company to open an office on the Bund in 1846 sealed its reputation as a sophisticated location in which to establish commercial and professional enterprises.

"I'm surprised that Trinity Court Enterprises doesn't conduct business here," Tom commented to Miranda as she walked the Bund like every other tycoon in her element. But her classy, business-like demeanor was a contradiction to her true feelings.

"It wouldn't be that easy," she countered. "The brokering that my lawyers would have to do in order to open an office here would be intense, a senseless undertaking given the fact that I want to relieve myself of Trinity Court Enterprises, not make it bigger." Miranda was more determined than ever to divest herself of all her holdings, no matter how attractive the international business scene appeared. "The only thing I look forward to now is a peaceful life on the Fetch."

"And I can't wait to get you there, sweetheart," Tom assured her.

That night, the couple attended a garden party at the American School for Children in Shanghai, where they socialized with fellow American citizens who lived and worked in China and whose children attended the school. Miranda was struck by the school's lack of basic supplies, prompting her to pledge five-million dollars, to be used at the headmaster's discretion. Hardly able to thank her enough, he promised that the money would be put to good use as he gratefully opened a bottle of champagne, drinking a toast to the school's new benefactress. Tom knew that it was time to get his generous fiancé back to their hotel before she drank too much and gave away 'the entire store at once,' as he put it.

From Shanghai, Miranda and Tom traveled to Hangzhou, China's 'paradise on earth'. They immersed themselves in the tranquility of West Lake, a garden-style park. Surrounded by scenic mountains and splashed with lush green islands, West Lake easily lived up to its reputation of beauty and charm. The couple rented bikes and leisurely cycled along the tree-lined walkways dotted with pagodas and arched bridges. After a short cruise on the lake, they strolled hand-in-hand, continuing to drink in the exquisiteness of the manicured grounds.

"It's so peaceful here," Miranda said, enjoying the quiet. Tom, too, thought that it was one of the most alluring places they had seen so far.

"This is surely one of God's greatest masterpieces," he commented. "It's almost as serene as the Fetch."

Next, they cruised the scenic Li River between Guilin and Yangzhou, taking amazing photos along the way. The natural beauty of the river's landscape an inspiration to Chinese artists for years, its striking presentation of hills, cliffs, and bamboo groves was a breath-taking rival to West Lake's. There were farming villages along the river too, and Miranda took sheer delight in the many villagers who waved as their boat passed, she and Tom waving back at these simple people who humbly lived their lives in this stunning setting. *How fortunate they were,* she thought.

"What do you think of the Chinese people so far?" she whispered in Tom's ear as he continued to take photographs and happily wave back at the villagers. It was, by all means, a rhetorical question, for Miranda already knew that he was simply enchanted.

The tour taking them next to Guangzhou, Miranda and Tom strolled through the many markets that filled the city streets, some of them selling antiques, others local handy crafts, while still others animals for slaughter. Their tour guide warned them that the people of the region were known for killing and eating anything that could be trapped or caught by local farmers in their fields, his caution not making it any easier to look at the animals not yet dead at one local food market. Miranda found it beyond disturbing to see the suffering animals in their cages, some of them with snapped limbs still ensnared in jagged-tooth claw traps. What was particularly upsetting was seeing animals considered to be domesticated in western culture, particularly the cats and dogs, which would wind up on somebody's dinner table that evening. However, the sight of a shackled red fox, bloody and squirming in agony, was too much for Miranda to bear. The couple would quickly exit the market and its black muddy grounds infused with the stench of dying animals, but not before passing a large barrel of black snakes slithering in and out of their open container. Miranda and Tom were relieved to have finally made it to the sidewalk away from the revolting sights of the market, an abomination of unthinkable cruelty. Unable to get the stench of the gruesome place out of her nostrils, disturbing images of suffering animals would haunt Miranda for the rest of the day.

Coming upon the famous Snake Restaurant, the couple would again be reminded that the eating culture of Guangzhou was completely foreign to that of their own, especially given Miranda's discerning palate as a connoisseur of haute cuisine. After carefully examining the long black snakes hanging in the restaurant window, patrons would choose the one that they wanted cooked for their meal and wait patiently while the reptile was taken off its hook, cleaned, chopped into pieces, and thrown into a wok. These were the same black snakes that they had seen slithering in and out of that barrel in the market, a disgusting sight that Miranda couldn't get out of her mind.

"Have you ever eaten snake before?" she asked Tom.

"I tasted rattler once, but I wasn't impressed, being a man who prefers steak to anything else. I certainly would never eat one of *these* bad boys," he said, gesturing towards the hanging snakes. They quickly walked away, not at all sorry to be leaving Guangzhou the next morning.

Headed next for the ancient city of Xian, Miranda and Tom were excited to finally see the famed Terracotta Army in person, one of the greatest archeological sites ever found. Discovered in 1974 by farmers digging a well, the life-size models had stood underground for more than 2000 years, protecting and defending their emperor while bringing him into his next life. Each soldier displaying different facial features and expressions, the vast army, as a whole, represented an ancient artistic triumph never seen before. Students of archeology from all over the world flocked to the site every year, volunteering to assist in the continual unearthing of the soldiers, Europeans working in this part of the extensive pit, Americans working in that part, and so forth.

The couple descended the stairs into the great pit and looked into the faces of as many of the soldiers as they could.

"This one looks like my Uncle Jeb," Tom laughed.

"Each one is meticulously sculpted…it's beyond my comprehension," Miranda commented. They would both appreciate the astonishing existence of what they were looking at, still explained only in terms of scientific conjecture as to how or why they even existed at all.

Beijing, China's modern imperial capital, was next on the itinerary. Here, another one of Cranston's telegrams caught up to Miranda:

Five-million to the Malaysian School for Orphaned Girls **STOP** One-million to the International Federation of the Red Cross earmarked for the Maldives **STOP** Trinity Court mansion and property sold for one-hundred-eighty-seven-million **STOP** Textile Factories Incorporated made offer to buy Trinity Court Enterprises for six-hundred-million **STOP** Think you should accept offer **STOP** Let me know and thanks for the bonus **STOP** Congratulations on your engagement **STOP** Keep going **STOP**

Miranda answered Cranston's telegram immediately:

Accept offer of six-hundred-million for Trinity Court Enterprises immediately **STOP** Compile list of charitable organizations in the U.S. that could be potential recipients of proceeds of six-hundred-million **STOP** Start the ball rolling in the establishment of a Non-Profit Trinity Court Foundation with the one-hundred-eighty-seven-million in proceeds from the sale of the mansion and property **STOP** You deserved the bonus **STOP**

Never before imagining that she would ever relay such instructions to her attorney, effectively signaling her intention to give away *all* of her money, Miranda visibly shook as she sent her telegram to Cranston.

"Are you all right, darlin'?" asked Tom.

"I am," said Miranda, unsure at first until she gathered herself. "This is really happening, isn't it?"

"It sure is, darlin'," said Tom, "but don't you worry...I'll take care of you for the rest of your born days." He wrapped Miranda in his tight embrace, making her feel safe and secure. She was now ready to see Beijing.

The couple couldn't help but smile at the difference between Beijing and Guangzhou. Even Xian had been primitive in comparison to this modern city of palaces, where, in imperial times, common people were forbidden entry into the sprawling Imperial Palace, hence the name Forbidden City. Home to the Ming and Qing Dynasties, no less than 24 emperors had occupied its eight-thousand rooms until 1911. Ranking now as one of the most important palaces in the world, it is considered to be a museum of cultural and historical significance, proudly showcasing its imperial relics. Now a far cry from the secluded residence once forbidden to most, Miranda and Tom would walk within its walls just as the emperors did all those years ago.

"Look at the pomegranate trees," said Miranda as they walked the grounds around the palace. "I would love to just reach up and pick one."

"I wouldn't do that if I were you, darlin'," cautioned Tom. "Remember, we're not in Kansas anymore," he said in playful gest.

"I love the carved dragons and other fierce-looking creatures on the roofs of the buildings," Miranda said, pointing to the intricate wooden carvings that looked down upon the palace and its grounds.

"They were meant to protect the wooden structures from fire," said their tour guide. "You can imagine why fires were a concern in the Forbidden City, which was built entirely out of wood." Miranda marveled at the majestic red and yellow palace buildings as she and Tom walked paths identical to those of the long past emperors, trying to imagine one of these magnificent edifices on fire, the dragons having failed to do their job.

From the Forbidden City, the couple traveled next to the Great Wall of China, a one-hour ride from their hotel in the city, where the best-preserved sections of the wall existed, drawing tourists from all over the world. Stretching across Northern China from the Hebei province in the east to the Gansu province in the west, the Great Wall can be seen from space as it serpentines its way through no less than 15 provinces. The longest wall in the world, originally built to protect China from the invading nomadic groups of the Eurasian Steppe, is a series of fortifications made of stone, brick, and wood and allows visitors to look out at some of the most breath-taking mountain scenery in the world. This foremost symbol of China, rebuilt and preserved over many centuries, took Miranda's breath away as it came into view, causing her eyes to swell with tears and her throat to tighten. She felt as though she were in the presence of something glorious…and far more sacred than any temple they had already seen. She was simply overwhelmed. There, the couple made a special purchase together: a blue and white silk rug that they would take back home to the Fetch.

After visiting the Great Wall, Miranda and Tom went to a nearby zoo where they observed the delightful antics of Giant Pandas before heading back to their hotel in Beijing. That evening, they would eat Peking duck, a sumptuous meal, if only for Miranda.

"Do you think this is one of the ducks we saw hanging in that store's window this morning?" asked Tom, picking at his food.

"No doubt," Miranda smiled. "Don't you like it?"

"I never look at a dead cow before eating steak," he said, looking a little squeamish. "Besides, there are ducks waddling all over the Fetch. They live in the big lake on the property and I've grown fond of them…like you would a pet."

"You're a big softee, you know that?" Miranda smiled, leaning over and gently kissing Tom on the cheek. Pushing his plate away, he blushed, quickly ordering a dish of beef chop suey from a passing waiter.

The following morning, Miranda and Tom boarded the luxury tour bus destined for the Summer Palace, China's largest imperial garden. A royal summer resort during the Qing Dynasty, the magnificent layout of the Summer Palace combined the natural hills and open waters of its surroundings with great palaces and halls, courtyards and pavilions, temples and bridges, and gardens and other displays. Wide open and airy, unlike the Forbidden City, the Summer Palace gave the emperors of long ago the peace and serenity they so desired amidst its architectural masterpieces and artistically-manicured grounds.

Miranda and Tom would board a small boat and cruise around Kunming Lake, enjoying the scenic view that had wrapped around them in full splendor. Their stay in China almost at an end, they would have one more day to see Beijing at their leisure before reluctantly boarding a bus that would take them to the Tianjin International Cruise Home Port, where the *Cavalier* awaited their return.

Miranda and Tom got up early the next morning, dressing and eating quickly, so that they could take in as much as possible that day before having to leave the most fascinating city in China. Armed with a map, they stepped out onto the street in front of their hotel, immediately overwhelmed by the sight of hundreds of bicyclists, probably on their way to work or market, whizzing by along with the cars. In the park across the street, a large group of people performed Tai chi.

"What a nice way to begin your day," said Miranda, marveling at the meditation exercise.

"It looks sort of silly to me," said Tom.

"They say it promotes inner peace," Miranda countered. "If that's the case, I should be doing Tai chi every morning." She wasn't kidding.

The couple made their way around the city, looking at the buildings, stores, sporadic small parks, and other places that were normally found in a large, modern city. There was even a McDonald's on one block, where Miranda and Tom ate lunch.

"At least I know what's in a cheeseburger," Tom said facetiously.

Making their way to Tiananmen Square, they snapped numerous photos as they stood underneath the massive image of Mao Tse-tung that loomed large over the city square and its visitors. Designed and built in 1651, it was now four times its original size, capable of holding 600,000 people.

"This place is *massive*," said Tom, amazed at the sheer size of it. And, although there was nowhere near a crowd of 600,000 people in the square that day, the size of the multitude was almost as overwhelming to Tom as the number of pedestrians who daily walked the Bund in Shanghai.

As they exited Tiananmen Square and continued to stroll, Miranda and Tom witnessed the beating of an elderly man by a policeman with a billy club…for stealing a loaf of bread. Having sunk to his knees, the old man sustained continual blows to the head, all the while holding on tightly to his precious loot, unwilling to let it go. It was a wild abuse of power, robbing the old man of all human dignity. Miranda watched in horror as Tom pulled her by the arm, dragging her away from the spectacle.

"I can't let him continue to do that without saying something," said Miranda naively, looking back at the cringing old man.

"Don't you dare," Tom ordered. "You hold no sway here, darlin', and, like I've said to you before…we're not in Kansas anymore." Miranda looked at Tom sadly, knowing that he was right. The two looked back to see that the policeman had let the old man get up and stagger away with his bread after having finished beating and humiliating him senselessly. It was time to go back to the hotel. Miranda had seen as much of Beijing as she cared to see that day.

That night, as she packed their belongings on her own good time, Miranda brought to mind all of the wonderful places they had visited and the amazing things they had seen in the last three weeks. She also thought about some of the awful things they had seen that she would prefer to forget, like the gruesome market in Guangzhou and the beating of the elderly man near Tiananmen Square. Maybe Tom was right. Maybe the Chinese people were, ultimately, the hard-core communists of his daddy's reoccurring dream. Miranda knew, though, that it wasn't right to generalize. After all, they had been treated like royalty their entire stay, never feeling less than privileged to gain insight into one of the most beautiful and ancient cultures on the face of the earth. Nevertheless, before they departed for the Tianjin International Cruise Home Port the next morning, where the *Cavalier* awaited their return in order to take them to South Korea, Miranda wired Cranston to send ten-million dollars to the International Asian Foundation for the Prevention of Cruelty to Animals, earmarked for China, and ten-million dollars to the Human Rights Council of Asia, an organization that worked to alleviate human rights violations in China; an almost impossible task, given the country's authoritarian posture and refusal to give its citizens fundamental human rights. And, of course, there was the five-million dollars that she pledged to the American school in Shanghai.

"Are you ready to move on, darlin'?" Tom asked.

"I'm ready," Miranda sighed, finding her sudden melancholy a surprise. It had been a wonderful visit, but, as the saying went, she wouldn't want to live there.

Chapter 26
Forget the Bad Dreams

Too many people spend money they haven't earned, to buy things they don't want, to impress people that they don't like.
-Will Rogers

The following morning, feeling thoroughly satisfied with their visit to China yet looking forward to moving on, Miranda and Tom traveled by bus to the Tianjin International Cruise Home Port to board the *Cavalier* for a full day of relaxation before arriving in Incheon, South Korea.

"Well, darlin', I can't say that I'm sorry to be relaxing once again in the comforts of the *Cavalier*," said Tom. "China was beautiful, but I'm looking forward to eating a steak and bathing in my own tub."

"I agree," Miranda concurred. "Speaking of which, would you care to join me in my private swimming pool for an enjoyable afternoon of bubbling blue waters and a bottle of champagne?" She gently nibbled Tom's ear as they sat on the deck of the ship sipping cocktails while enjoying the gentle breezes that blew in from the bay as they headed out into the Yellow Sea.

"Now you're talking," said Tom, placing an arm around Miranda's shoulders as they stood up and leisurely strolled the deck, smiling at the other passengers who were quick to resume their many activities onboard the ship. Picking up a cocktail shrimp here and a beef kabob there, the couple stopped intermittently to watch a shuffleboard tournament, rock climbers scaling an immense wall onboard the ship, and a few Olympic hopefuls practicing their flips off of the high diving board before going back inside the magnificent *Cavalier* to relax.

Ordering a bottle of chilled champagne as soon as they got back to Miranda's penthouse suite, they quickly undressed and got into their white, terrycloth robes as they waited for room service. Their bare feet sinking into the plush carpet, Tom took Miranda by the hand and led her to the nearby couch. He held her close and gently nuzzled her neck before tenderly kissing her lips.

"This beats walking around that gruesome market in Guangzhou, doesn't it?" Tom asked.

Lightly massaging her back as he resumed his tender kisses, Tom slowly opened Miranda's robe and gently reached in, wrapping his arms around her soft, warm body before lovingly caressing her. She trembled at his touch, hair-raising goose bumps suddenly appearing on her arms and fluttering butterflies in her stomach. Tom made her feel like a teenager again, only better and without the angst. Suddenly, the doorbell rang. The two gazed into each other's eyes and smiled. It was difficult to stop what they were doing.

"I'll get that," Miranda said, closing her robe while letting out a long sigh. "It's the champagne." Indeed, and it was accompanied by a small basket of exotic fruits and a plate of teacakes, pastries, and chocolates. Bringing the champagne and various delicacies into the large bathroom with them, Miranda and Tom picked up where they left off, making love in the warm, bubbling blue waters of the small pool as they drank champagne and ate sweets. She wouldn't care if they spent the remainder of the cruise that way, unbothered by the rest of the world, but there were other places to see and more money to spread around. It was Miranda's intention to go home entirely broke.

Docking in Incheon the next day, the couple looked forward to touring there for several days before heading up to Seoul. Walking in the land where his father had fought all those years ago, where the Chinese had made such a lasting impression as to haunt the old man's dreams for years, Tom took in the sites with wide eyes, his father never far from his mind.

176

"I wonder what Daddy must be thinking, looking down and seeing me here in Korea," Tom thought out loud, his sudden apprehension over being there obvious to Miranda.

"I'm sure he would love to be here with you to show you around and point things out," said Miranda. "Remember, history has a lot to teach us." Tom knew that she was right about that, but he continued to wonder about his father, whom he figured might just be casting his strong disapproval of the visit from on high. As though he had gotten caught with his hand in the cookie jar, Tom felt as though he were a little boy all over again, expecting his father to, somehow, reprimand him.

First, they strolled along tree-lined sidewalks in Songdo Central Park, a similar space to that of Central Park in New York City, where they enjoyed sculptures and artwork before finding a café on the eastern side. There, they sipped soju and snacked on fried rice cake skewers, content to watch the many young families that romped about on the green grasses, they too enjoying their day in this relaxing park. Later, as they watched the canoes being rowed gently around the lake, Miranda and Tom talked about the future.

"The first thing I'll do is teach you how to ride a horse," Tom promised.

"Will I have my own horse?" Miranda asked.

"You certainly will, darlin'," Tom answered with pleasure, now knowing what to get her as a wedding present.

That afternoon, they visited Jeondeungsa, a Buddhist temple located in Ganghwa-gun, before driving to the centuries old Gwangseongbo Fortress, a historic site famous for the many battles that had taken place there, especially the American invasion of 1871. The next day, they traveled to Wolmido Island, located one kilometer off of the coast, where they visited the Korean Traditional Garden at Wolmi Park and walked the promenade after attending a show at a puppet theatre in Performance Square.

"I vaguely remember Daddy talking about Walmido Island," said Tom, squinting his eyes in an attempt to recall past conversations. Their tour guide overheard his comment.

"In 1950, the United States Army bombed Wolmido Island for five days because it was occupied by many North Korean

Army soldiers at the time. Several hundred civilians were killed," said the tour guide. "Did your father fight in the Korean conflict?"

"Yes, he did," said Tom cautiously, not sure where the tour guide was going next with his comments.

"Then, I am particularly happy to welcome you here…in honor of your father," the tour guide said, extending his hand in a gesture of friendship. Never one to pass up a hearty handshake, Tom shook the tour guide's hand and smiled. After that, no other words were exchanged…nor did they need to be.

That evening, as they prepared to leave for Seoul, Tom was noticeably introspective.

"What do you think your father is thinking now?" asked Miranda, gently putting her arms around her quiet cowboy.

"I think he's thinking that maybe it's time to forget about the past and the bad dreams…to just have a good, peaceful rest," said Tom, throwing a pair of clean socks into his suitcase. "You were right, darlin'. History sure does have a lot to teach us, and today I learned that sometimes you have to look backward, and make your peace with it, before you can move forward. Do you know what I mean?"

"I think so," said Miranda quietly, her arms still around Tom.

"Today, I was welcomed here in honor of my father and I'd like to think that Daddy approved." Tom choked back his emotions.

"I'm sure he did, sweetheart," Miranda assured him. "I'm sure he did."

The next morning, a comfortable tour bus took them on a short ride to Seoul, the largest city in South Korea. There, traditional Korean culture existed in a modern city, drawing tourists from all over the country and the rest of the world. Known for its palaces, temples, art galleries, museums, and much more, Seoul was, indeed, the cultural center of South Korea, where Miranda and Tom would spend several days sightseeing. Feeling that his father was somehow walking beside him, the city took on a magical aura to Tom, unlocking a past which his father had rarely spoken about, but had clearly manifested itself in his nightmares. Tom hadn't felt this close to his father in years, finally understanding him and all that he stood for as he and Miranda continued their visit in the Land of the Morning Calm.

First, they went to the Gyeongbokgung Palace, the main royal palace of the Joseon Dynasty. Built in 1395, it was home to the Joseon kings and their governments before it was destroyed by Imperial Japan in the late 16th century. The grandest and most beautiful of all the Korean palaces, it was reconstructed to its original form, additionally housing the National Palace Museum of Korea and the National Folk Museum within its walled complex. It was a fine display of ancient Korean culture, much like the Imperial Palace of the Forbidden City.

Next, they toured the nearby Jogyesa Buddhist temple before visiting the Changdeokgung Palace, also built in 1395 by the Joseon Dynasty. Although a beautiful palace as well, of greater interest to Miranda and Tom was the Huwon or large garden to the rear of it, originally built for the royal family and palace women.

The couple leisurely strolled the perfectly-manicured grounds of the Huwon, often called the Biwon or Secret Garden, enjoying its ponds, colorful flowers, traditional pavilions, and trees, some of them over 300 years old. They sat at one of the pavilions in the area of the Ongnyucheon, or Jade Stream, drinking bokbunja and eating filled pancakes and dumplings.

Finally, rounding out their day of sightseeing, the couple went to Bukchon Hanok Village, a traditional Korean village containing many structures and alleyways. Originally, this residential neighborhood was home to the nobility of the palaces and the many high government officials of the Joseon Dynasty, until wars and other issues in the region forced the quartering of commoners.

"Tomorrow, we go to the War Memorial of Korea before leaving for Taiwan," said Tom. "I hear it's impressive, memorializing the entire military history of the country."

"As Americans, we sometimes don't think beyond the Korean War," said Miranda.

"No, we don't," smiled Tom, "but, frankly, that's the part of the Memorial that I'm most anxious to see. The rest is just gravy on the beef, as far as I'm concerned."

"You sure can turn a phrase," Miranda laughed. "Maybe someday I'll get you to say, 'the rest is just vegetables in the salad'." She smiled after making what she considered to be a clever comment, but Tom didn't appreciate the joke.

"A word of caution, darlin': don't ever stand between a man and his beef," he warned light-heartedly, shaking a friendly finger at Miranda. Tom was already well-aware that his fiancé would attempt to change his diet after they were married. No cattle rancher would ever stand for that. Besides the horse, he would also turn over to her, as a wedding present, the outright ownership and responsibility for a small herd of cattle. If she intended on becoming a cattle rancher's wife, then she would have to stop thinking about beef as though it were repugnant. He wasn't about to allow the Dakota Fetch to become a tearoom and sewing club, so to speak.

Opened on the former site of the army headquarters, the War Memorial of Korea had six indoor exhibition rooms and an outdoor exhibition center. In galleries were rows of black marble monuments that honored those who died during the Korean and Vietnam Wars, as well as policemen who had died in the line of duty. The plaza had an artificial waterfall and in the center stood the Statue of Brothers, a well-known symbol of Korea's disunity. Thousands of items—including weapons and other equipment, paintings, and sculptures—were displayed in six different halls, each with its own theme. Many larger weapons could be found outdoors, around the main building. Of course, the hall commemorating the Korean War was of particular interest to Tom.

"Look at all the guns and knives," he commented, pointing at the various weapons in the case. "Daddy left me a knife just like that one over there." Tom's remark would prompt Miranda to take pause, this suddenly granting her a delightful notion.

Before leaving for the Incheon South Korea Cruise Port, where they would board the *Cavalier* for Taiwan, Miranda picked up her messages at the hotel, among them the latest telegram from Cranston:

Trinity Court Enterprises sold for six-hundred-million **STOP** List of charitable organizations compiled for your review upon your return **STOP** Have filed legal documentation for the establishment of a Non-Profit Trinity Court Foundation **STOP** Ten-million to the International Asian Foundation for the Prevention of Cruelty to Animals, earmarked for China **STOP** Ten-million to the Human Rights Council of Asia **STOP** Five-million to the American School in Shanghai **STOP** Keep going **STOP**

With her own thoughts about a wedding present for Tom swirling around inside her head, Miranda excitedly answered Cranston, the idea to honor Tom's father having come to her at the War Memorial of Korea:

Immediately dispatch attorneys in Japan to Seoul **STOP** Have them arrange twenty-million dollar donation to the War Memorial of Korea, earmarked for the Korean War Hall for renovation and upkeep **STOP** Donation to be made in the name of Winston Cosborn Dakota, on behalf of all those Americans who fought in Korea, with a plaque bearing his name to be displayed on the International Walk of Memorials **STOP**

Wouldn't Tom be so surprised...and pleased? The visit to Taiwan would seem anticlimactic, now that Winston Cosborn Dakota could have a good, peaceful rest for himself, his work here done and his legacy now complete.

Miranda and Tom would be in Taiwan for several days, spending their entire visit in the capital of Taipei. Their exquisite hotel, furnished with all the luxurious amenities a visitor could possibly desire, compensated for their having to leave the *Cavalier*, even though their heavy itinerary would only allow for brief sleep there and nothing more.

"Are we *really* going to be able to visit all of these places in only three days?" asked Tom, looking at the daily planner over Miranda's shoulder.

"I suppose so," answered Miranda. "Everything seems to be well-organized, right down to the last minute."

"You'll have to peel me off the floor to get me back on the ship," quipped Tom.

"With pleasure, sweetheart," Miranda answered. "You won't get away from me *that* easily."

"Nor would I try," Tom assured her, planting a quick kiss on Miranda's lips before the couple would begin their whirlwind tour of Taipei, stamina and good humor the key ingredients to a successful stay there.

For the next three days, Miranda and Tom were totally immersed in Taiwanese culture, history, politics, and food, an interesting and impressive learning experience that they would carry with them for a long time. They visited the National Palace Museum, one of the largest museums in the world, containing hundreds of thousands of Chinese artifacts; they toured the Presidential Office Building that housed the Office of the President of the Republic of China; they walked about the Chiang Kai-shek Memorial Hall built to honor the late president; they shopped and ate coffin bread and beef noodle soup inside the impressive Taipei 101, formerly one of the tallest buildings in the world; they walked around the Shilin Night Market, the largest night market in the city, where they tried oyster vermicelli and ice-cream dorayaki; and they visited the Mengjia Longshan Temple, one of the oldest temples in Taipei. They also attended a theatre performance and walked around a street festival outside of their hotel where they feasted on spring rolls, pig's blood cake, sanbeiji, and pork balls.

"It's a wonder we haven't gotten sick yet, darlin'," said Tom after downing another pork ball.

By the time they arrived at the Keelung Cruise Port Terminal to board the *Cavalier*, they were exhausted…and still quite full. Grateful that Manila was over 700 miles from Taipei, Miranda and Tom decided to unwind from the last three extremely hectic days in the royal-blue waters of Miranda's swimming pool, and this time they would remain there in luxuriant privacy until the *Cavalier* docked in Manila. Eating and drinking little, they relaxed and digested, throwing off the after-effects of the previous three days in readiness for their next stop, where they would get back on the sightseeing treadmill…all over again.

After docking in Manila, Miranda and Tom began their seven-day visit to the Philippines, where there was plenty to enjoy. They first visited the capital, Manila, where they shopped in the traditional Quiapo market, purposely staying away from the modern malls of the city. A street market surrounding a centuries-old church, Quiapo overflowed with local delicacies and typical Filipino handicrafts. There, they tried takoyaki balls, stir-fried garlic beef, and pulutan while perusing the over-abundance of religious goods in the booths and on the tables that surrounded the church. Tom bought Miranda a small cross that they would later have blessed by the priest on the *Cavalier*, a rather rotund but jovial man whom they had befriended at one of the all-night buffets on the ship.

Over the next five days, the couple would walk around the rice terraces in Ifugao and the Mayon Volcano in Albay before taking a comfortable yacht with a private tour guide down to Cebu, a cultural center of the Philippines. There, they would visit the chapel that housed the famous Magellan's Cross, the foremost symbol of Christianity in the Philippines, as well as the nearby Basilica Minore del Santo Niño. Fortunate to be there at just the right time of year, they attended the religious feast of Santo Niño de Cebu and observed the colorful Sinulog dancing in the streets, both important cultural elements of the Sinulog Festival. Impressed by the good works of the Basilica to stem the poverty that existed there, especially in the depressed area of Northern Cebu where hundreds of malnourished children lived, Miranda pledged ten-million dollars to the Ecclesiastical Province of Cebu.

Afterwards, their yacht took them to the white sand beaches of Boracay where they relaxed for a day before heading up to the town of Taal to visit the Minor Basilica of Saint Martin of Tours, the largest church in the Philippines and, in fact, all of Asia.

Their tour complete, they headed back to Manila to, once again, board the *Cavalier* bound next for Vietnam, but not before Miranda would contact the archbishop of Manila. Her admiration of the church's dedication to alleviate the suffering of the poor had manifested itself in the donation she had made to the Ecclesiastical Province of Cebu. Why not do the same in Manila, where she was sad to see families of squatters living in an alley behind her luxury hotel, placing the poor only a stone's throw away from the affluent?

After explaining who she was and why she was in the Philippines, Miranda informed the archbishop of her intention to donate twenty-million dollars to the Ecclesiastical Province of Manila, asking that the money go towards helping the poor families who lived there. Personally knowing many of those who lived out their daily lives in abject poverty, the archbishop was only too happy to discuss the dire problems that plagued the poor people of Manila and, without hesitation, graciously accepted Miranda's generous offer. She would never learn, though, of the archbishop's true feelings of doubt as to the legitimacy of her offer. Would the Ecclesiastical Province of Manila ever really see such a windfall?

"I would hope that a meal program might be put in place, especially for the children," Miranda commented.

"And perhaps building as many low-cost housing units as we can afford, the number depending upon how far your generous gift takes us."

"In that case, add another ten million dollars to my pledge," Miranda said decisively, "so that you can go that much farther."

Miranda would wire Cranston from her hotel room that afternoon before leaving for the *Cavalier*, docked and awaiting the return of her passengers in the Port of Manila:

Ten-million to the Ecclesiastical Province of Cebu **STOP**
Thirty-million to the Ecclesiastical Province of Manila **STOP**

The archbishop would soon find out that he had no reason to doubt Miranda's word, and, for the first time, she could not help but wonder: was she getting close?

Chapter 27
Previously Impossible

Don't think money does everything or you are going to end up
doing everything for money.

-Voltaire

The enchantment of Southeast Asia took Miranda's breath away, as she knew it would, the beauty and fascination behind these ancient cultures appealing to her passion for all things historical. The temples, museums, archeological sites, and lovely vistas replenished her soul wherever she went, but, in this part of the world so aesthetically different and in many ways mystical, she found herself gravitating towards people more so than she had in other places.

One country ravaged by years of war, another struggling to stem the tide of human trafficking, there were some serious issues plaguing Southeast Asia. With eyes and ears open, Miranda would take everything into account, for it was doubtful that she would ever pass this way again. Here too she might be able to make a difference.

Vietnam, no longer an integral part of the American stream of consciousness or the lead story on the nightly news, as it had been during the war years, was now a country joined with the world of nations but in many ways still licking its wounds. The poverty rate was high, especially in the rural areas where many people, particularly children, had little to no access to basic necessities; Vietnam could not adequately provide for its most vulnerable people, who lived well beyond government reach. No food and water, lack of sanitary conditions, and the absence of formal education were issues of particular concern in these areas, which told Miranda that there was much her money could do here, particularly for the children. Knowing this, she would quietly consider her options.

Thailand, on the other hand, had an entirely different problem. Miranda and Tom having heard about it in the Philippines, although giving it only vague attention at the time, the issue of human trafficking was already a social issue despicable to them on many levels, especially as it pertained to children. Brought to this beautiful country of Buddhist temples and royal palaces of kings past were the women and children who were sexually exploited, while people wanting higher wages were recruited to work in the fishing, farming, or construction industries, only to be abused by labor traffickers. Difficult to control, human trafficking from other countries to Thailand occurred regularly, as evidenced by the crowded boatloads of incoming men, women, and children who were forced into a life for which they had not bargained. Could she make a difference here too and how might she go about it? Miranda would quietly consider her options, if any, in Thailand as well.

Arriving at the port of Phu My on the South China Sea, a tour bus drove Miranda and Tom the 80 miles to their hotel in Ho Chi Minh City, where a telegram from Cranston awaited Miranda's arrival:

Twenty-million to the War Memorial of Korea earmarked, for the Korean War Hall arranged **STOP** Government officials gratefully accepted money and readily agreed to plaque **STOP** Ten-million to the Ecclesiastical Province of Cebu **STOP** Thirty-million to the Ecclesiastical Province of Manila **STOP** Keep going **STOP**

Keeping the first part of the telegram a secret from Tom, not to be revealed until the day of their wedding, Miranda was ready for their 10-day stay in Southeast Asia. She wasn't only looking forward to seeing the sites, but she was also determined to, somehow, leave her mark, encouraged by the words of inspiration found in all of Cranston's telegrams urging her to 'keep going'. She knew that there was much good work to be done here, but exactly how she would go about it would have to be determined at a later time.

Tourism in Vietnam previously impossible, the couple would visit many sites of historical and cultural value throughout the country. Before boarding an airplane at the Tan Son Nhat Airport for the former imperial city of Hue, Miranda and Tom spent two days in Ho Chi Minh City where they saw the Saigon Notre Dame Basilica, the Fine Arts Museum, and the Saigon Opera House.

They also enjoyed the spicy Vietnamese cooking there, considered to be one of the healthiest cuisines in the world for its use of fresh fruit, vegetables, rice, and fish. Even Tom had to admit that the food was good, despite its lack of fat and beef, but, once again, he warned Miranda straight out not to expect him to change his eating habits once they got home. A vacation was one thing…life on the Dakota Fetch was quite another.

"After this cruise, I don't believe I'll ever eat another grain of rice again," Tom said definitively.

After their stay in Ho Chi Minh City, they boarded a plane for Phu Bai Airport, located just outside the city of Hue where Tom showed particular interest in the former imperial capital. As the seat of the Nguyen Dynasty, it was home to emperors and, later on, the national capital. The immense citadel located on the north side of the Perfume River, surrounded by a moat and an impenetrable wall of stone, and encompassed the Imperial City, the Forbidden Purple City where the emperor once lived, and a replica of the Royal Theatre. There were other monuments along the river too, including the tombs of several emperors and the Thien Mu Pagoda, the official symbol of the city. Finally, along the south bank were numerous buildings distinctly French in their architectural style, all impressive and interesting elements of Hue's historical culture. These places along the river, combined with the Museum of Royal Fine Arts and its impressive collection of artifacts from the Imperial City, made the couple's visit to Hue a worthwhile learning experience.

"Getting to know Vietnam through the lens of history is so incredible to me," Miranda commented, "especially since I never knew much about it, outside of the war. Even then, my knowledge was sketchy at best, since I found it difficult to watch the news."

"That was a long time ago, darlin'. It's finally time to mend fences," said Tom, still in the conciliatory mood he had carried with him all the way from South Korea.

Rounding out their visit to Vietnam were trips to Phong Nha-Ke Bang National Park, known for its 300 caves and grottoes, including a cave considered to be the largest in the world and the caves located in the northern coastal region of Ha Long Bay. From there, Miranda and Tom took a helicopter to Noi Bai Airport, outside of Hanoi, where they boarded the plane that would take them to Bangkok.

Miranda was looking forward to Thailand, but she had unfinished business in Vietnam. Formulating the words in her head, she would wire Cranston immediately, instructing him to make arrangements to send twenty-million dollars to a fledgling orphanage in Hue and one-hundred-million dollars to a school and medical center currently being built in the Dien Bien Province. Satisfied with her choices, Miranda was confident that her money would make a difference in these rural areas…especially for the children.

After their plane touched down in Bangkok, Miranda and Tom checked into their hotel and immediately began to visit the historical and cultural sites in and around the city, for the length of their stay would be all too brief. Their hotel was luxurious and conveniently located, allowing easy access to all their points of interest, especially Thai restaurants with five-star cuisine.

"I'm starving," said Tom as the two entered a fancy little bistro. "If it can't be McDonald's, then I'm glad it's here," he said, ordering sautéed sesame beef and shitake mushrooms.

The migrant population obvious within the city, Miranda couldn't help but wonder if they were actually living out their dreams or had simply become victims of abuse stranded in a foreign land. For now, she would immerse herself only in the history and culture of Bangkok.

Their first stop, the Grand Palace and the Royal Temple of the Emerald Buddha, was the main temple to see in Bangkok. Built in 1782, it still remained the site of many ceremonial occasions, even though royalty was no longer in residence there. Nevertheless, its beautifully ornate construction was a testament to the grandeur in which the kings had lived centuries ago. Sharing the site of the Grand Palace was the Temple of the Emerald Buddha, which housed the representation of a meditating Buddha, carved from a single piece of jade. Dating back to the 15th century, the carving remains an object of solemn veneration, its robes changed three times a year only at the hands of the king, in accordance with the changing seasons.

Miranda and Tom, next, visited the Temple of the Reclining Buddha, located south of the Grand Palace on Rattanakosin Island. Classed as the highest grade of the first-class royal temples, it was built by King Rama I, whose ashes were enshrined there in the early 19th century. Largely expanded by King Rama III, the temple contains the largest collection of Buddha images found anywhere in Thailand, including the 150-foot long reclining Buddha. Also thought to be the earliest center for public education in Thailand, it also houses a school of Thai medicine where traditional massage is still taught and practiced.

That evening, Miranda and Tom walked through a merry street festival where people in colorful costumes danced, sang, and celebrated with good food. Here, the couple tried coconut griddlecakes and green papaya salad before heading over to the night market for rice noodle rolls and roasted duck on skewers. There, the locals, many of whom were families with babies in strollers, spent their time together laughing and chatting as they ate their way through the market, enjoying the many Thai delicacies so familiar to them.

Miranda couldn't help but notice, though, the dozens of children who roamed in and around the numerous stalls without the accompaniment of adults, some of them begging for food. Did they belong to anyone or had they been abandoned on the streets of Bangkok to fend for themselves? She also heard one of the vendors comment in passing that the children were not Thai, for they spoke Burmese and Khmer, among other foreign languages. This would tear at Miranda…and she wouldn't forget it. Their stomachs full, the couple headed back to their hotel having to wade through the hundreds of strolling people who had flooded the market. They would have to get a good night's sleep before boarding a plane early the next morning for Sukhotai, the capital of the First Kingdom of Siam.

"I'm as full as I can be," commented Miranda, trying to find a comfortable position as she lay on the bed. "I hope I can tolerate the plane ride tomorrow."

"A little bicarbonate of soda will do you a world of good," said Tom, pulling the box from his suitcase. "It's a staple at the Fetch."

"Oh, yes…the land of steak and potatoes," smiled Miranda.

"You mean, the land of *love*," said Tom, oozing with syrupy sweetness as he mixed the bicarbonate of soda into a glass of water. But, alas, not even the most ladylike of burps would ease Miranda's indigestion. She could only hope that their plane wouldn't hit turbulence.

Dating back to the 13th and 14th centuries, Sukhothai had a number of monuments and temples, all keen examples of early Thai architecture. With a triple wall and four gates the city protected these structures, which are today considered to be some of the most unique and treasured architectural achievements in Thailand's history. Here too the civilization of the early kingdom allowed various influences and ancient traditions to help mold its culture, making it one of the greatest societies of its time. Sukhothai meaning the dawn of happiness, they ruled the Thai Empire for approximately 140 years and today its monuments and temples stand as a testament to the culture and innovation of the people that erected them.

From Sukhothai, Miranda and Tom would fly to the site of Ban Chiang in the Udon Thani Province, one of the most important prehistoric settlements in South East Asia. Evidence at the site pointed to an early civilization in the region that farmed and made use of metal tools. Discovered in 1966, the settlement was also known for its red painted pottery, now found in museums all over the world. Besides visiting the settlement, they strolled through several museums in the area, all of them proudly displaying the ancient red pottery for which Ban Chiang had come to be known. Miranda fell in love with the red color and beautiful designs of the many jugs and pots they saw, not only in the museums but in the shops too. Tom bought her a gorgeous pitcher that caught her eye, making arrangements to have it shipped to the Fetch.

"Think of it as an early wedding present," he said. "It'll be waiting for you when we get there."

After flying back to Bangkok, Miranda and Tom prepared to leave for Singapore, the *Cavalier* now awaiting their return in the port of Laem Chabang on the Gulf of Thailand, two hours south of the capital. From there, the magnificent ocean liner would journey to the Singapore Cruise Center, where they would disembark for their final few days in South East Asia.

Leaving the hotel in a private cab, Miranda and Tom watched out of their respective windows the men, women, and children who walked the streets of Bangkok, the eventual distance of the cab rendering them faded and small.

As they continued their drive south, Miranda became pensive, thinking about the hundreds of people they had seen on the streets and in the markets, many of them children just wandering around with no one to hold their hand, buy them food, or tell them to go home. Perhaps there *was* no home for these urchins who seemed to haunt the streets of Bangkok, especially at night. Had they been brought to Thailand for an unspeakable purpose, only to have run away or been abandoned? Miranda had kept the human trafficking in her thoughts the entire stay, upholding a promise to herself to consider in her thoughts the entire stay, upholding a promise to herself to consider her options, mulling them over and over again until, finally, she had made up her mind in the cab ride out of Bangkok. She would donate five-million dollars to the American Center for Exploited Children in South East Asia, a watchdog organization that kept data on human trafficking and worked to rescue children who had been sexually exploited. If her pledge could make even a small difference by saving the life of just one child, Miranda would be elated, although it would be her fervent wish to save every single one of them. If only it were possible. Unfortunately, given the nature of the problem, she would never know the outcome.

After a few days of rest and relaxation on the *Cavalier*, Miranda and Tom disembarked at the Singapore Cruise Center, looking forward to some leisurely sightseeing over the next several days. The primitive, rural sites of both Vietnam and Thailand had tired them out and they were looking forward to a little less dust and a lot more modernity before going to India, the last leg of their long journey before heading back to Europe. She would immediately wire Cranston about the five-million dollars to send to the American Center for Exploited Children in South East Asia, as she was eager to put business behind her in anticipation of a much less hectic visit over the next several days. Although still awaiting her trusted lawyer's confirmation of her instructions concerning Vietnam, Miranda would revel in Singapore and think only of her future at the Fetch…now drawing closer with each passing day.

"When we get back, I'll personally escort you to Trinity Court, where you can pick up your things and say goodbye," said Tom.

"I don't think there's anything there that I want," Miranda said, shaking her head sadly after having already thought about it. "There's nothing at all that I've even missed, but I *would* like to say goodbye to my household staff. I'll also instruct Cranston to give each of them six months' wages from the proceeds of the sale of the estate."

"That's generous, darlin'," said Tom. "You'll be able to move to the Fetch with a clear conscience." He kissed her tenderly. "It won't be long now," he assured her.

Between the restaurants and hawker food stalls, Miranda and Tom enjoyed three days of cuisine at its most diverse; any kind of rice or noodles were Miranda's favorite, while Tom gravitated towards the beef dishes. They had time to sit down for a fancy meal in several fine restaurants, but choosing from the stalls was their favorite way to eat, affording them greater choice from a variety of international cuisines. They were inclined to eat at the Indian, Cantonese, and Vietnamese stalls, although Tom *did* run into a nearby McDonald's at one point, unable to resist his urge for a hamburger. They obviously never suffered from a lack of food as they immersed themselves in the sights and sounds of Singapore, a culturally engaging country with plenty to do. More importantly, they were having fun.

Attending a Chinese New Year celebration two blocks from their hotel, Miranda and Tom were most delighted by the endless, colorful processions and lion dances. While there, they happily accepted mandarin oranges from well-wishers as they snaked around the many stalls feasting on buttery pineapple tarts, spiced cakes, rolled egg biscuits, coconut cookies, spicy shrimp rolls, and sweet pork jerky. It was a joyous street scene, the people steeped deep in their revelry, and it was a great way to spend a few hours.

"Life on the Fetch won't be *this* raucous," Tom commented. "I hope you won't be bored after seeing all of this."

"I can't *wait* to begin my peaceful life with you on the Fetch," commented Miranda as she squeezed his hand, "and, no…I won't be bored." The reluctant heiress had already had all of the excitement she could ever want, far beyond what most people ever experienced in a lifetime.

"Well, outside of a few rodeos that take place on the ranch every year, life just pretty much saunters along there," said Tom with a smile. "I can't wait to get back…with you by my side."

"I don't think I ever sauntered, not even once in my life, until I met you," she lovingly joked. Life at the Dakota Fetch couldn't come soon enough.

Having had enough of the Chinese New Year celebration, the couple walked for many blocks until they reached the quaint, more traditional neighborhoods of Singapore. They peered in store windows, admired the architecture of the buildings, and observed the people on the streets until they reached their destination: Chinatown. There, they bought souvenirs on Pagoda Street and did a walking tour of the many Hindu temples, Chinese temples, and mosques, all within close proximity to one another. There were people celebrating the Chinese New Year in these neighborhoods too, the streets ablaze with color, especially red, and an over-abundance of Mandarin oranges. And, of course, there were the many commonplace hawker stalls.

The next day, Miranda and Tom visited the National Museum of Singapore, the oldest museum in the prosperous island nation and an architectural icon. Here, they learned about Singapore's past and present as they walked through the Singapore History and Living galleries. It was an interesting and informative testament to this culture and, like all of the other places they had visited throughout the world, seeing this museum was the chance of a lifetime. After that, they visited the Singapore Art Museum, which housed contemporary artwork from all over South East Asia. Not really Miranda's cup of tea, she would always prefer classic Renaissance paintings to modern art, but she enjoyed the exhibits nevertheless.

"Now I can say that I've seen the best of South East Asian contemporary art," she said, never one to shy away from a learning experience.

That night, they would go to a safari park and explore the rainforest there at dusk, both of them having a wonderful time.

"The last two days have been so full, but I can keep going!" Miranda exclaimed. "So far, Singapore has been such fun!"

With only one more day there before having to leave for India, the couple chose to go to Gardens by the Bay, a conservatory complex. There, they visited the Flower Dome, a glass house with seven different gardens, a colorful flower show, and an olive grove—all of these plants indigenous to the Mediterranean and other semi-arid tropical regions. They also visited the Cloud Forest, with its 138-foot Cloud Mountain, both situated along the edge of the Marina Reservoir. They marveled at the Supertree Grove—made up of vertical, tree-like structures technologically outfitted to mimic the function of real trees—and walked the Skyway for a panoramic, aerial view of the Gardens complex.

"It's time to leave, darlin'," said Tom. "We have to board the *Cavalier* by 8:00 this evening."

"I wish we could stay in Singapore a little longer," Miranda lamented.

"It's been fun," Tom admitted, "but it's time to move on." He'd been looking forward to India for a long time, but it was also obvious that Tom's attitude had changed, for the sooner this cruise was over, the sooner he would have Miranda, all to himself, at the Fetch.

When they went back to the hotel to pick up their luggage, Miranda found the long-awaited telegram from Cranston sitting on the desk in their room:

Twenty-million to orphanage in Hue **STOP** One-hundred-million to school and medical center currently being built in Dien Bien Province **STOP** Five-million to American Center for Exploited Children in South East Asia **STOP** Only one-hundred-million left at your disposal **STOP** Keep going...but slow down **STOP**

Miranda's heart pounded and it would do so all the way to the Singapore Cruise Center, for she no longer had to wonder. She was, indeed, getting close.

Chapter 28
India

Many people take no care of their money till they come nearly to the end of it, and others do just the same with their time.
-Johann Wolfgang von Goethe

After four days of travel over seas of varied temperaments, the Arabian Sea extending the calmest, most placid waters, the *Cavalier* docked in magnificent Mumbai, the couple's welcoming passage to India. Wrapped in the rich culture of old Bombay, Mumbai was a treasure chest of architectural jewels, from the Gateway of India to the Chhatrapati Shivaji Maharaj Vastu Sangrahalaya to the ISKCON Temple in Juhu…and Miranda and Tom would see them all. Throughout their four-day stay, they would also immerse themselves in the epicurean delights of the region, especially enjoying the presentation and delightful tastes of vada pav, panipuri, and the various types of kebabs that would satisfy Tom's penchant for meat, their stomachs surprisingly tolerant of the new cuisine.

"I believe that my stomach has developed a steel lining," Tom said kiddingly. "Nothing seems to bother me. I hope I haven't spoken too soon," he added sheepishly.

There were many other foods too that they would have a chance to taste as they made their way around Mumbai, visiting many sites of cultural interest before leaving for Agra. One of these was the Elephanta Caves, located on the island of Gharapuri in Mumbai Harbor. The Elephanta Caves, a group of sculpted caves consisting of two Buddhist and five Hindu caves with rock-cut stone sculptures, had been dated as far back as the 5th century. Carved out of solid basalt rock and carefully painted, the caves were architectural and sculptural masterpieces, the main cave serving as a Hindu place of worship until Portuguese rule began in 1534. After having been severely damaged and neglected throughout the centuries, the main cave was later restored, much of the original artwork preserved.

Miranda and Tom walked through this incredible network of caves enthralled by its many intricate sculptures dedicated to the Lord Shiva. These carvings were yet another historical example of artistic brilliance, and Miranda was grateful for having been given the opportunity to see them. Clearly this, which was now an amazing legacy so culturally significant to the region, would more than likely have remained unknown to anyone destined to never visit India. After their walkthrough, the couple left the caves in awe, having had an experience they would long remember.

Next, they visited the Kanheri Caves located in the forests of the Sanjay Gandhi National Park on the outskirts of Mumbai. These caves contained Buddhist sculptures, paintings, and inscriptions dating back to the 1st century. Found on a hillside, Miranda and Tom would have to walk up rock-cut steps in order to get into the complex, containing no less than 109 caves in all. At one time utilized as monasteries, the caves were an important Buddhist settlement where monks lived, meditated, studied, and worshiped. The many carvings of Buddha were beautifully intricate, again another testament to the reverence and artistic brilliance of that long past culture. That night, Miranda and Tom shared a meal of Dahipuri, Ragda-pattice, and Pav Bhaji before departing for Chhatrapati Shivaji International Airport, where they would board a plane headed for Agra. They were giddy in anticipation of their next stop: the Taj Mahal. Little did they know of the impact it would have on their hearts, and their very souls.

Upon seeing the ivory-white marble mausoleum, Miranda was moved to tears, for there stood the greatest testament to eternal love the world has ever known. Commissioned by Shah Jahan after the death of his favorite wife, Mumtaz Mahal, the Taj Mahal complex was built to house her tomb, along with a mosque, guesthouse, and formal gardens. Surrounded on three sides by sandstone walls but open to the river, the structure was considered to be the most excellent example of Mughal architecture in India and a representative of the illustrious history of the imperial court and the undying love of one shah for his Persian princess. It took some 20,000 artisans to complete the construction of the mausoleum, its surrounding buildings, and garden by 1648, then and now considered to be the greatest jewel in India's treasure chest, recognized and admired worldwide.

The tomb, a white marble structure topped by a large dome and gilded finial, is the central focus of the Taj Mahal. Framed by four minarets, each standing at 130 feet tall, it houses the graves of both Mumtaz Mahal and Shah Jahan, not in the main chamber but at a lower level. An image of the mausoleum can be seen reflected in the pool found in the center of the garden. Miranda sat for a photograph, the majestic Taj Mahal behind her in the near distance. The image took Tom's breath away.

"You look so beautiful sitting there, darlin'," he said, clicking off one picture after another. "You and the Taj Mahal belong together…two priceless jewels."

"But it's a tomb," Miranda countered, "a place built out of grief. Do you really think I *belong* here? Say, are you trying to bump me off before we even get married?" she joked.

"It's magnificent and beautiful, representing the deep love and devotion between two people," said Tom, still clicking away, "and all of those things remind me of you."

"Well, as long as you put it that way," said Miranda, "then I guess I'll allow it." Tilting her head, she smiled lovingly at Tom as she stood up and turned around, staring at the overwhelming majesty of the Taj Mahal one more time before she and Tom would walk around the garden and explore the other structures. It was a sight never to be forgotten. Miranda would tuck it away deep in her memory…and her heart…forever.

Remaining in Agra for four days, the couple visited other important Mughal sites, historically impressive and culturally significant in their own right. The Agra Fort, completed by Shah Jahan in the 17th century, was made entirely of red sandstone, it too a beautiful example of Mughal architecture. The tomb of Akbar the Great, completed in the early part of the 17th century, had the 99 names of Allah inscribed on it. The deserted city of Fatehpur Sikri, built by Akbar in the 16th century, was considered to be one of the most illustrious cities in the Mughal Empire. The Itmad-ud-Daulah Tomb, a lavish structure built in the 17th century, was known for its detailed carvings and inlay work. The Mankameshwar Temple, one of four ancient temples dedicated to Lord Shiva, where it is said that the Shiv lingam is covered by silver metal, is believed to have been founded by Lord Shiva himself. The Ram Bagh, built by Babur in 1528, is considered to be the oldest Mughal garden in Agra. And the holy city of Vrindavan, is home to thousands of temples dedicated to Lord Krishna.

Besides appreciating the Taj Mahal and the other important Mughal sites that surrounded it, Miranda and Tom enjoyed the distinct cuisine of Agra as well, the Mughal influence reflected just as much in the food as in the architecture. Mughal foods, usually prepared with fruits, vegetables, and grains, were typically seasoned with pungent spices. Tom enjoyed the creamy kormas and steak-like pasandas, but good-naturedly tried Puri-Aloo and Kachori, two of the most famous vegetarian dishes in Agra, just to please Miranda. They also indulged in a couple of typical rice preparations, such as Lucknowi Biryani and Zarda, along with several varieties of kababs, such as Shami Kabab, Kakori Kabab, and Gulnaar Kabab. Tom's favorite dish in this region was Kundan Kaliya, a mutton preparation with gravy and saffron, while Miranda adored the Kachori and rice, meat never essential to her diet, as far as she was concerned. On the night prior to leaving Agra, they dined on Nehari Khaas and Murg Mussallam, their final taste of Mughal cuisine before boarding a plane that would take them to Jabalpur Airport and their next destination: Kanha National Park.

This vast national park was the largest expanse of protected land in Central India. Also known as the Kanha Tiger Reserve, it safeguarded a number of Bengal tigers, Indian leopards, sloth bears, barasingha, and Indian wild dogs within its boundaries. It was speculated that the forest characterized in Rudyard Kipling's *The Jungle Book* was based upon the forests of Kanha National Park. These forests, interspersed with meadows or open grasslands, were also home to wild cats, foxes, jackals, swamp deer, and gaur. Deer, antelope, langur, and wild boar were also prevalent, while striped hyena and the sloth bear were only seen now and then. Also living there were nocturnal animals such as the hyena, jungle cat, and civet, along with 300 species of birds, including the black ibis, crested serpent eagle, and white-eyed buzzard. Reptiles included pythons, cobras, and vipers, while there were many species of turtles as well. Although wild Indian elephants no longer roamed the area, these massive creatures would carry Miranda and Tom on safari.

Staying in the core area of the park for four days, the couple went on no less than six safaris, each time riding on the trusted back of an experienced elephant.

"There's the tiger," Tom whispered as he clicked off his camera in quick succession. "The elephant knows just how to block it from walking away. Fascinating," he remarked, still speaking in a low whisper. Miranda was taken with his sense of wonderment.

The elephants took the couple through the forests twice a day for three out of the four days that they stayed in the park, these safaris typically two hours in duration. Luckily, they spotted a tiger three times over three days, a frequency often unheard of, as their large transport lumbered through the flora of the lush forests. They saw a leopard too, along with many deer, foxes, and wild boar. And when they looked up in the trees, the birds were a spectacular sight.

"Look at that pretty red one," Miranda pointed, bringing her rented binoculars up to her face. Her smile couldn't get any broader.

Facing a vast meadow with jungle all around, Miranda and Tom stayed at the compound of the Baghira Log Huts, their guide warning them not to wander out at night.

"Remember where you are," he said, pointing a finger. "An attack by a tiger or leopard is not out of the realm of possibility. If any such animal should come around the huts at night, we will sound an alarm." He smiled slightly, for he knew that he had gotten Miranda's attention.

"I won't put a single toe out of the door at night," she assured the guide, feigning fright. In reality, she was absolutely enchanted with the place. Tom just laughed.

"This is all just so *fantastic*," he said with a big grin, shaking his head.

Indeed, during their stay, they would look out on the meadow at nightfall in search of wildlife, usually over drinks and a leisurely dinner of poha, malpua, seekh kababs, jalebi, or whatever else the chef had managed to cook up that night. It never took long to catch sight of the many deer, bison, foxes, and wild hogs that sauntered about in search of food and drink. Miranda made good use of her binoculars, a small watering hole in the near distance always a draw for thirsty animals at sunset. She was more besotted with the animals than she ever thought herself capable. When their stay at the park was over, Miranda and Tom were sorry to leave, feeling fortunate, nonetheless, to have seen yet another region of India that they would never forget.

After flying back to Mumbai, they packed up their belongings in readiness to go back to the *Cavalier*, their time in India now over. Once on the ship, they would slowly travel across the Arabian Sea over to the Red Sea, then up through the Suez Canal, taking only a brief peek at Egypt before finally heading out into the Mediterranean. There, they would stop for a few days' respite on the island of Corfu in Greece before cruising up to Monte Carlo for a luxurious stay on the Cote d'Azur before departing for home.

"The way I figure it, we should be sitting pretty on the Fetch in about one month," said Tom. "Can you believe it?"

"It's all I've been thinking about," said Miranda. "I can't wait. What kind of wedding would you like?" she asked.

"Something festive and lively…soon after we get back," said Tom decidedly. "We can get married right in the main corral, maybe even on horseback. What do you think of that?"

"I would like that just fine," said Miranda smiling warmly, excited to be thinking about the wedding once again after four days on safari. "I've been thinking about something else too, sweetheart," she said. "Since the gold in India is so beautiful, perhaps we should buy our wedding rings right here in Mumbai."

"That's a fine idea, darlin'," said Tom, sorry he hadn't thought of it himself. "We'll shop at that fancy gold center down the block from our hotel before leaving for the *Cavalier* tonight.

"And there's one more thing," said Miranda, taking in a deep breath and then holding it.

"You sure have been doing a lot of serious thinking today," said Tom, furrowing his brow with concern. "Okay…out with it, darlin'. What else is on your mind?"

"I'll be wiring Cranston before we leave to send one-hundred-million dollars to the National Organization for the Preservation of Indian National Parks and Wildlife Reserves." She was breathless after saying it. Tom was flabbergasted.

"Are you sure, Miranda?" he asked, surprised at her final philanthropic gesture. "That's the rest of your money, isn't it?"

"It is…gratefully," she confirmed, "so, without reservation or regret, I am finished." And just like that, Miranda's disposal of her fortune was finally, and irrevocably, complete.

Part Three

"He who loses money loses much; He who loses a friend loses much more; He who loses faith loses all."

Eleanor Roosevelt

Chapter 29
Home at Last

Money can't buy friends, but you can get a better class of enemy.

-Spike Milligan

By the time they reached Monte Carlo, there was already a telegram waiting for Miranda, her faithful lawyer never one to mince words:

Endowment to the National Organization for the Preservation of Indian National Parks and Wildlife Reserves on hold **STOP** Please reconfirm your intention to send such a large donation to said organization **STOP** Will await your advisement before taking any further action **STOP** Final decision is yours **STOP** Only verifying that I correctly understood your instruction **STOP**

For some reason, Cranston's telegram brought a smile to Miranda's face, even though she was slightly perturbed that he was questioning her instruction.

"So, Cranston thinks that I'm crazy too," she said, knowing full well that he would never think such a thing.

"Crazy? Why?" Tom asked.

"For making that large donation to the national parks in India," she said.

"I'm sure he doesn't think that you're crazy," Tom reassured her, "and neither do I. It's just that it was such a large—"

"I think I'll call him," Miranda interrupted. "I'll assure him over the phone that he didn't misunderstand my instruction and that I'm not *crazy*...just tired," she sighed. "I want to put this awful life of mine behind me. I'm ready for a new life...with you," she said, looking lovingly at Tom as she picked up the phone from its cradle. He believed her too, never having doubted for one moment her desire to spend the rest of her days with him, and not because she wanted to get away from Trinity Court, but because she really loved him. And he loved her...so much.

"Your new life has already begun, darlin'," he said softly. "We're almost home."

And indeed they were. Miranda *did* call Cranston from Monte Carlo that afternoon, verifying that he had correctly understood her instruction, but within a matter of days, she and Tom were back at Trinity Court, where she was able to speak to him personally. So much had changed in her absence.

"Cranston, I'd like you to meet Tom, my fiancé," she said, the two men shaking hands.

"I'd like to personally thank you, Cranston, for all you've done for Miranda over the last eight months," Tom said graciously. "Her mind was always at ease knowing that you were taking care of the financial and legal matters at this end."

"I was just doing my job," Cranston said modestly.

"It was more than that," Miranda chimed in, putting a hand on her lawyer's arm. "You're a good friend, Cranston. Tom and I have talked about it and, well, if you should ever want a job on the legal team at the Dakota Fetch, you've got one," said Miranda sincerely.

"Thank you, Miranda, I'll certainly keep that in mind," Cranston said, clearly grateful. "But, until all of your finances are settled, and that might take some time, my presence here is required."

"Well, at least you'll come to the wedding," said Tom. "Surely you can get away for that."

"I would be delighted," said Cranston with a tinge of melancholy to his voice, truly sorry to see Miranda go. Their attorney-client relationship, as well as their friendship, had been long and steady. He would miss her.

Trinity Court looked like a different house, all of the furniture covered with crisp white linens, while the paintings were off the walls. Miranda would take several of her cherished masterpieces, sending the rest to a museum. She showed Tom around the impressive mansion, pointing out the various rooms and offices, first in one wing and then the other. It wasn't until now that he fully understood the extent of her wealth, displayed with such extravagance at the ostentatious Trinity Court, and exactly what she was giving up just to be with him. He had seen equal splendor only on the *Cavalier*.

Before they would go outside to walk the grounds, Miranda peeked inside Colin's suite of rooms, then Landon's. She knew that the boys were not in residence, still awaiting their trial, but she could almost see them in her mind's eye pacing the floors, as they often did, conducting their questionable affairs while vainly attempting to appear vital to the family business. Miranda had to accept that they were gone from her life to be put on trial for what they had done to her…and others. Their many transgressions too numerous to count, their criminal minds beyond redemption, she needed to forget about them. She fervently hoped that Tom would never have to make their acquaintance.

When they finished walking the grounds at Trinity Court, Miranda and Tom came back inside to find the entire staff, 65 in all, lined up in the Grand Entrance Hall to say a final farewell to their madam, someone for whom they had always felt a deep devotion and respect, especially after learning what she had been through at the hands of her two sons. Many would shed a tear as she thanked them for their service, Cranston assuring her that they had been given generous compensation, just as she instructed.

Certain that she had gathered all the clothes and other belongings that she would ever need or desire, Miranda and Tom left that evening for the Black Hills where the Dakota Fetch awaited their arrival, many of the ranch hands in attendance to meet the lady who had stolen the heart of Cosborn T. Dakota.

Naturally, Miranda was nervous at first, but as soon as she got to the Fetch, her fears quickly dissipated with the early morning fog, the sun rising over the hills just as they arrived. She shook hands with everyone on the ranch that morning, no matter what their position. All of them men, they were as gracious and gentlemanly as could be.

"Boys, this is my fiancé, Miranda Grimes. She and I are to be married right here on the Fetch within the next couple of weeks. Treat her with the same respect that you do me, not only because she'll soon be my wife, but also because she'll be the head cowgirl around here!" Tom shouted as the ranch hands whooped it up, clapping their hands and throwing their hats high up into the air. Miranda immediately felt as though she belonged, as though she had been a part of the Dakota Fetch all her life. "And now, it's time to show you around the place, darlin'," Tom said, taking her by the hand and leading her into the wide-open spaces of the Fetch. They walked around the corrals, meadows, and barns of the peaceful ranch, the realization finally sinking in that life as they each knew it would never be the same again. There was no looking back now.

"I hope you can learn to love it here the way I do," said Tom as they strolled through the main corral still holding hands. "This is where we'll be married, right here in the main corral," said Tom. "I've held many festive and happy occasions in this corral, but this will be the most festive...and by far the happiest."

"I already *do* love it," said Miranda, feeling quite comfortable in her new home. "And *you're* here. It's all I could ever want," she said, kissing Tom passionately.

"Just the same, darlin'," Tom began seriously, breaking free of their embrace, "I've asked Cranston to have your name put on the deed of the Dakota Fetch. If anything should happen to me, this place will be all yours. That way, I can rest easy knowing you'll be well taken care of." Miranda didn't want to talk about such things, especially right before the wedding, putting her at a loss for words. Besides, she was desensitized to the notion of inheriting *anything* further in her life. Having to respond, she acknowledged Tom's gesture as simply as she could.

"If that's the way you want it, sweetheart," she said.

Miranda and Tom would discuss their plans, leaving much of the preparation to Tom's secretary, who relied daily on Miranda's approval and consent to move forward.

The next two weeks were a blur of anticipation and planning as the couple had their blood tests, created a menu, and sent out invitations. Tom arranged for steaks to be cooked over charcoal fires set in large kettledrums and corn on the cob to be boiled in nearby pots. In the meantime, potatoes would bake in the ground, much like in the lovo in Fiji, and a champagne fountain, kegs of beer, and cases of wine would prevent the guests from becoming parched. Tom ordered fresh Maine lobster to be flown in to the Fetch as a special surprise for Miranda and asked the chefs to cook as many rice and vegetable dishes as possible, although he hoped that his bride would eat a nice, thick, juicy steak.

Miranda, for her part, would make sure that the main corral was all set for the event, having it properly decorated and outfitted with the necessary tables and chairs. The fences and tables were swathed in white and pink streamers and tulle, while carnations and roses, arranged in large horseshoes, hung around the perimeter. A large archway of balloons, through which the couple and their guests would enter and exit, stood over the entrance to the corral, now a most lovely sight. She would also arrange for the musicians with the help of one of Tom's ranch hands who frequented most of the barn dances in town. Not surprisingly, Miranda didn't feel the need to invite anyone other than Cranston. As a matter of fact, he would be the one to give her away, effectively quashing Tom's initial plan to be married on horseback. Finally ready to tie the knot, they would await Cranston's arrival the following morning.

In the meantime, that afternoon, Cranston hurriedly packed, feeling an acute sense of panic. How would he tell Miranda the bad news and how would she react to it? He couldn't possibly tell her before the wedding, because it would spoil the entire day. He knew his client well, and this sudden turn of events was certain to cause her pain and emotional distress, perhaps for days. Even *he* was so jittery about it that he would have to breathe deeply and take a tranquilizer before boarding a plane for the Dakota Fetch that evening. No, he would wait until after the reception to tell her, but it would be difficult not to say anything about it all day long. He would force a calm demeanor, hoping that would belie his fears, and pay particular attention to suppressing the slight facial tic that always plagued him during times of undue stress. He was determined that his manner mustn't inadvertently give him away on such a special and well-deserved day for his friend. After all, as a lawyer, he should know that these things happen all the time and for Miranda's sake he must assuage his disbelief. *Breathe, breathe, breathe,* he kept saying to himself.

By the time Cranston arrived at the Fetch the following morning, the wedding was nearly at hand, Miranda feeling cool and collected while Tom nervously paced the expanse of the large barn off of the main corral.

Wearing an ice-blue dress that matched the color of her eyes, a single necklace of pearls adorning her slender neck, Miranda looked breathtakingly lovely and quite sure of the step she was about to take. Tom wore a black tuxedo and the same black cowboy hat that he had worn the first time Miranda ever saw him: through the peephole of the door to her penthouse suite on the *Cavalier*. Wiping beads of sweat from his brow, Tom's best man would take him by the arm into the main corral, the 75 guests already swept up by the air of romance and sympathetic toward his wedding day jitters. It was a perfect day for a wedding too, the sky bright and the air crisp, scented with the fragrance of carnations and roses.

Cranston slowly walked Miranda into the main corral, her arm loosely linked with his, as she smiled at her guests, the band playing a sleepy country version of the *Wedding March*. Kissing her gently on the cheek, he placed Miranda's hand in Tom's, whose trembling seemed to have subsided now that the big moment was here. Exchanging short personal vows that they had written themselves, the couple was married by the local justice of the peace in a matter of 10 minutes, after which time the women clapped loudly while the men threw their cowboy hats high up in the air. As they were being showered with rice, Mr. and Mrs. Cosborn T. Dakota made their way across the main corral, through the large archway of balloons, and into the house for a little privacy before the festivities began. Once inside Tom's private library, they fell into each other's arms and kissed passionately, Miranda's eyes pooled with tears. Finally…they were married.

"I love you, darlin'," said Tom, "and I'll take good care of you for the rest of your life."

"I love you too," Miranda answered breathlessly, and that was all she could say. Her life would now be perfect…or so she thought.

The couple gleefully exchanged wedding presents in private, the gold wedding bands that they had purchased in Mumbai glistening on their fingers. Miranda told Tom about the twenty-million dollar donation that she had made to the War Memorial of Korea in honor of his father and about the plaque that would bear his name to be displayed on the International Walk of Memorials. Touched beyond words, Tom's chest heaved slightly with emotion as he tried to control himself. She also gave him a set of gold cufflinks and a 10-gallon hat, white in color.

After Miranda was finished presenting her gifts, Tom took her out into one of the side corrals where a tan and white filly meandered about, eating hay while lazily swooshing flies with her tail.

"She's all yours," said Tom with a smile from ear to ear.

"Oh, Tom!" she exclaimed. "My very own horse!" Miranda was thrilled, naming the animal Cavalier right on the spot, not only for the ship that had brought them together, but for the carefree life that she and her new filly would have on the Fetch.

Tom also gave Miranda a leather saddle emblazoned with her new initials and walked her out of the corral towards a side meadow where a herd of cattle, now belonging to her as well, grazed en masse.

"Oh, Tom," she said somberly. "I could never sell those animals for slaughter."

"You can do whatever you want with them, darlin'," said Tom. "They're all yours too!"

After going back inside to unpack the red pottery that he had bought for her in Thailand, along with the blue and white silk rug that they had purchased together in China, Tom gave Miranda one final wedding gift: a diamond bracelet.

"It's the most beautiful bracelet I've ever had," she said, unable to take her eyes off of it.

"Then let's get back to our guests and show it off," Tom said excitedly, placing an arm around her shoulders as he walked her towards the door. The ceremony finally over, they would emerge from the house ready to celebrate, their guests greeting them with a standing ovation and round of applause.

Cranston stood in a corner of the corral, biding his time, as the rest of the guests ate, drank, and danced. Smoking a cigar and sipping on a beer, he observed from afar the merry occasion that would last well into the night. Miranda and Tom danced the entire evening, never taking their eyes off of each other, as the dazzling white and pink lights illuminated the main corral. They occasionally slowed down to socialize with the guests who were dancing around them, but, for the most part, they held each other closely, twirling and waltzing to the continuous music of the band. By midnight, Cranston was feeling sloppy, having had four or five beers and a couple of glasses of champagne. Unable to keep his mouth shut any longer, he tapped Tom on the shoulder.

"Would you mind if I cut in?" he asked the groom.

"Not at all," Tom said, handing his bride over to the drunken lawyer.

"Cranston, where have you been?" asked Miranda, a little tipsy herself. "We haven't danced together once all evening."

"You've been having such a good time that I didn't want to interrupt," said Cranston, holding Miranda at a respectable distance as they slowly waltzed around the corral, "but I have something important to tell you that can't wait any longer."

"Well, what is it?" she asked, not really paying attention to him as she waved and smiled at any guest looking her way.

"Miranda, the boys have been let off on a technicality," said Cranston. "A mistrial was declared early on and they're now out of jail." She didn't seem to comprehend what he was saying. "They're free, Miranda," Cranston said, looking her straight in the eye, "no longer locked up." She stopped dancing and looked at Cranston in disbelief.

"What do you mean? Are you telling me that they're no longer behind bars?" Miranda asked, her eyes wide with fright. Finally…she got it.

"That's exactly what I'm telling you," said Cranston.

"Where are they now?" she asked.

"That's the thing," said Cranston, "no one knows. They seem to have disappeared, but word on the street is that…they're looking for you."

The band continued to play one song after another while the guests danced and drank champagne, unaware of the somber news that Cranston had just given Miranda. The white and pink lights illuminating their faces, the now rambunctious crowd laughed uproariously while stepping lively around the main corral, often lifting their glasses in an occasional toast. Miranda slightly stumbled into a dark, private corner and sat in a chair, Cranston right behind her.

"Are you all right?" he asked her.

"I'm frightened, Jim," she said, her hands trembling as she lit a cigarette. "I'm frightened." For Miranda, the party was now…over.

Chapter 30
Over Her Shoulder

When it is a question of money, everybody is of the same religion.

-Voltaire

The next morning, Miranda lay on her bed with a cold cloth over her brow, the wedding reception now a frightful memory. All the guests gone, with the exception of Cranston, who was packing his things in order to catch the next flight out, the house was quiet while the main corral was still decorated in pink and white, a reminder of what took place there the night before. No matter what he said to her or how much he tried to soothe her, Tom could do nothing to relieve Miranda's anxiety.

"Darlin', I'm telling you flat out that neither of those boys will *ever* step a toe on this property without being caught and throttled by one of my men," said Tom, trying to ease Miranda's mind.

"You don't know them, Tom," she said, lighting up another cigarette. "If they can't somehow get to me, then they'll hire someone who can."

"I'm here to protect you, darlin', along with all of my ranch hands who even *I* wouldn't want to meet in a dark alley. Now, if *that* doesn't calm your fears, then maybe I should just hire a bodyguard," Tom concluded, grasping at any straw that might quell Miranda's fear. "Would that make you feel better?" he asked in a gentle tone of voice, speaking to Miranda as though she were a fragile china doll that would break into pieces at any moment, for he knew that the news about her two sons had rendered her emotionally brittle once again. Cranston stood unobtrusively in the hallway listening to the conversation.

"That might not be a bad idea, if you don't mind my saying," he interjected, slowly walking into the bedroom, not quite sure if he was overstepping his bounds, now that Miranda was a married woman. "I can take care of that for you when I get back to Trinity Court. I know some of the best security teams in the business."

"I'd appreciate that," said Tom, massaging Miranda's shoulders. "And I want you to know that *you're* always welcome here, Cranston. Good friends like you are hard to find." Cranston nodded and backed out of the room modestly, too embarrassed to watch Tom massage Miranda's shoulders any longer. "I'll contact the right people as soon as I get home," he assured the two of them from the hallway. "And, Miranda, if I should hear anything about the boys, anything at all, I'll get in touch with you immediately."

"Thank you, Cranston. I know that I can always count on you…that *we* can count on you," she corrected herself, reaching a hand out to him from the bed. He quickly walked back into the bedroom from the hallway, gently squeezed her hand, and bent down to kiss her cheek.

"I really must go," he said. "I don't want to miss my flight. I'll call you in a couple of days. Please…try to relax." Cranston turned to Tom and shook his hand.

"May I bring you to the airfield?" asked Tom.

"No, thank you, that won't be necessary," said Cranston graciously. He bid a final goodbye before immediately leaving the house, for it would take him the better part of an hour to get out to the airfield. Tom was relieved that Cranston was protective of Miranda's safety too. If there was anyone who could uncover what Colin and Landon were up to, he could.

In the days that followed, Miranda slowly got used to her new home, although she instinctively looked over her shoulder whenever she was in one of the corrals or meadows. Every rustling of the bushes or swaying of the trees caused her to snap her head around, expecting to find her sons watching her after having infiltrated the Dakota Fetch.

"I get the feeling that I'm being watched," she said, the hair on the back of her neck standing straight up.

"You're *not* being watched, darlin'," Tom said a little impatiently, taking her by the hand. "Now, don't you think you're carrying this thing a little too far? I told you that you're perfectly safe here. You need to trust me," Tom said pointedly, staring intensely into her frightened eyes.

"I *do* trust you," Miranda said, "but why hasn't Cranston been able to hire a bodyguard?"

"I told you what he said when he called a few days ago," Tom reminded her. "He's doing his best, but he's having trouble finding someone who is able to come to the ranch right away. He said he can have someone out here in a couple of weeks and I told him that you would be just fine until then."

"I know," said Miranda, "but—"

"No buts," said Tom firmly. "In the meantime, you're going to continue to explore your new home, get to know your cattle, and learn how to ride your horse. I'll be with you the entire time," he finished softly, placing two gentle hands on her shoulders before kissing her tenderly.

"All right, sweetheart," Miranda said resignedly, melting up against him, "as long as you're with me." She let out a long sigh as her head lay on his chest. There was so much on the ranch for her to enjoy, but, right now, she was simply a bundle of nerves.

Miranda did indeed continue to explore her new home, particularly enjoying the horses. She spent many hours with Cavalier, grooming and petting her lovingly before getting up the nerve to mount her. The pretty filly would be, by far, the best wedding present that Tom had given Miranda, for it proved to be therapeutic, soothing her unsettled nerves and giving her something pleasant to do. Though a little awkward at first, she was comfortable in her new leather saddle as she trotted around the corrals, her backside usually feeling the effects later in the evening when she would attempt to sit down to dinner.

"Don't worry, your ass will get used to it," Tom would laugh.

He taught her how to properly tend to *all* of the horses, and, in no time at all, she was the one saddling them up first thing in the morning for the working ranch hands. Even though she showed just a passing interest in the cattle, Tom knew that Miranda had found her niche with the horses, her knowledge and interest growing more every day, as her confidence and happiness seemed to re-emerge. She adored riding, sometimes cajoling Tom into the saddle two or three times a day to walk around the corrals or trot around the meadows.

She rarely looked over her shoulder now, having finally let down her guard in the bucolic setting of the Dakota Fetch…and this is where our story began.

"Let's ride over to the meadow with the wildflowers!" Miranda called out to Tom over her shoulder, Cavalier taking her through the gate of the main corral at a brisk pace.

"We were just there yesterday!" Tom roared back with laughter, his horse obediently following.

The meadow with the wildflowers, as Miranda liked to call it, was actually the high meadow in the northeast corner of the ranch and indeed filled with colorful, oddly-shaped flowers that attracted pretty butterflies and bumblebees. Surrounded on three sides by an elevated ridge, the high meadow was the perfect place to ride, for it was quiet and private, unless, of course, someone was looking down at it from the ridge. Miranda rode her beloved Cavalier at a leisurely pace while, at times, holding hands with Tom, who rode his trusty steed alongside her. They laughed together and made their plans, Miranda far more relaxed than she had been in days.

"I'm so glad you're feeling better, darlin'," said Tom. "It's nice to see you smiling again."

"I feel much better," said Miranda, flashing Tom the smile that he loved to see. "You were right, sweetheart. I had no reason to worry so much."

The couple rode on a little further before dismounting their horses. Miranda always liked to pick the colorful flowers in this meadow while Tom walked to the perimeter inspecting the trees. He carved their initials into a large oak, prompting Miranda to giggle like a young schoolgirl. They turned over every rock, busy little rodents scurrying from underneath, and delighted in the butterflies flitting about overhead before sitting in the soft grass to have a leisurely chat.

"This is one of the prettiest pieces of land on the property," commented Miranda as she looked around. "It's too bad that the house wasn't built here."

"That can easily be remedied," said Tom like a foxy little boy with something up his sleeve.

"Really?" she asked quizzically. "What do you have in mind?" She felt her heart thump in her chest as a broad smile brightened her pretty face. *Could he possibly be thinking about…?*

"How would you like to live on this meadow?" Tom asked, sure that he already knew the answer to his question. "I can build us a nice, little house that would be far enough from the main compound to give us plenty of privacy but close enough to—" Miranda wouldn't let Tom finish his sentence, jumping on top of him and smothering his face with kisses.

"Are you serious?" she squealed. "You would do that for me?"

"Of course I would, darlin'," Tom laughed, kissing her back. "I would do *anything* for you, as long as it made you happy."

"I would be the happiest person on earth if we could live on this meadow!" Miranda assured him with a loud exclamation.

"You would be in charge of the architectural design and all of the furniture, as long as the place doesn't end up looking like Trinity Court," Tom warned, only half-kiddingly. "I have a good friend who's an architect and I bet that if you work closely with him, he could build us a beautiful home, something that would please you beyond your wildest dreams." A worthwhile distraction, Tom knew that this undertaking would dominate most of Miranda's time, taking her further away from any lingering worries about her two sons.

"I have so many ideas swirling around inside of my head already," Miranda said excitedly, rearing to take on the project. "Think about all the striking examples of architecture that we saw on our trip. I could combine the best features of each one!"

"Now hold on…I don't want to live in a Chinese palace or a Buddhist temple," Tom cautioned. "Whatever we build, it must uphold the beauty and integrity of the Fetch."

"It will, Tom, I promise," Miranda pledged, determined to make the project a monumental success, something of which Tom would be proud.

The couple got back on their horses and proceeded to ride back towards the main house, Miranda too excited to sit in the grass any longer. She would now look at the meadow in a different way, turning her head from side to side in order to take in the contour of this handsome piece of property, the place where she and Tom would happily live out their days. The horses walked slowly along as the couple continued to chat.

"Isn't this the most beautiful meadow you've ever seen in your entire life, Tom?" Miranda asked, breathing in the fresh air. "And what a place to build a home!" she tingled all over with excitement, Tom having given her the best gift of all.

"It sure is beautiful, darlin', but I can't say that I like that high ridge," he said, pointing at the long, narrow land elevation above them.

"That won't interfere with the house," Miranda assured Tom, unaware of his concern that anyone could have access to the ridge and, hence, the property down below. He would keep that to himself for the time being, not wanting to appear too worried, now that Miranda's fears had substantially diminished.

Almost at the perimeter of the meadow, Miranda and Tom slowed down to maneuver their horses, one behind the other, before entering the trail that would take them back to the main corral.

At the same time, unbeknownst to them, a shadowy figure moved along the high ridge, inconspicuously watching them while walking quickly across the narrow elevation to keep up with the pace of the horses. Having walked as far as possible, the figure stood witness as Miranda led Cavalier onto the trail first, Tom not too far behind.

Suddenly, a loud shot rang out, causing both horses to unexpectedly rear up, throwing their riders to the ground. Feeling stunned and not quite sure of what she had just heard, Miranda slowly got up and stumbled over to Tom, who still lay on the ground. Shaking him hard, she couldn't arouse him, causing her to wonder if his neck had been broken in the fall. Horrified, she crawled behind his lifeless body, only to quickly discover the truth: Tom had been shot in the back.

Chapter 31
What Goes Around

They, who are of the opinion that money will do everything,
may very well be suspected to do everything for money.
                                                    -George Savile

"Miranda, I got here as quickly as I could," said a breathless
Cranston, taking brisk strides into Tom's private library. As
dozens of people milled around her, Miranda sat expressionless
in a corner chair, utterly shocked at what had happened. She
stared at her friend vacantly before speaking:

"It's too late, Cranston," she said, her voice devoid of any
inflection. "Tom is gone. Landon and Colin have won, taking
from me my only chance at happiness."

"We'll find them...and they'll pay dearly this time,"
Cranston said, angrily spitting out his words. "Did anyone find
the gun that shot Tom?"

"Yes, up on the ridge," Miranda said, her voice now barely
audible. "It was a rifle...the same one that Landon used to keep
in his bedroom closet."

"How do you know that?" asked Cranston.

"I *should* know...it had his initials carved into the stock,
just as I had custom ordered before giving it to him for his
birthday five years ago," said Miranda in utter despair. "I can
only wonder why, in heaven's name, it was Tom who was
murdered...and not me," she said, finally breaking down.

"We might never know the answer to that," replied
Cranston, draping an arm around her heaving shoulders. He
could say nothing more that would, in any way, ease Miranda's
grief, deciding instead to mill around with the rest of the
company. Feeling helpless, his heart went out to her, but he

would have to wait until the time was right before further asserting himself into the situation. Perhaps she would ask him to settle Tom's estate…or find the whereabouts of her sons. In any case, he would do whatever she asked of him. He always did.

The days of mourning that followed Tom's death were arduous for Miranda, her dreams tragically shattered by a bullet, suddenly plunging her into an unspeakable depth of grief. She found herself making funeral arrangements for a man she had married only a short time before; she had to choose the right casket, find an appropriate burial place, and arrange for a proper service to be held on the ranch in the main corral, the same place they had celebrated their wedding only weeks before.

That night, after the house had emptied itself of the many guests who had come to express their condolences or simply hang about the place, as though their presence was necessary or somehow desired, Miranda aimlessly walked through the empty rooms, unsure of what to do next. She could no longer revel in the beauty of the high meadow, make plans to have a new house built there, or find pleasure in tending to the horses. The Dakota Fetch had lost its charm and, now that it was hers, she had no idea what to do with it.

The service that took place was solemn and respectful, Tom's coffin ceremoniously positioned in the middle of the main corral, high on a bier, for everyone to see. Draped in the same flag that normally flew over the Dakota Fetch, the coffin was circled by his favorite steeds, their heads bowed in seeming despair. Well over a hundred mourners passed by as Miranda sat silently and watched, a black veil covering her face. This place, decorated in white and pink only weeks before, was now plunged into the dark, gloomy colors of mourning; the organ music especially reverential, drowned out only by the collective sound of weeping. Cranston had come back to attend the memorial service and, in the days that followed, Miranda would lean on her friend for support.

"I'm so glad that you've decided to stay for a while, Cranston," said Miranda, blowing her nose with an overused tissue as they sat in what was once Tom's private library; her favorite room in the house now.

"I'm happy to stay," he said, placing a hand on her shoulder. "I'll do whatever it is you want me to do. If you want me to handle Tom's last will and testament, or settle any other legal matters connected to the estate, then you need only to ask me. I'll do anything…anything at all that might ease your burden at this time." Cranston's consolation meant the world to Miranda.

"I'm lucky to have you," she said, her eyes welling up with tears again.

"I'm just so sorry that I couldn't get a bodyguard out here sooner," Cranston commented softly, shaking his head back and forth.

"That wasn't your fault," said Miranda quickly, "and I don't want you to give it another thought."

"Thank you for understanding, but I fear that my nights will continue to be restless until I've completely reconciled the issue within myself," said Cranston, appearing to blame himself for Tom's death. Miranda put her hand on his and squeezed gently.

"How long have we known each other, Cranston?" Miranda asked out of curiosity.

"Now, let's see," Cranston said slowly, raising his eyes to the ceiling and putting a hand to his chin as he calculated, "Landon was a baby, but I don't think that Colin had been born yet when I was hired by Trinity Court," he said, squinting his eyes, "so that would make it somewhere around 30 years."

"You know me better than anyone," said Miranda, "even better than Tom had known me. And I'll never forget how you rescued me from the Mountain Valley Sanatorium and got me back on my feet at the beach house, not to mention the fact that you were instrumental in having all of my rights restored." Miranda went on and on as Cranston moved in closer.

"Like I said before," Cranston affirmed, his voice now in a low whisper, "I would do anything for you, Miranda. As a matter of fact, why don't I stay on at the Fetch indefinitely? After all, you once offered me a job here," he reminded her. "That way I can help you…and take care of you," said the lawyer, moving farther into Miranda's personal space. "We could be together all the time and—"

"Hold it right there, Cranston," came the abrupt intrusion into the private library. "Before you start making plans with

Mrs. Cosborn, you might want to tell her a few things." There, with his hands in his pockets, stood the detective who had followed Cranston up to Cloudy Mountain all those months ago...the same detective who had arrested Landon and Colin.

"Detective, what are you doing here?" asked Miranda with evident surprise.

"Ask Cranston, Ma'am," said the shrewd detective, giving the lawyer a chance to talk. But Cranston wouldn't take the bait.

"I have no idea what you're talking about, Detective," said Cranston, obviously rankled. "You've come at a most inopportune time...Mrs. Cosborn has just lost her husband."

"I know that," said the detective. "My condolences, Ma'am," he expressed, tipping his hat to Miranda. "Would you care to tell her *who* killed her husband?" the detective asked, turning once again to Cranston.

"She *knows* who killed her husband, Detective," said Cranston through clenched teeth. "Landon killed Tom. His gun was found up on the ridge."

"Detective, what's this all about?" asked Miranda. "What are you trying to say?"

"Let me explain, Ma'am," he said. "Would you mind if I sit down?"

"No, of course not...go right ahead," said Miranda, gesturing towards the chair directly across from her. The detective sat down, making himself comfortable while Cranston sat in a corner, his face suddenly blanched white.

"I must begin with a confession," he started sincerely, folding his hands and leaning forward in his chair in order to speak more intimately to Miranda. "Following Cranston had become such a part of my daily routine that I never stopped. Even after I arrested the boys, I found his habits to be fascinating entertainment. Never could I have imagined that he would do something...pernicious."

"What is *that* supposed to mean?" Miranda asked with an edge to her voice.

"You have a lot of nerve," Cranston interrupted before the detective could answer Miranda's question. "You had no reason to follow *me*."

"I must admit that it was boring until Landon and Colin Grimes were let off by that dirty judge…what a travesty," said the detective, shaking his head.

"Well, what about it?" asked Cranston. "I fail to see the connection between *their* release and you're following *me*."

"After Landon and Colin were released from jail," the detective continued, "they immediately flew to Bolivia, where they still remain, their repeated attempts to muscle their way into a factory in La Paz once owned by Trinity Court Enterprises still unsuccessful, although they continue to try…according to my source. It's my guess that they'll come home once they've finally realized that they're irrelevant players who no longer carry any clout, but that's neither here nor there. It was at this time that I followed Cranston with even greater interest, because—"

"Wait a minute," interrupted Miranda, now standing. "Are you telling me that my two sons have not been in the country since their release?"

"Yes, Ma'am, that is exactly what I'm telling you. Please, sit down," said the detective, gesturing towards Miranda's chair. She gave Cranston a long, hard look before sitting back down. "As I was saying," he continued calmly, "it was at this time that I followed Cranston with an even greater interest, because one particular habit had become quite curious."

"And what habit was that?" asked Cranston, looking at the fingernails of his right hand.

"His trips here to the Dakota Fetch had become more and more frequent, ten or 12 times just in the last month," said the detective, directing his answer to Cranston's question at Miranda. Suddenly, turning to the lawyer, he commented, "I must say, old man, that you made it much harder for me to follow you, since I had to take a plane to do it."

"You must be mistaken, Detective," said Miranda. "Cranston has only been here twice, the first time for my wedding and the second time for Tom's funeral service…not the ten or 12 times that you say."

"Well, I've only told you *in part* about the one particular habit that had become quite curious," said the detective, lighting the cigarette that Miranda had put in her mouth.

"Spit it out, Detective," said Miranda, who by now was getting quite impatient. "What the hell are you telling me?"

"When he came here, he never notified you," said the detective, indeed spitting it out quickly. "He stayed in a lodge about 30 miles from here at night, while during the day he would canvas the Dakota Fetch, becoming familiar with the property…and your routine. After a half a dozen visits or so, he gravitated time and time again to the elevated ridge that surrounds the high meadow in the northeast corner of the ranch. I watched him there…while he watched you and your husband ride around that meadow day after day." Miranda looked at Cranston with shock and horror. "He knew the ridge, your routine, and had access to the gun that belongs to your son…who has an airtight alibi."

"Why, Cranston?" Miranda managed to ask. "Why?" He slowly stood up from his chair, no longer looking at his nails but looking straight at Miranda, his eyes burning into hers.

"All those years," he said bitterly. "All those years that I took care of you and protected you. I rescued you, literally and figuratively, over and over again. And what did I get for it? Maybe a pat on the back or a bonus check," Cranston lamented. "Not once did you think that I might love you, that I might want a future with you. That I might want to take care of you…for the rest of your life. You never gave me a chance," he said grievously, burying his head in his hands. "You never gave me a chance."

"I had no idea," Miranda said to the detective, once again in shock over the senseless death of her husband…at the hand of her friend. She stood up and aimlessly wandered about the room as the detective put Cranston in handcuffs.

"James Cranston, I am placing you under arrest for the murder of Cosborn T. Dakota. You have the right to remain silent…" he said as he led the now exposed lawyer out of the house. Miranda watched through a window as the detective put Cranston in his car.

"I'll be damned," she whispered to herself. "I'll be damned."

Several months would pass before the reading of Tom's will, during which time Miranda tried to regain some semblance of order in her life. No longer having her usual confidant to turn to, she depended upon Tom's entourage of friends and business associates to guide her through the lonely days and answer any legal and financial questions that she might have. Her losses had been monumental over the last year, her doctor, her sons, her husband, and now Cranston, all vital to her in their own way and for different reasons.

Cranston had been the only man she had ever truly leaned on until she met Tom, always painfully aware that her two sons were of questionable character. Could she have misled her friend into thinking that their relationship might be something more? How was it that she never picked up on that? Even Tom, who was usually a pretty good judge of people, was oblivious to the true nature of Cranston's intentions. It seemed doubtful, maybe even hopeless, that she would ever again find another man to trust…or love.

The day came for the reading of Tom's will, a day which Miranda had dreaded for a long time. Even though it would finally lay to rest the legal and financial questions that swirled around the ranch—many of Tom's associates still resentful of the advanced position of power and wealth in which he had placed Miranda before his death—it would be the last remnant of Tom's life for which she would have to endure the tiresome palaver of his staid legal team before finally getting on with her own life.

At least a dozen men of high position at the Fetch were seated in the private library, many of whom Miranda didn't know personally. A group of four lawyers read Tom's will out loud, small pieces of the livestock enterprise going to every one of the men in attendance. With the exception of $10,000 given to each of the faithful domestic servants who had been with Tom for many years and the horses bequeathed to several devoted ranch hands, Miranda would inherit everything: the ranch, the businesses associated with it, and all of Tom's cash and investment accounts. After everyone had left the room, with the exception of Miranda, the lead attorney made a final, telling comment.

"Mrs. Cosborn, you are now a prosperous woman, having inherited…a fortune," he said, at which time he closed his briefcase and departed, leaving Miranda to her thoughts.

Ironically, she was back to where she had started, once again…a wealthy heiress.

Suddenly, the doorbell rang, jarring Miranda from her deep contemplation. She rose unsteadily from her chair to answer the door, most of the help having been given a sorely needed day off. Who could it be now? It was her sole desire to be left alone…today of all days. Slowly opening the large oak door, she stood frozen to her spot, gazing in horror at her uninvited guests. Her life having gone full circle, she could no longer hide from her past.

"Hello, Mother," said Landon, Colin standing sheepishly behind him. "We're home."